AN ECHO OF FIRE

AMBER LYNN NATUSCH

An Echo of Fire - Fireheart Book One
© 2023 Amber Lynn Natusch

Print ISBN: 978-1-959010-08-1

Published by Amber Lynn Natusch
Cover by Franziska Stern
Print Formatting by The Madd Formatter
Editing by Kristy Bronner

http://amberlynnnatusch.com

PROLOGUE

The sky was cast in ash and fire—everything around me burned. Mother lay on the ground next to me, unmoving, her bright red wings stained with blood and soot. Even though I was only four years old, I understood that she wasn't just sleeping. Somehow, I knew she'd never hold me again. Never tell me how much she loved me.

I stepped out into the blood-coated streets and slipped several times, trying to navigate the battlefield in little more than bare feet. I saw movement at the far end of the road; a figure cloaked in smoke and dust. But I could see wings in that silhouette, and that was all I needed. I ran as fast as my little legs could carry me, hurtling toward the unknown with reckless abandon.

Because I was afraid.

Because I was full of hope.

The air seemed to split, allowing a mountain of a male to step through, his black wings tucked into his back. Behind him were two others. The three of them fanned out to take in the carnage. They hardly even noticed my approach until I was only yards away, not slowing. I skidded to a halt just before I slammed into them and looked up at each one, smiling. Then my eyes fell on the leader, and my heart leaped in my chest.

I had seen his face a handful of times before.

My father had returned.

"Baba!" I screamed, latching onto his leg. He reached down to pull me off, and I gripped it tighter.

He said something to the others—words I was too young to understand—then slowly bent down to look at me.

"What is your name, child?" he asked, his dark eyes fixed on me. Had it been so long since I'd seen him that he had forgotten me? Then I looked down at the blood and dirt caked all over my body and I understood.

"It's me, Baba." I tried to wipe my face clean so he could recognize me. "Ariel…"

His brow furrowed. "Where is your mother, Ariel?"

I looked back down the road toward the remains of our home and pointed. His dark gaze followed my gesture, then he nodded.

One of the other men bent down and spoke into my father's ear, the two of them looking me over—especially the oxblood wings tucked in tight behind my back. The ones far darker than my mother's.

"She comes with us," my father said, picking me up.

"Kade—"

"She comes with us, and that is final," he snarled at the one who had dared challenge him. The man lowered his gaze and took a step back to allow my father and me to pass. I wrapped my little arms around his neck and held on tight as he took to the air.

We flew until the sun began to rise and the mountains grew tall, until we arrived at what looked like a village, though it was far different from the one my mother and I had

4

lived in. Warriors walked around everywhere, their black wings spread wide and bodies strapped with weapons. This was to be my new home, I thought. Baba and I would live here together forever.

He took me to a building filled with children. They ran around like wild animals, shirtless and covered in dirt and blood. They fought and played and screamed with delight and pain and everything in between. Mikroús polemistés, he called them. His little warriors. It was then that I realized I was the only girl. The only girl in a crowd of little boys destined to be mikroús polemistés. The only pair of deep red wings in a sea of black ones. I was different, that much I knew.

What that really meant, I would come to learn over time.

As soon as my father left, the others circled me like predators, moving closer with every step. One of the bolder ones reached out and tugged at my wing, stretching it to the point of pain. I cried out, and another one punched me in the face. I fell to the ground, sobbing, and they began kicking me, shouting words I didn't understand. Names I couldn't comprehend until I was older. I called for my father over and over again, but he never came.

Someone else did instead.

A boy, only a couple years older than I, tossed the others out of his way as though they weighed nothing. He didn't stop until the blows quit landing and only he stood in front of me. He reached his small but mighty hand toward me, and I took it.

"My name is Hemming," he said, a faint accent to his words—one different than my mother's. Than mine.

"Ariel."

He looked at my wings and nodded, understanding in his pale eyes. "Welcome to Daglaar, mikros drakos."

Then he walked away, the others parting to let him pass.

From that day forward, the boys in the camp thought twice before messing with me outside of our training. Because I was Hemming's mikros drakos—*his little dragon—and whatever he was had them all running scared.*

Years later, that would include me, too.

Present Day
ARIEL

I ran through the silent halls of the manor on light feet, ducking from shadow to shadow to make sure I wasn't caught. It was clear from the tone of my father's letter that it wouldn't end well for me if I was. The Midlands were no longer safe for me.

The front door was the nearest exit but also the most conspicuous. With no time to debate the merits of finding another way out, I darted toward it. When I reached the heavy wooden doors, I pressed myself flat against them and calmed my breathing so I could hear whether I'd been followed. I was greeted by eerie silence, which put me more on edge than ever. Instead of weighing what it could mean, I pulled the door open just enough to slip through, then closed it gently.

The dead of night greeted me, its inky black sky peppered with stars and a bright blue moon; the light that would help guide me on my journey. That and the blessing stone in my hand.

My blood-red wings snapped open, stretching before I could take to the sky. But first, I needed to get off Kaplyn's property. It had long been warded against flight, and for good reason. There was history between my father's country and his, and it was not pleasant. At least not until the treaty. As I sprinted for the front gate, I wondered what treachery had forced my father to send the note telling me to flee. Whatever the reason, it was clear that the truce between the Nychterídes and Neráides had fallen.

And I was officially an enemy in Neráida lands.

I stuffed that worry away and threw open the wrought-iron gate. The second it snapped shut, a bloodcurdling sound rang out through the night. I looked back to see iridescent green eyes lurking in the shadows near the manor, staring in my direction. With a jolt of fear, I took to the sky, wings beating hard and fast.

And those green eyes followed.

I looked back to find the night swirling behind me, the billowy tendrils curling into the shape of something massive and winged. The shrill cry it made as it neared made my heart stop dead in my chest. Whatever it was, it was after me, but for what purpose, I didn't know. I had no intention of finding out, either.

With that thought to motivate me, I pushed harder, following the pull of the blessing stone, trusting Delphyne's trinket to guide me through the dangers of the Midlands to what I desired. But even it could not save me from the creature gaining on me. I prayed to the gods that Delphyne hadn't turned on me too; hadn't sent me off with a beacon for the monster chasing me to follow.

"Aaaaaaaaaaariellllllllll," it cried, its mangled caw

butchering my name—but it knew it, and that was a grim sign indeed, for names had power in the Midlands.

I felt my wings slow with every drawn-out syllable.

"No, no, no!" I yelled, panic shooting through my limbs. I tried to think of the tricks Kaplyn had taught me during our training sessions—the ones to ward off the magic of the Neráida—but my mind was too gripped by fear to focus. As I slowed to a crawl, the beast gaining on me with every second, my survival instincts finally kicked in and cleared my head. I screamed my name backwards as loud as I could: "*LEIRA*!" The second the word left my mouth, the tether holding me back snapped, and I surged forward.

The creature screeched in frustration.

"I won't let you take me alive!" I shouted over my shoulder. "I am the daughter of Kade, General of the Nychteríde army. I will return to him or die, and not by your hands!" The powerful beat of wings that had chased me for miles ceased. Through a break in the clouds, I saw a massive raven hovering in the air, staring at me with those piercing green eyes. "Tell Lord Kaplyn I know of his plans to betray me," I yelled at it.

With a sharp dive, I sped toward the ground, my wings tucked in tight behind me. No other had ever been able to match my speed when I did that, and I doubted the bird was any different. If I could put enough distance between us, I knew I'd be all right. With the moonlight to guide me, I weaved my way through trees and buildings until far in the distance, miles and miles away, I could see a dark forest of pine and fir trees—the trees of Daglaar. My father's land. My home.

A final cry from the raven echoed through the Midlands, sounding my escape.

I poured on speed and didn't stop until I reached the border.

2

ARIEL

RIEL,

YOU CANNOT TRUST KAPLYN. GET OUT NOW!

I LOOKED DOWN AT THE NOTE IN MY HAND, THEN BACK AT THE warded divide between the Midlands and Daglaar. In the four years I'd resided in the Midlands, I had received weekly letters from my father. And then those letters had stopped. A week had gone by. Then two. Then three. Then that final fateful note had arrived and sent me fleeing without a second thought.

A blast of cold mountain air rushed through the woods and caught my oxblood wings, snapping them wide. I may have only been half Nychteríde, but that half craved the blast

11

of freezing air to ride. My wings twitched, begging to take flight again.

It was time to go home.

With a steadying breath, I reached over my back and pulled my staff from between my shoulders. My father had given it to me as soon as I was old enough to wield it. I may have been escaping newly hostile territory, but the one I was returning to would not be much better; not after what had happened to me the night my father sent me to Kaplyn for safekeeping. Or so he'd thought.

What a difference four years made.

I was older, stronger, and wiser now, but that didn't mean that the feelings of those residing in the training camp had changed. Despite what Delphyne thought, I wasn't foolish enough to believe otherwise. Kaplyn's seamstress—and mother figure to me—had warned me against returning for that reason.

"Have you forgotten what they tried to do to you? Why your father brought you to the Midlands?" she asked me. "They broke you, Ariel, and they will try again, given the chance."

I looked down at the thick brown leather pants and halter she'd crafted for me and felt a pang of fear and guilt in my heart. They'd always been her way of telling me she loved me. Apparently enough to let me flee without alerting her lord. Enough to give me the blessing stone to keep me safe.

"This will help guide you to what you desire and send you on the safest path possible," she said, her voice low and full of resignation as she placed the shiny black stone in my palm. "It will also guide you back, should you ever desire that."

With sadness in my heart, I gripped my staff tightly in one hand and the stone in the other and stepped through a hole in the wards. Come mischief, mayhem, or certain death, I would learn why my father had sent that letter—what trouble the Nychterídes now had with the Neráides.

If I didn't, I feared I might meet the fate I'd narrowly escaped the last time I was in Daglaar.

I ran through the woods with as much stealth as my weary body could muster. I knew there would be warriors patrolling the border—likely more now that the treaty had fallen—and that could prove problematic. I didn't know what allies, if any, I still had in Daglaar, and I had no intention of finding out the hard way. I knew from past experience that assumptions could kill, like assuming your best friend would never press a blade to your throat while those that would see you dead cheered him on.

Getting to camp undetected and quickly was the name of the game.

Since the day I'd arrived in Daglaar, I'd never been fully accepted by the Nychterídes as a people. Being of mixed descent, I strongly resembled their Minyade enemies, from my colored wings to my paler skin (though it shared the same olive undertone as theirs) to my light sage-green eyes. Those differences came with a price.

Most in the settlement and the villages beyond had tolerated me because I was the general's daughter. Their loyalty to him was strong because he'd been the one to restore Daglaar after the gods had cursed our people and turned their backs on us. He'd taken a lawless, barren land, given it order, and created an army capable of protecting it. For over one hundred years, he'd kept the Nychterídes fed and safe. For this, he was their general—their leader—a king without a crown. In return, he only ever asked for three things: loyalty to Daglaar; loyalty to him; and loyalty to the Nychterídes.

It was that final request that seemed undermined by my existence.

Many of the warriors in camp resented me, for various

reasons. For being part Minyade. For being a female trained to fight instead of to serve them. For being Kade's daughter. I would often hear rumblings from those I trained with about how favored I was; how the *half-breed* received special treatment, from the food I ate to where I slept. How I lived in relative luxury compared to them in my father's home on the mountainside. In retrospect, perhaps they had a point, but I'd been too young and naïve then to see it. After living on Kaplyn's estate, I realized their grudges seemed somewhat valid. Perhaps Father should have let me live with them.

I wondered if it would be one of them I'd encounter on my way to the settlement. Father would have the younger soldiers patrolling the border—soldiers my age. The possibility that one of them could have been involved in the attempt on my life was not lost on me. If I was caught, they'd undoubtedly finish what they started four years earlier and dispose of my body before anyone even realized I'd reached the woods.

My return home would be cut short.

So I continued in silence through the woods with my staff drawn and my senses sharp.

Halfway to the mountain, I heard the crack of a branch underfoot. I hid behind a tree and surveyed the woods but saw nothing. Not willing to wait for disaster to strike, I took off at a sprint, less focused on stealth and more on speed.

The closer I got to camp, the more certain I became that I was being followed. Footfalls far heavier than my own echoed through the trees. The ground shook with every step as they grew louder and nearer, an ominous sign at best.

Fear drove me forward, pushing me hard. I hadn't come all that way to be stopped so close to my destination. I would see my father. There was no other option.

Only yards from the tree line that opened to the clearing at the center of camp, I dared a look back. Darting from shadow to shadow was a massive Nychteríde, gaining on me. I could not see his face, but it didn't matter. He was no ally, that much was clear. All I needed to do was make it to the clearing. Once there, I could find my father.

I broke through the trees to a familiar sight. Rows of tiny stone cabins rimmed the base of the mountain. Black-winged warriors were scattered throughout the camp. Their collective attention turned to me the second I came into view; weapons were drawn in an instant.

"Baba!" I shouted, still running from whoever had been chasing me. I was fast and in motion, two things that would work in my favor, but not forever. I needed to find a friendly face in a sea of potential enemies.

Fifty yards away stood the large stone building that housed the training area where I'd spent so much of my childhood. I breathed a small sigh of relief as I bolted toward it, knowing that if my father wasn't there, then Baran, the warrior entrusted to train the Nychterídes, should be. He could deliver me safely to my father. It was my best shot at making it to him fully intact.

I threw open the thick metal-covered door and ran into the vast space to find neither Baran nor my father anywhere in sight. What I did find was a group of warriors I knew all too well. The ones who'd tormented me growing up.

Fear spiked in my veins yet again.

From deep in the crowd, Tycho stepped forward. There was no love lost between him and me. Our mutual dislike had begun the day I arrived in Daglaar and he shoved me to the ground in front of the others. I doubted his temperament had improved much since then.

"So the Minyade's returned…" he said, twirling a broadsword in his hand. "You look good, Ariel."

He was much larger than he'd been when I last saw him. I

tried not to focus on that as he walked toward me. "You look the same. Possibly uglier."

He snarled and clenched the pommel of his sword. "We'll see how good you look once I'm done with you."

He ran at me, weapon poised to strike. I threw my pack aside and clutched my staff, ready to parry his blow. It was carved from a special tree from the Midlands, its wood immune to both fire and steel. Wood strong enough to damage a warrior with skin of stone like the Nychterídes possessed—one of their greatest defensive traits.

I called forth my scales, gifted to me by way of my mother's blood. In a cascade of iridescent armor, they covered my skin. Tycho hesitated for a moment at the sight. "Minyade whore," he muttered to himself before raising his sword again.

"*Tycho!*" someone shouted from the far side of the room, and my heart dropped to my gut. I'd have recognized Hemming's voice anywhere. I dared to let my gaze drift from the enemy before me to find him storming toward us, his narrowed grey eyes full of fury. "She's *mine*."

I held my breath as he pushed his way through the crowd, his formidable frame even larger than I remembered. Broader. Stronger. I took a breath to steady myself for the danger to come—for him to try to finish what he'd started before I fled Daglaar.

Hemming gave Tycho a challenging look, then whispered something that made him stand down. Tycho said nothing as he took a step back, relinquishing his position as well as his weapon to Hemming. But his silence belied his rage. Tycho wanted another shot at me too, but like last time, it had been stolen by the male standing across from me.

My childhood protector.

My best friend.

And the one who'd tried to kill me.

3

ARIEL

I thought I'd adequately prepared myself to see Hemming again—the one I'd idolized as a child. The one who'd betrayed me when I needed him most. I'd had just over four years to do it; that should have been enough. But standing there, looking at him, I knew it hadn't.

I couldn't move. Couldn't speak. It was as if the night I'd fled Daglaar was occurring all over again. The hatred in his grey eyes. The tension in his square jaw. The aggressive way he'd pushed his way to the head of the pack to get to me. My childish hope that maybe that night had somehow been a misunderstanding died the moment I started reliving the attack in my mind, my body frozen by fear and disbelief, and I wondered how I'd ever been so wrong about him.

Moonlight glinted off the blade pressed to my throat, and all I could do was stare at the ice-blue reflection. It kept my mind from breaking. The reality of the situation was too much for it to bear.

Hemming leaned in closer, and I dared a glance at his eyes, hoping to see some sign of the boy I knew in them. All I found was a cold grey stare. I swallowed hard as the sharp edge of his dagger bit into my skin, the cheers of Tycho and the others surrounding us urging him on. But he was in no hurry to end me. For reasons I couldn't fathom, he took his time, the pressure of his blade slow and steady.

"Why?" I asked. The word squeaked past my lips, barely audible.

I never did get an answer.

Instead, the roar of my father's anger echoed through the forest. His soldiers dragged Hemming off to his fate—a grim one, I was certain—while Father tucked me into his side and rushed us out of the woods and, eventually, out of Daglaar to the Midlands.

"Have you forgotten how this works?" Hemming asked, staring at me as though I'd lost my mind. The harsh cut of his features snapped me back to the present.

"Of course not," I replied, anger in my tone. I would need that anger if I was to defeat him. That and the help of the gods. "Where is my father?"

"Not here," he said, surveying the room.

Without warning, Hemming lunged with lightning speed. I parried his strike and stepped aside to let his momentum carry him past me, followed by a blow from my staff to his back. When he turned to face me, his eyes were narrowed and ferocious.

"Trying to finish what you started?" I asked quietly enough for only him to hear.

He said nothing in response; he just raised his weapon.

Again, Hemming shot toward me, and I slipped right to avoid having half my face removed. He followed up with two more passes, forcing me back toward the crowd. I sidestepped him, following through with a blow to his head. The crack of my staff against his jaw set him off balance, and I caught him under the chin with an upswing, knocking him backward. The inside of his mouth bled, and he spat red at the ground, anger flaring in his eyes.

We exchanged blows for what seemed like forever, until we were both tired and panting like dogs. He shoved me back when our weapons locked once again, and I tucked into a roll to keep from cracking my head on the stone floor.

"Why did you return?" he asked before advancing again.

"My reasons are my own," I replied. His sword sliced past my head again. I smiled when I ducked and slammed the end of my staff into his gut in response. "As were yours the last time I saw you." He cursed under his breath and began circling me. "Do you think you have the balls to actually do it this time? Or will you hesitate again and get caught?"

A low growl escaped him and he charged, his weapon lowered. I launched into the sky, but it was too late. He jumped and caught my legs before I could fly over him. We crashed to the ground with such force that it knocked my staff from my hand, and my head ricocheted off the stone. For a moment, I saw two Hemmings hovering over me, blades in their hands. But I only felt the tip of one pressed to the scales on my throat.

"Your blade won't pierce them," I said, pushing up into the weight of his sword.

Something flashed in Hemming's eyes as he stared at me —at the burgundy stone resting in the notch of my neck. The sharp tip of his sword hooked the cord of the necklace, and he lifted it gently as if he were inspecting it. The present he'd given me for my birthday years before.

"Enough!" My father's deep voice bellowed from deep in the room.

"You shouldn't have come back," Hemming said, his voice low and threatening and solely for me.

"I said *ENOUGH*!" My father's order echoed off the walls, forcing everyone back a step away from the arena.

With a flick of his wrist, Hemming sliced the cord, then withdrew his weapon and walked through the crowd toward the door. It slammed behind him, punctuating his exit.

"*Ariel...*" Father said. He stared at me, sprawled out on the dirt floor of the training room, shock in both his voice and his expression. But it was present for only a second before a scowl settled on his face and the brusque tone he used with his soldiers returned.

"Baba—"

"Get up." I did as he asked without question. I quickly tucked my broken necklace away as I picked up my weapon. It was only then that I saw Father's most trusted lieutenants behind him, a wall of dark olive-skinned warriors I'd known since I was a child. The mixed expressions on their faces were more than I could bear. "Let's go," Father muttered under his breath, leading the way through the mob that parted to let us by. I ignored their hateful stares as I passed. The second we were outside, Father ordered me to go to the house and wait for him there. That I would explain myself in a minute, but first, he had something he must do.

Full of emotions I couldn't name—couldn't process—I walked away, too weary to fly any more than I had to. Just as I reached the base of the mountain, I looked back to see my father talking to someone in the distance. His sizable frame blocked the other male from view until he turned in my direction and pointed, his face red with anger.

Hemming stood beyond him, still staring at me with cold rage in his eyes.

And murder in his heart.

HEMMING

She's back...

I watched as Kade disappeared into the sky, headed for his home—his daughter—but not until he'd warned me to stay away. Threatened that I would not fare as well as I had last time if I so much as breathed the same air as Ariel while she was in Daglaar. That my strength as a soldier and rank in his legion would be of no consequence, affirming what I'd long known: I was disposable.

The bastard half-blooded sons of the Nychterídes always were.

Anger and frustration flowed through me as I stormed off to my stone cabin. I slammed the door so hard the sole window in the building rattled. For minutes, I stood there, trying to calm my breathing. Apparently, the window wasn't the only thing that had been rattled. Ariel's surprise appearance had my mind going a thousand directions at once. Emotions I'd long since stored away sprang to the surface with a fervor I resented, and I collapsed onto my bed, arm slung across my eyes, an attempt to block the image of her lying below me in the training room from my mind. Silence permeated my home, and I'd never been happier to live alone.

I'd been on my own since I'd been ripped from my Nychteríde mother's arms. As soon as I was weaned, I'd been taken to the camp to be raised a warrior. She was branded an outcast and left to fend for herself in a village far away; I never saw her again. My Neráida father—whose heritage gave me the pointed ears that branded me a half-blood—was unknown. I'd never met him, but I hoped to one day.

I wanted to carve his heart from his chest while it still beat.

With a sharp exhale, I flipped onto my stomach and buried my face in the bed. My father was yet another thing I didn't want to think about. But the second I forced his blank face from my thoughts, Ariel was there again, a barrage of memories slamming into me all at once. No matter how hard I tried, I could not escape them. She was the thorn in my side I couldn't remove. We had unfinished business, and it festered like a wound that would never heal until I dealt with her.

5

ARIEL

My room was exactly as I'd left it, though cleaner. Given the way Baba and I had dashed out of there the night we fled Daglaar, I knew he'd tidied it since then. The handstitched quilt of vibrant red and burgundy was neatly draped across my bed instead of strewn across the floor. My dresser was tucked perfectly under the window, no drawers ripped from it or hanging open. The bloodstains on the wood floor were no longer visible, the sheepskin rug that had lain previously at the foot of my bed now placed over them. And the tapestry of my family's story once again hung above my bed. I'd refused to take it with me when I left.

Taking it, above all things, would have spoken to the permanence of my arrangement far too much for my liking.

As a child, I would make my father tell me the tale of that tapestry every night until my eyelids grew heavy and sleep took me. There was such comfort in knowing where I came from. Both my mother's and father's sides.

23

I flopped down onto the bed and stared up at it as dusk settled in around the mountain. Brightly colored silks wove together to create an image so intricate that I still couldn't understand how it had been created. It was if the gods themselves had given it to us: a gift. A reminder. The image of three women falling from the sky, arms outstretched as if they were about to take flight, stared back at me as my mind stirred.

The tapestry told the story of how the three tribes of Archigi came to be. The sun at the top represented the gods. They'd called forth three of our female ancestors to join them, but to join them meant to serve them in every way—to be their slaves. The women banded together and refused when sex was demanded of them. For this, they were cast out of the skies. But as they fell, one of the gods took pity on them and granted them wings. Instead of crashing to the earth below, they soared down, their newly acquired appendages carrying them to safety.

Along their descent, they were separated, each landing on a different part of the continent, creating the three countries that existed now: Daglaar, the mountainous region of the west; Anemosia, the rocky shores of the east; and Mesigi, the vast, lush lands between. For centuries, there was peace, until one day that god who had taken pity on them returned. He went to each of those women and demanded an offering for having saved them—an offering in the form of a child.

The female from Mesigi, terrified of incurring his wrath, gave him what he asked, handing over her only son. The one from Anemosia had no child to give, but instead gave herself to spare a plague on her people. The female of Daglaar, too strong and proud to comply, was cursed. Both she and the people of her lands became the Nychterídes—Bats of Stone —*gargoyles,* if you dared to insult one. The one from the east, regardless of her sacrifice, was cursed as well, her

24

people becoming Minyades—Dragons of Fire—*drakos*. And the female from Mesigi, who gave her only son, was blessed by the gods, her people transformed into Neráides—Favored Ones—*fae*, as they later became known, long after they distanced themselves from their language, their roots, and anything that reminded them of who they had been before the magic was bestowed upon them. When they began to refer to their country as the Midlands instead of Mesigi. That magic ran deep and transformed their land into something to envy—something to covet.

The hatred amongst the three countries ran deep.

The Great War had happened long before I was born—long before Kade took charge of the Nychterídes army—but the image of it in that tapestry was so vivid and real that some nights, as a child, I wondered if blood might drip onto my bed while I slept. If I might wake to bodies strewn about my room.

I closed my eyes and rolled to my side, suddenly tired from my journey. My exhaustion most certainly had nothing to do with my botched fight with Hemming or the fact that nothing between us had changed in four years. It was just plain old weariness from my travels, I told myself over and over until the lie began to ring true.

Almost.

A knock on the door pulled me from my thoughts, and I sat up just as my father walked in.

"Ariel…what are you doing here?" he asked, doing his best to remain calm when it was clear from the set of his shoulders and steel in his tone that he wasn't. "Kaplyn was supposed to keep you away."

I looked at him curiously. "You told me to come." I fished the letter out of my pocket. "You sent me this."

His brow creased as he took the paper from me and opened it. "This is my writing, but I did not write this."

Angry eyes soon met mine. "Tell me everything about your escape. Leave nothing out."

I did as he asked. I swore he didn't breathe while I told him of the dark raven creature. By the time I was finished, he looked like he wanted to tear my room apart. "This is fae magic," he growled, crumpling the letter in his hand. "Someone sent you this to draw you out. To try to kill you—"

"We can't know that—"

"It was a well-laid plan. Keep my letters from arriving until you were desperate enough to act when you finally received this one."

I wanted to argue but couldn't. There was too much logic to be found in his words.

"And accusing Kaplyn of being untrustworthy kept you from going to him about this note."

"Yeah…" I muttered under my breath. "So what do we do now? Surely I've caused trouble with Kaplyn, leaving the way I did."

He turned his sharp gaze to me. "I will get word to him. He needs to know what is going on in his lands."

With nothing helpful to add, I merely nodded in agreement.

After a few deep breaths, the tension in his shoulders slowly disappeared, and he walked over to my bed. He motioned for me to stand and I did as he asked, bracing myself as he reached for my shoulders. He held me at arm's length so he could take me in. It had been an eternity since he'd last seen me—much had changed in that time.

"You look good, Ariel," he said, gripping my arms. "Strong."

"We trained every day, just like you wanted," I said. "You should have seen me a year ago when I turned eighteen and my scales emerged. I shot fire across the fighting circle at

Kaplyn," I said, giggling at the memory. "He barely dodged it in time."

Father choked on a laugh, and I looked up to find him shaking his head at me, a tiny smile on his scarred face. "My *mikros drakos*…so full of fire."

I smiled in return. "That I am."

"Tell me, how did the fae lord take that turn of events?"

"Once his shock wore off—and he made sure all his parts were intact—he laughed so hard he fell to the ground. Tears rolled down his face until Delphyne came out to see what all the commotion was about. One look at the two of us and she stormed back into the mansion, mumbling about our childish behavior." I smiled at the memory. "I think she was just angry that she had to replace his scorched fighting tunic—it was some of her best work."

"Kaplyn has always had a kind way about him," my father said under his breath.

"He does, and I've come to enjoy my time in the Midlands, but…"

Sharp brown eyes met mine. "But what?"

"I miss you."

"Ariel…" My name was a warning.

"Maybe I could stay for a bit since I'm here? See if things are better now?"

"Did they seem better when Hemming had his sword at your throat?" he asked, his tone full of anger. "Has today not reminded you of why we escaped in the middle of the night and flew to Kaplyn's manor in the first place?"

"Of course, but things are different—"

"Different how?" he asked, cutting me off.

"I'm older. Smarter. Stronger—"

"And so are those that would see you harmed."

"My fire-breathing and Minyade scales are powerful weapons against the Nychterídes."

"And their resentment and anger toward you are just as powerful, Ariel."

I let out a sigh and plopped down on the edge of the bed.

Father sat down next to me and placed his hand upon mine. "I'm sorry I could not come to see you." His hand tightened around mine. "It was not easy bringing you to Daglaar as a child, Ariel. Many questioned my judgment—my loyalty—at first. It took years to make them see that you were an asset to our army, or would be once you came of age. When you left..." He cut himself off for a beat, his brow furrowed with worry. "When you left, it looked like you had turned your back on your people—like you were a traitor to the Nychterídes."

"But I *am* Nychteríde—"

"Not enough," he said sadly. "Not enough for them."

I nodded, unable to meet his eyes. Whatever blood we shared was irrelevant in the eyes of others because of my paler skin, lighter eyes, and wings that were not the shade of the Nychterídes. Who my father was, how hard I trained, or how many enemies I could one day slay on a battlefield would never matter.

I was not one of them.

"Things have been...complicated since you left."

"I thought they were supposed to get better."

"They have, in some ways. Less so in others."

I turned and placed my other hand on top of his. "Tell me."

He took a deep breath. "There has been word about the Minyades...they are planning something."

"They're always planning," I countered. "That's what you've always taught me. That the Nychterídes will never be safe until they are all dead."

His shoulders slumped slightly as he looked at my burgundy wings—a clear sign of my Minyade heritage. "Not all of them, Ariel," he replied, pushing my wavy brown hair back from my face. "But you being here—it will not help the tensions in the camp. I did all I could to address the rumors about your disappearance, but there is only so much I can do to truly change their minds. If I deny it too vehemently, it does not reflect well on me. You know there is a difficult balance to strike when in power. If I let you stay, it will be like asking them to accept their enemy, and that is something they will not do. I know that now. I was a fool to have ever believed otherwise."

I leaned away from him. "Are you ashamed of me, Baba?"

"No! Never—"

"Did you send me away because I remind you of a mistake you made?"

He stared at me as though I'd slapped him. "It broke my heart to take you away from Daglaar, Ariel. Away from me. It hurt to imagine you happy with Kaplyn and his people—to think he could keep you safer than I could—but at the time, it was the truth. Now I am not so certain…"

"I love Kaplyn," I said, wrapping my hands around his wrists, "but he is not you, Baba. He never will be."

My father nodded, a sheen forming in his eyes. He quickly got up and headed for the door. "I will make contact with Kaplyn and demand a meeting. Until we know how to deal with this matter, you will not be returning there."

"So I can stay for now?"

"I see no other way," he said, frustration in his voice.

I stood and began taking off my weapons, ready to make myself at home for however long I could. I reached into my pocket and pulled out the blessing stone, placing it on the table next to my bed.

My father's eyes went wide. "What is that?" he asked, rushing over.

29

"Delphyne gave it to me before I left. She caught me packing—I lied about why I was leaving, of course. She gave me the stone and said it would guide me to you safely."

"Don't let anyone here ever see it, do you understand?" he asked, panic in his tone.

"It's just—"

"You know how the Nychterídes distrust the magic of the fae! How it reminds them of the past and the hardships we've endured every day since the gods turned their backs on us!"

"All right," I said, stuffing it back inside my leather halter. "I'm sorry."

"If you are seen with that, Ariel, the suspicions about you being a traitor will be confirmed. You will be branded a spy and executed on sight. It will be outside my power to stop it because that is the law."

I swallowed hard and fastened the button of my pocket. "Do they know where I've been all this time, Baba?"

"I do not know," he said, pulling himself up to his full height. He looked every bit the general he was in that moment; every inch the being the others feared. "But that is not information they need."

I flopped down flat on the bed and stared up at the tapestry, focusing on a small depiction of a couple inter- twined at the bottom—the only pleasant image it boasted.

"My return has made a mess of things, hasn't it?"

His silence spoke volumes.

"What's done is done, Ariel. I will not throw you out of Daglaar tonight, no matter the repercussions. I want to enjoy whatever time I get to spend with you before you return to the Midlands." He pulled me up and hugged me. His hand smoothed my long, wild hair, and it reminded me of how he'd comforted me when I'd woken at all hours of the night as a child, calling for my mother. "But you cannot attend the solstice celebration tonight—it won't be safe."

I opened my mouth to argue, then thought better of it. I focused on a different issue instead. "What about Hemming, Baba?" I asked, my cheek pressed to his chest.

A rumble echoed through his stony chest beneath the leather. "He will not be a problem."

6

ARIEL

I remained in the house per my father's order, though the sound of the drums echoing up the mountainside called to a part of me I couldn't describe. They beckoned me to come down. The solstice celebration had officially begun.

It had always been my favorite night of the year as a child; it was the most joyous event for the Nychterídes. I lasted three songs before I found myself disobeying my father's order and skulking through camp toward the women rushing about, platters of food in hand. I stole one off a table and carried it around as though I were helping, when really all it did was serve as a camouflage of sorts—a poor one, but one nonetheless.

Most of the women who had come from the nearby villages were wives of various warriors. They were civil enough to my face when they realized who I was, but I heard their whispers when they thought I was out of earshot. Rumors of why I'd really left were rampant and laced with

33

salacious theories. One woman went so far as to call me a whore to the fae lords, until I whipped out my staff and placed the end of it under her chin. She seemed disinclined to speak negatively about me after that. Nychteríde women understood the threat of violence better than most. They knew when to be silent.

Generations of being blamed for the gods' curse drove that point home.

The warriors started to arrive, the call of the drums impossible for even them to deny. I didn't want to get caught so early on, so I found the woman in charge and offered to retrieve another barrel of wine from the storage cellar carved deep into the side of the mountain around the far side of the settlement. She merely nodded, a silent dismissal. I thought she and the others were just happy to be rid of me.

The area leading to the cellar was hilly, with rocky outcroppings that grew taller the closer I got. I remembered playing on them as a kid, learning to trust my wings as I'd jump off and glide back to the ground. You could see the ocean in the distance if the sky was clear—I used to stare at it for hours growing up. Hemming and I both did.

The thought of him soured the moment, and I moved along.

The cellar door was fortified to keep animals out, but never locked. I was confused when I found chains hanging from the handle. "What is this?" I said to myself. I let out a frustrated breath, then turned to go back and get the key to unlock it. It would have been nice if the woman had mentioned I'd need one. I couldn't help but wonder if that had been intentional.

I turned to walk away from the cellar through the tunnel formed by a crevice in the mountain and found Tycho standing there leering at me, his friends behind him. "Forget something?" he asked, dangling a ring of keys from his finger.

"Apparently, but since you have those, I'll leave you the honor of fetching the wine for the celebration."

I started to walk past him, but he threw an arm out to the rock, blocking the way. "That's women's work," he said. His eyes drifted down my body, then back up again. They were filled with lust and hatred—a deadly combination.

"I'm a warrior, not a woman. And I am your general's daughter. You would be wise to remember that, Tycho."

He leaned in toward me. "And you would be wise to remember that your father is not here."

I clasped my hands behind my back and attempted to look bored, a charade to gain me access to the only blade I had— the tiny knife tucked into the back of my pants. "What do you want, Tycho? Do you want to fight me? Angry that Hemming stole your chance yet again?" His eyes narrowed and his features tightened. "I don't fear you, no matter how much bigger or stronger you've gotten."

He pressed closer, and I wrapped my hand around the hilt of the knife, ready to strike. The blade was made of obsidian —the only material that could penetrate the stony skin of the Nychterídes.

"I don't want to fight you, Ariel," he said, his lips at my ear. "There are so many more fun things I could do to you instead…"

"You sound a little too confident in your skills," I replied.

"I've had a lot of practice in the past four years."

"I'm sure you have. The women in the villages are not at all particular, nor are they able to defend themselves against unwanted advances. But I am."

"Maybe that's what I want," he whispered. "To have to work for it." His breath on my face made me cringe, the reek of ale filling the air between us.

I trailed my free hand lightly down his bare arm toward the hand that held the keys. His eyes widened at my touch, his breath catching in his throat. "Then you shall have it," I said, leaning into him. I brushed my chest against his and pulled the knife free behind me.

In one graceful motion, I snatched the keys, pushed him away, and swiped the blade across his chest. With a boot to the stomach, I drove him into his friends, the group stumbling back a step. I rushed to the door and unlocked it. In a flash, I was inside. It took a second to find something to jam the handle, but once I lodged a broom through the mechanism, I knew I was safe—at least for the time being.

Tycho raged outside, pounding on the door, screaming about how I was going to die when he saw me again. They weren't entirely empty threats; I wasn't dumb enough to think that. But I knew the celebration was far too public for him to try anything. If I could wait Tycho out, knowing someone would come for the wine eventually, I would be fine.

With the noise he was making in the background, I walked through the vast room, looking for something to eat while I waited. I found a stash of salted meat and pulled out three pieces. The strong, smoky scent soon filled the space as I found a place to sit. The barrel of wine I'd come to retrieve made the perfect seat.

As I moved to sit down, I noticed something small and flat and covered in dust on the barrel. I picked it up and wiped it on my pants. Even in the dim light of the cellar, it sparkled as if it were in full sun. That was the beauty of an Azure of the Sea stone. It shone like a bright blue star no matter what.

I flipped the prize jewel of the Nychterídes over in my hand, wondering why it was tucked away in the cellar. It was too precious for that. It deserved to be worn and adored, and I knew the perfect person for that job. A slight little Neráida girl with equally blue eyes and a heart of gold. It would make the perfect "I'm sorry" gift for Sophitiya when I returned to Kaplyn's manor.

I'd left without saying goodbye—a nearly unforgivable offense to a seven-year-old.

I hoped the stone would help make amends.

It was dark in the cellar, with only the cracks in the door to let light in. I managed to find a lamp in the crowded space and breathed a spark into it. Fire erupted within, illuminating the room. It was harsh at first, so I dimmed it until it was tolerable, then held the stone up to it, smiling at its beauty. It was the exact color of Sophitiya's eyes. I could practically hear her giggle with delight, the way she would when I gave it to her. Then I tucked it away in my pocket for safekeeping.

Mice skittered about as I made my way back to the barrel, but the sound of their feet on the stone was not the only noise in the cellar. Something else moved behind me. Something that made far too much sound to be a rodent of any size.

Something with boots and clothing—and twitching wings.

"Hello?" I called, lifting the lamp in search of whatever lurked in the darkness. In the very back of the room, I saw a metal door I couldn't remember ever having seen before, tucked between two storage shelves. I shone the light toward it, and the scuffing of feet on rock echoed off the walls. "Who's there?"

At the top of the door was a narrow slat barely large enough to fit my hand through. I walked over to it and held up the lamp to look inside. When I laid eyes on what that door kept hidden, my heart fell to my stomach.

Three males, skin fairer than mine, sat cowering from the light. Each one had brightly colored wings caked in dirt and dust. *Prisoners*, I thought. *Minyade* prisoners.

"Dear gods…"

"Food," one of them whispered, his voice so hoarse that it cracked when he spoke. I raced over to the bag of meat and grabbed a handful of pieces. There was no water, but there was wine, so it would have to suffice. I threw the food through the tiny opening, then tried to figure out how to get the wine to them. As I ran toward the barrels, the keys that hung from my hip jingled.

My gaze slowly drifted back to the door and its tiny lock near the latch.

"Who are you?" one of them asked, his eyes flashing in the opening of the door.

"I think the better question is, who are *you*?" I replied, suspicion setting in. "And why are you here, in Daglaar?"

I looked up to find eyes as blue as the sky staring through the hole in the door. The second he saw my wings—my coloring—those bright eyes widened. "*You*...you are one of us..."

"My mother was Minyade, but I was raised here, with my Nychteríde family."

"Help us," another weak voice begged.

"I'm trying to get you wine to drink, but it won't fit through this hole, and I can't open the door." I carefully tucked the keys into the back of my pants, not wanting my lie to be so plain.

It was only then that something dawned on me—something dark and terrifying and destined to haunt my dreams—a question I feared the answer to, but needed to know all the same. "Who brought you here?" I asked, meeting those blue eyes again.

"A soldier. I do not know his name."

"Where did he find you?"

"They caught us when we breached the border."

"You attacked the Nychterídes?" I asked, disbelief in my tone. He shook his head. "Then why? Why did you come?"

38

A voice from deep in the cell rang out, its timber far deeper and stronger than the other two. "We came for the child…"

My body went numb in an instant. "A child? What child?"

The shuffling of feet sounded behind the door and the blue eyes disappeared, replaced by yellow-green ones. Shrewd eyes. Sharp eyes. The eyes of a seasoned warrior.

"A child who is no longer a child. One of great importance to our kind." Those eyes narrowed. "One with wings the color of dried blood…"

His words seeped into my mind, slowly taking hold. "*Me*…you came for me…"

"You must free us," he said, thrusting his skinny arm through the opening, his filthy hand reaching for me. "You must free us now!"

I backed away from the metal barrier between us. "I…I can't…"

Pounding on the cellar door silenced us both.

"Who is it?" I asked, looking over my shoulder into the darkness. When nobody responded, I told the prisoners to be quiet, then walked over to the broomstick I'd wedged into the door handle. "If you don't tell me who you are, this door will remain locked."

"You will open it, or I will tear it off," Hemming replied, his irritation plain.

I looked back at the door to the cell that housed the Minyades—my mother's people. I wondered if they were even strong enough to fly if I did free them. I knew they wouldn't make it past Hemming unless I distracted him. My mind swam with possibilities, none of which seemed feasible given the circumstances. I needed more time. I needed more information.

And I needed to get rid of Hemming.

"You tear that door off and you'll be greeted by a wall of fire. Better make sure to keep your mouth closed—"

He pounded again. "Ariel!"

I ran back to the prison cell. "Listen, I don't understand what's going on or why you've been locked away down here, but I'm going to find out. I'll try to come back tonight. I promise."

Green eyes stepped up to the door. "Remember why we came," he said, his words a warning, "and remember who you are."

The pounding turned into the sound of wood groaning as Hemming started to do as he'd promised: rip the door from its hinges.

"For the love of the gods…" I held my knife in my hand and took a deep breath before I pulled the broomstick from the handle and opened the door. "Move!" I held the blade in front of him to make sure he saw that it was obsidian. He instantly obeyed my command and stepped back a pace.

"Why are you barricaded in here?" he asked, his expression as stony as his flesh.

"My father will come looking for me if I don't return soon." A blatant lie, given that my father thought I was at home. But Hemming didn't know that, and it sold the story well.

"That's not what I asked you." He folded his arms across his chest and stared at me, silently demanding an answer.

"I came to get wine. Tycho followed me to get *something else*, so I got waylaid."

His harsh expression tightened, his brows knit together in irritation. "Is that why he was bleeding and cursing the blood moon when he returned to the celebration?"

I smiled. "He was warned, as you will now be: touch me and I will bury this blade in your side."

"You shouldn't be here," was his only response. Those

words from his mouth still felt like a gut punch, and I hated myself for letting them get to me.

"I'm starting to come to that conclusion," I said under my breath. He stared at me, the pale light seeping through the clouds highlighting his hard features. He was so much bigger than when I'd left. Broader. Taller. More handsome, which seemed nearly impossible. But there was an anger in his eyes that hadn't been there when we were younger. Anger and resentment. "Follow me back to the party and I'll gut you, got it?" I said, keeping my shoulders squared as I circled him. Then I backed away, unwilling to take my eyes off him, and headed toward the celebration.

"Tycho will kill you, Ariel."

"He'll try," I countered. "Just like you did."

I sprinted just far enough to clear the rocks, then took to the air, knowing Hemming couldn't catch me there. I'd always been the faster flier. And in that moment, I couldn't have been more thankful for that edge.

7

ARIEL

Hemming returned to the party with a barrel of wine, and I smiled with satisfaction from deep in the shadows. He dropped it next to the table of food, glared at me, then disappeared into the woods. One less angry warrior for me to worry about. I was too preoccupied with the three Minyades I'd found in the cellar to focus on who might try to kill me next.

The clearing was packed with father's soldiers, both young and old, and their families. The unwed women from the neighboring villages were allowed to attend, though most refused. It wasn't a place for anyone wishing for her virtue to remain intact.

With a mug of wine in hand, I moved through the group in search of my father. Solstice or not, he and I had some things to discuss; things he certainly wouldn't be in the mood for, but I wouldn't take no for an answer. I had wine in my veins and burning questions about Minyade prisoners in my head.

I saw his most trusted lieutenants clustered together near the food and made my way over. Erwan and Adrik were laughing at one another—as they often did—their dark, unbound hair blowing gently in the wind. Erwan was my father's second in command and Adrik his third. They'd always been my favorites growing up. They both grinned when they saw me approach.

"I'm sorry to interrupt," I said, "but have you seen my father?"

"Not sure where the old goat's wandered off to," Erwan said with a laugh.

"It's good to see you too, Ariel," Adrik said, wrapping his arm around my shoulder.

I shook my head, embarrassed by my behavior. "It's always nice to see you, Adrik."

"When did you get here?" Kolm asked as he approached with two cups full of wine. He drained the contents of one, his eyes never leaving mine.

"Asks Kade's favorite spy," Erwan scoffed. "Remind me: how did you ever get that title, anyway?"

Kolm merely shrugged and awaited my answer.

"I got here this morning. It's a long story…"

"She arrived to much fanfare," Adrik added. "We found her in the training area with a blade to her throat. Seems she's gotten lazy in her time away."

"Who did you fight?" Omar asked, walking up to the group. I nearly jumped at his arrival. He was shrewd, deadly, and adept at torture techniques that could turn the stomach of even the most hardened Nychterídes. He did the things that must not be traced back to my father. I had always been scared of him as a child. It was hard not to retreat a step under the weight of his gaze.

"Hemming," I replied. For a moment, nobody spoke.

"Did you at least knock the piss out of him before he got you?" Caelum asked, peeling an apple.

"Not like I'd hoped to."

He smiled at me, the puckered scar slicing through his mouth stretching. "Missed opportunity if you ask me."

I took a sip of wine, wanting the Hemming talk to come to an end. "Hey, Omar. Have you seen my father?"

He jerked his head toward the training building on the far side of the clearing, then turned to Kolm and started talking.

"Thanks," I replied. "I'll see you guys later."

The deep sound of the drums got lighter with every step I took toward my father. I wondered why he was hiding away during the greatest celebration the Nychterídes boasted.

As I approached, he stepped outside with Baran at his side. "Baba!" I shouted, running toward him. Baran gave me his usual disapproving look, then walked away.

My father looked murderous. "What are you doing here? Why aren't you at the house?"

"I just wanted a drink," I lied for the second time that night. Given the furrow of his brow, he, unlike Hemming, saw right through it.

"You need to go," he said, ushering me away from the party.

"What were you talking with Baran about?" I asked, thinking of how concerned he had looked.

"Baran had news for me," he said, hand on my elbow to steer me. "It appears Kaplyn has agreed to meet us, but only in the Black Forest. We leave at first light tomorrow."

The Black Forest… I cringed at the thought. Some of the oldest, nastiest creatures in the Midlands roamed there—things that I did not wish my father to meet. He read the concern on my face and hugged me lightly. "It will be fine, Ariel. Adrik will accompany you to Kaplyn's manor, where

Shayfer will await your arrival. You are to stay under strict watch until Kaplyn returns, is that clear?"

"Yes, Baba."

He stopped just shy of the mountain and looked down at me. "Good. Now, let us not think about tomorrow. Tonight, let me enjoy the fact that you are here and safe." I smiled up at him, but he could clearly see it was only for show. "What's bothering you, Ariel? Is this about the celebration? We already spoke about why—"

"I need to ask you something," I said, interrupting him.

Concern etched his brow yet again. "What?"

"I…I went to the storage room tonight to get more wine, and—"

His mouth pressed to a thin line. "And *what*?"

"Baba, why is there a prison cell in there? I don't remember seeing it before."

"We did not need one before you left." His answer was curt and cold, and given his expression, all the explanation he planned on giving.

I ignored his hint and pressed further. "Why do we have prisoners at all?" The Nychterídes, as a rule, didn't keep prisoners. We interrogated them and dispatched them when they were no longer of use. That was our way, which begged the question: why change those methods so suddenly, and why for those particular prisoners?

"Because we had intruders."

"But you kill those—"

"We kill *Neráida* intruders. These, as I'm sure you already know, are not Neráida."

"Baba, they're half dead. How could you treat them this way? At least in killing them, you show them respect."

"Because they have information I want. Until they give it to me, they will live in that hell."

"Information about what?" I asked.

46

His body went still as stone. "I cannot discuss this with you, Ariel, but I need you to trust me. Whatever you think is going on—whatever they may or may not have told you—they cannot be trusted. You need to stay far away from them, understand?"

"But Baba—"

"No, Ariel!" His raised voice made me wince. He never yelled at me. Never. Seeing me shy away from him yanked him from his anger, and he reached out slowly to pull me to him. "I'm sorry. I should not have shouted. Forgive me."

"Always."

"I need you to trust me—trust that I cannot tell you. Not until I know more, all right?"

"All right."

"That would be the greatest solstice present you could ever give me."

I hugged him tighter. "But they said they were looking for a child with blood-red wings who was no longer a child, Baba."

"And I said they cannot be trusted, Ariel. Please, please remember that."

I considered his words—considered the situation as a whole. My father had never imprisoned anyone before. He was brutal, but fair and honorable, and had always done right by me. If he said that his methods were necessary, then I would believe him. Because he was my father and I loved him.

Because he would never lie to me.

I watched him retreat toward the celebration as the drums echoed off the slopes of the mountain and shook the earth beneath my feet. Alone, away from everyone, I slowly began to sway until that was no longer enough. I had to move—to let the driving beat carry me through the shadows and across the camp, body gyrating as though there were no other choice. As though that were what it had been built to do.

I could feel eyes on me as I did, a stare filled with hatred and jealousy and lust. But all I cared about was the wine in my hand and the beat of the drums thrumming through my body. I was at home for solstice for the first time in four years. Home with my father. And even if I had to leave the next morning, that reality could not taint the feeling of rightness coursing through me as I danced my way closer to the mountain.

Closer to my home.

HEMMING

S he watched her father return to the celebration with a bright smile for him before he walked away, leaving her alone in the darkness. But that smile never reached her eyes. She was haunted by something—probably what had happened with Tycho. And with me. *Good*, I thought. It's about time.

Her father caught my eye across the clearing and glared daggers at me. I drank my wine and headed back toward the tree line. My presence wasn't welcome—he viewed me as a threat. But I wondered if he saw all the others, their combined malice looking for a chance to strike her down. There was no lack of it now. *The Minyade whore...the Neráida spy...* She had many names when the general wasn't around to hear them. Names they wouldn't dare say in his presence. But those that shared those sentiments grew bolder every minute she remained. If she didn't leave, she would die. It was only a matter of time. Kade's anger toward me blinded him to the

49

reality that I was not the greatest threat to her. If he didn't see it soon, his beloved Ariel would be dead by sunrise.

From the shadows, I watched her, my eyes raking over her every curve—following her every move—as she danced alone by the mountain. She was a fool to behave this way, to not lock herself away in her house and await her father's return. She didn't realize what the others in the camp said about her. How they planned to ruin her as soon as they had a chance.

I held my post until the drumming ceased and her body stilled. Standing there, highlighted in the moonlight's blue glow, she looked over her shoulder, the red highlights in her hair like an icy fire burning down her back. She pinned her pale green eyes on the trees until they found me.

I stepped forward into that eerie blue glow, and for at least five breaths, the two of us just stood and stared at each other. I wondered if this would be the moment she chose to confront me about what I'd done—how I'd driven her from Daglaar—if she'd had enough wine for the loathing I'd seen in her eyes to spill over, letting her true nature through. To turn her into the killer she truly was.

Ariel had always been two sides of a coin. With a flip, she could change.

Without warning, she turned and walked toward her father's home in the sky. She unfolded her blood-red wings and took flight, letting the wind carry her along the mountain wall until she disappeared from sight. She'd be safe for the night; safe for the time being. But tomorrow was a new day, and with it would come new threats.

And her father would not be there to save her.

9

ARIEL

The celebration was long over, but darkness still loomed when I stole away from the house into the sky. Before I could leave Daglaar for what would likely be the final time, I had one last thing to do; something I should have done before I left the first time.

I swooped down to the camp below, then darted between the cabins on silent feet until I stood below Hemming's window. He would still be sleeping, which I was counting on. His window never latched fully, so I levered it open as quietly as I could, then hauled myself through it.

He stirred when I landed in the modest open space, and I gripped the dagger in my hand tighter. If he woke, there was no question what he would do—how he would react. Not after all I'd seen since I returned.

I crept across the room and placed the parchment on the small table next to his bed. Atop it, I laid the necklace he'd given me years ago. The one I'd never removed since the day I received it.

I didn't need it anymore. It no longer symbolized what it once had.

As I left, I stopped to look at him. His face was always so peaceful when he slept. A stray lock of dark brown hair lay on his cheek, and I fought the urge to sweep it aside and kiss his forehead—to kiss him goodbye. But you don't kiss your enemies, and though my mind fought hard to refute it, that was what he'd become. My enemy.

I sneaked back to the window, crawling through it to land on the ground below without a sound. I surveyed the area to make sure I was still alone, then flew back up to my father's house and climbed into bed. I lay there for a while, my thoughts too loud for sleep to take hold. I thought about the Minyades in the cellar—about why they'd come. Then I remembered my father's warning that they could not be trusted. Though I may have loathed their treatment, I understood it, and I was unwilling to free them until I knew more about the truth behind their search for me. If my father couldn't—or wouldn't—tell me, then I'd have to find another way.

Someone needed to explain why the Minyades had come for me.

≈

FATHER ENTERED MY ROOM EARLY IN THE MORNING, LONG before the sun was up.

"It's time to go now." I sat up and rubbed my sleepy eyes. "Adrik will accompany you to Kaplyn's estate. You are to follow the stone's direction and not deviate from it, understand?"

"Yes, Baba—"

"Promise me, Ariel!" he said, gripping my shoulders hard. "Swear it on your mother's bones."

"I swear it. I swear it!"

A look of relief that only parents ever wore overtook his countenance. "Good. Now get up."

I groaned as I hauled myself out of bed. He grabbed my few belongings and stuffed them into my pack for me. Flashes of the night we fled Daglaar assaulted my mind, and I ran to him, throwing my arms around his massive frame. Even fully grown, I could not wrap my arms all the way around his broad shoulders.

He hesitated for a moment, then dropped my pack and hugged me back. "You will see me again, Ariel. You are blood of my blood. You saved me from a darkness that threatened to consume me. I could never truly let you go..."

"I love you," I whispered into his chest.

"I love you too, and I'm grateful for the little time we've had together. But we must go now." Every muscle in his body eased as he hugged me once more; then, without another word, he walked out of my room. The door clicked shut behind him, closing me in with my sadness and the knowledge that I would not see him for a long time—maybe ever again, despite what he'd said.

Because he'd said the same when he left me with Kaplyn.

I hurried around my room, collecting the remaining belongings strewn about. With a final look back, I said goodbye to my room one last time. My gaze drifted up to the tapestry hanging from the ceiling, and I walked over and cut it down. I rolled it up and stuffed it into my pack.

I couldn't bear the thought of leaving it behind again.

My father and Adrik waited for me outside, and together,

we wound our way through the woods separating the mountain from the border. We traveled in relative silence until we finally reached the point where our paths would diverge. With one last hug, my father strode south, headed to where his lieutenants waited in the distance. He looked over his shoulder only once and gave the slightest of nods—a goodbye, an apology, and an order all wrapped into one.

"It's going to be all right, Ariel," Adrik said, placing a gentle hand on my shoulder.

"I know…"

We stood and watched until my father disappeared into the trees. Once he did, Adrik and I continued our journey on foot. The forest was too densely packed to fly through easily; we were earthbound until we reached the border. Once safely across, we could take to the air.

The sun threatened to overthrow the moon as we ran toward the Midlands, the faint golden glow in the east guiding us.

"Kade said that you have something to help navigate the Midlands when we get there, but that I shouldn't ask too many questions about it—or see it."

I choked on a laugh. "I feel like you're begging to with a statement like that."

I glanced over at him, his warm smile looking back at me. "You know how I love a little mischief…"

I stopped and reached into my pocket. I pulled out the black stone that looked so innocuous—so powerless—but I knew it wasn't. I could feel its magic coursing through me, getting warmer and warmer by the second, until it was so hot that I nearly dropped it.

"Can I hold it?" he asked, reaching toward where it lay in my palm. It flared with a surge of heat. A message of sorts. A warning.

I looked up at Adrik with narrowed eyes as I tucked the

stone into my pack. "It's better if you don't. You know how the Nychterídes are about fae trinkets," I said, using my father's words as a joke and a shield. Something was wrong, but I couldn't tell what.

"Yeah," he said, his smile belying his hurt, "maybe it is."

I opened my mouth to apologize, but it was cut short by a spray of blood. It coated my face, and I scrubbed it off to find Adrik staring at me with wide, empty eyes. The blood-coated tip of an obsidian blade glistened at me as it poked through his chest.

When the blade was ripped free, Adrik's body fell to the ground, his dead eyes staring up at the one who'd taken his life. Tycho merely smiled at what he'd done. And what he was about to do.

I whipped my staff from my back, ready to wield it against him. Then the rest of his entourage emerged from the tops of the trees, dropping to the ground one by one, and my stomach sank. Disbelief and terror shot through me as I realized what was going on. We'd been ambushed. Adrik had died simply because he'd been with me.

Anger boiled in my veins, eclipsing my fear.

I scanned the woods to see what I was up against. I expected to face a handful of bitter warriors looking for a shot at revenge. What I was not prepared to find was a small army of variably ranked soldiers circling me with swords longer than I was tall, ready to behead me with a single blow. Skilled or not, I was in trouble, and I knew it.

"Going somewhere?" Tycho asked, his sneer as menacing as ever as he stood before me.

"This is treason, Tycho. Do you have any idea what happens to traitors?" I replied, ignoring his question.

"No. But I imagine you will sooner than later."

I looked at Adrik's cooling corpse, and rage burned

through my veins. "You're a *coward*," I seethed. "You have no honor."

"The only way you're leaving here is in pieces, you know," he said, my words having no effect on him at all.

"Tiny, mutilated pieces," another male added. He was behind me, and I didn't dare look back to see who it was. Tycho was leading this attack. He was the one to watch.

The one to kill first.

"You should have gone with your father," Tycho said, taking a step toward me, weapon drawn. "It's as though he left you behind for slaughter on purpose. Like he orchestrated this end..."

"He'll pluck your wings with his bare hands just for saying that."

"He's a fool where you're involved."

"That much is true," I agreed. "He'll have Omar start torturing until someone tells him who came after me."

"He'll never know what happened to you."

"Now who's the fool?" I asked, daring a step closer to the wall of male before me. "You killed Adrik. You've left a trail of blood. If I die, he won't rest until he knows every detail."

For the briefest moment, Tycho looked concerned, but then he regained his bravado. "That's if he returns from his trip..."

Ice slid down my back, his words undoing me. "He will return just fine."

"Perhaps. Or perhaps something awful will happen to him on his journey to the Black Forest. There are many traps for our kind when crossing the Midlands. One wrong move and your wings could be shredded to bits. It's a long fall from those heights. Long and deadly."

"He knows how to navigate the Midlands."

He leaned in closer. "Maybe it isn't the Midlands he

should fear. Maybe we aren't the only ones that disapprove of his adoration for you."

I couldn't breathe. "No one would dare," I said, my words barely an exhale. "Attempting to usurp him would be madness."

Tycho merely shrugged, toeing Adrik's body. "It takes a little madness to do the impossible."

Truer words had never been spoken. And as I gathered myself, prepared to fight for my freedom so I could save my father or die trying, I clung to Tycho's sentiment.

"Then my odds are looking pretty good at the moment."

Before he could blink, I swung my staff in an arc, burying it in the side of his face. He staggered back a step or two and raised his sword, but I was already slashing at him again, aiming for his arm. The staff crashed down with such force that it knocked his weapon from his hand. But I had no time to celebrate that small win.

The others were coming for me.

Though I was far smaller than they, I had speed and agility that they lacked. In a blur of motion, I wielded my staff against them, the hum it created as it whirled around me the background noise of our battle. It shuddered in my hands as it met its targets over and over again, but even with my speed, they were closing in on me too fast. Once they did, my weapon would be rendered useless. A hand-to-hand battle with a Nychteríde would be the death of me.

And a painful one at that, given the hatred they possessed.

Just before their circle entombed me, I planted my staff and used it to launch myself over their heads. With a tree at my back and all of them before me—at least the ones still standing—I had a fighting chance, for the time being. All I needed to do was get to the border. Once I could take to the sky, I would lose them. I had a blessing stone to guide me through the Midlands. They, however, did not. Navigating the wards there without one would be a death sentence for them.

If I was lucky, their hubris would lead them to follow me —and never return home.

Ten were still armed and approaching. I assessed the situation quickly and formed a plan. If I could cut a path through the middle, I could make a run for it. Our speed on land was comparable, but I wasn't wounded. With only a few pursuers, I had a chance at making it.

"You can't win," Tycho said, spitting a mouthful of blood at the ground, "and do you know why?"

"Why?" I asked, matching their approach with a sideward retreat.

"Because you are a woman. And they are only good for one thing."

My blood began to boil, a fire building within me at his insult. It spread through my body until it could no longer be contained. Flame the likes of which I had never seen erupted from my mouth and drove them back. None of them had ever actually faced the enemy before. The orange glow of fire danced in their widened eyes as they looked upon that which they'd been taught to hate.

I could feel my scales erupting from my body, unfurling like an impenetrable shield of armor along my skin. They glistened in the light of dawn, the golden shimmer distractingly beautiful. But it didn't distract them for long. They were soon upon me in force, slashing their swords at me to no avail. They were all but useless against me now.

With a dive, I tucked and rolled between them and took off at a sprint, not looking back to see how close they were. Because I wasn't invincible against them, and I knew it. Kade had taught me the weaknesses of my kind, just as he'd taught them. If they caught me and held me still, they could kill me with a blade under my arm—or another delicate area far less appealing. Those were a dragon's most vulnerable places, and I had no intention of exposing either to Tycho's army.

I hurtled through the trees, jumping over anything in my way. I was so close to freedom I could practically taste the sweet air of Kaplyn's country manor.

A low branch snagged my pack and yanked me to a halt. Panic shot through me—I wouldn't survive long without its contents, but I wouldn't survive long if I couldn't get free, either.

"Dammit!" I shouted, slicing myself free. I turned to run but found Tycho right there. He slammed into me like a rogue wave and drove me to the ground. Once pinned under his weight, there was nothing I could do but pray to the gods of my father and beg for mercy, because I knew Tycho would show me none.

"You were so close," he said, his breath hot on my face. I felt the tip of his blade drag along my scales, the scraping sound echoing through the forest. "But like I said, you can't win. So now the question remains: how should I do this?" His dagger slid along my torso, headed for the tender area beneath my arm. "Here?" he asked, his tone playful but deadly. The blade took an abrupt turn, dragging between my breasts as it headed lower and lower. "Or maybe here?"

My body raged but I remained still. Bucking against him would only do his job for him. Instead, I waited for him to lean closer.

"What are you waiting for?" I asked, lifting my head toward him. I saw the others standing behind him, their expressions taut with sick anticipation.

Tycho smiled at me, pressing his forehead against mine as the blade poked hard enough to break skin.

He'd taken the bait.

In a flash, I locked my lips to his and breathed fire through his body. He didn't have time to do anything but react as one would when they're being cooked from the inside out. He tried to withdraw from my hold, but it was iron against his retreat. The dagger was lost in his struggle to live, and as soon as I realized it, I cast him aside, jumping to my feet, but the others were ready for me. Two of them wrestled me against a tree and held my arms high above my head while the others restrained my feet.

I breathed fire wildly to no avail—I didn't have the advantage anymore. Tycho, half dead but still alive enough to want to take my life, staggered over, smoke billowing from his mouth and nose, his body smoldering. The stench was almost enough to do me in.

"You bitch!" he spat, coughing on those words that escaped on a wisp of smoke.

No amount of wriggling or fighting could free me, and I knew it. My fate was sealed the second I saw him pull the grey Daglaarian steel blade from its sheath.

"I'm going to do this slowly," Tycho said as the dagger bit through the soft flesh of my underarm, sliding in through muscle until it met bone. He wiggled it until he found the space between my ribs and continued to press it further, heading for my heart. I fought hard not to cry out against the pain, but eventually failed. The searing flesh was too much to bear.

"Good," Tycho seethed. "Let the steel of our mountain burn you like you burned me." I could feel how dangerously close to its target his dagger was. Another inch and I would be dead. "Any last words?"

I started to answer him but stopped short when I saw something move in the trees at his back. Something was lurking in the cover of the forest. Something stealthy and silent. Something that had tracked us.

"No," I said, feigning confidence, "no last words. Just a warning."

"Oh yeah? What's that?"

I smiled. "Watch your back."

He laughed aloud and shook his head—then it flew through the air, ripped clean from his body.

I barely had time to register what had happened before Tycho's blood rained down upon us all, spurting from his neck as his body fell to the ground. The Nychterídes holding me to the tree abandoned that task in an attempt to defend themselves against their attacker, but two fell before they got their chance. The other two darted off into the woods together, headed for the camp. Following close behind them was the one who had saved me.

I fell to the ground next to Tycho's corpse and gritted my teeth as I slid his dagger from my chest. Blood flowed from the wound, and I did my best to staunch it, but it spilled out between my fingers. I pulled my hand away and breathed on it, the tiny fire heating my scales until they glowed amber. With a deep breath, I prepared myself for what I had to do.

"On three," I said aloud, counting slowly. "One...two..."

I pressed my fingertips to the wound, screaming while it cauterized. Sweat rolled down my face as I choked back the vomit threatening to escape. It took a breath or two before I calmed myself enough to fumble my way to my feet, relying far too heavily on the tree at my back. I needed to get out of there before anyone else came for me. The screams of Tycho and the others would have been enough to alert Father's sentinels. Reinforcements would be on their way. I needed to get a head start on them.

Them and the mysterious shadow creature that had saved me.

10

ARIEL

I removed the blessing stone from my pack and stuffed it in my pocket, then turned to run, but a heavy hand on my shoulder held me back.

I turned to find Hemming frowning.

"Explain," he said, shoving the note I'd left for him in my face. The one with a single line scrawled upon it: *You were right.*

Hemming didn't even spare a glance at Tycho's corpse lying beside us in a pool of blood, like he wasn't at all surprised to see it. Then I noticed the blood covering his bare chest and arms, and his lack of surprise suddenly made sense.

"What have you done?" I asked him, ignoring his question. "They'll kill you for this—"

"*Explain,*" he said again, unfazed by my horror.

"I shouldn't have come back," I replied, echoing the words he'd spoken to me in the sparring arena.

His eyebrows drew together. "Then you should go before the others arrive."

He released me, and I took a step back. For the first time since I'd returned, I could not find a hint of anger in his expression.

"You did this...but *why*? *How*?" He said nothing in response, and a queasy feeling settled in my stomach. "To save *me*?"

My heart stopped in my chest when I watched him nod slowly. Nothing in that moment made sense, fueling the panic rising within me. Maybe I couldn't begin to fathom his motives for coming to my aid, but I didn't really care. The part of me that craved the relationship we'd had before everything went wrong clung to the hope that maybe a remnant of it still existed—that not all between us was lost. And it was unwilling to let it go.

"What will you do?" I asked, scared for the boy I'd grown up with now encased in the massive male before me. The one who'd once been my best friend. The one who would be executed for treason.

"I'll be fine."

I shook my head. "You won't be fine. They killed Adrik for helping me, Hemming! You think they won't do the same when they find out you did too?" My words didn't permeate his stony armor. He remained stoic, waiting for me to leave. "Something's going on here. You can either stay here and die," I said, the cool calm of my voice barely covering the desperation I felt, "or you can leave now—with me—and help me find my father before it's too late." Again, he didn't budge. I took a step toward him. "Someone is going to kill my father in the Midlands, Hemming. If you won't save yourself, then help me save your general."

Hemming's eyes went wide. "What are you—"

"I don't understand any of this, but Tycho implied something awful was going to happen to him—that there's a coup forming against him—and I can't let that happen." The blessing stone flared in my pocket. "If helping my father isn't motivation enough, then maybe the promise of something else will be…" Again, the ancient Neráida stone warmed my skin—the stone that could help guide me to whatever I sought in the Midlands. Like the father that Hemming had never known, but had always wanted to find one day. "I'll help you find your father. Give you the vengeance you've always craved."

He stared at me, shock overtaking his countenance. "*How?*"

The snapping of trees announced the arrival of the cavalry; we were out of time. It was act or die.

"There's no time to explain," I said, daring a glance beyond him as I strapped on my pack. "Are you with me?" He stared at me for a moment before nodding once again. Then we took off at a sprint just as the others came into view.

Feet pounding against the forest floor, we finally broke through the wards at the border. We were in the sky seconds later, leathery wings flapping with a determination I'd never known. Never needed before that day.

Some of Father's soldiers pursued us until the path became too treacherous. Once two had been taken out by the invisible traps set in the air, the rest turned back, reminded of just how deadly the Midlands could be. They knew that traveling them ill-prepared was nothing short of suicide.

I pulled the blessing stone from my pocket and held it tightly in my hand. The feel of the smooth surface as I stroked it calmed me. I could feel it directing me through the air every time I thought of my father.

"Stay close!" I yelled at Hemming, who flew directly below.

I was small enough that I could position myself between

his wings, provided we beat them in unison. That posed a challenge, given that mine were far shorter and less broad than his, but he knew how dire the situation was and altered his pace so we could navigate the magical traps as one. I wasn't willing to have him at my back. Regardless of the fact that he'd just saved me, I couldn't afford to trust him.

Not yet, at least.

We flew like that for hours, neither one speaking until I felt the deep perimeter of magic weaken. We'd made it through the worst of the faes' defenses. I placed my hand between Hemming's shoulder blades to get his attention, and he looked back.

"Down there," I said, pointing to the forest of black far below. I surged ahead of him and dove toward it. From our position in the sky, it looked like an inky lake, but I knew what it was. I'd been there with Kaplyn before. And though it was full of creatures who preferred to remain undisturbed, it was where my father had gone, so it was where we, too, would go.

I wove through a small break in the canopy with Hemming tight on my heels. We landed in a relatively clear patch of woods, but once our feet touched down, it felt like the trees moved closer. I looked up to find a wall of darkness where we'd just entered the forest. Light was scarce, so I gathered some wood and quickly made a torch.

With one tiny breath, we had a fire. As it roared to life, the trees shied away.

For a moment, the two of us just stood there, staring at each other. It was clear that I hadn't fully thought through my plan to save Hemming as he'd saved me. I hadn't wanted him to die a traitor's death at the hands of those we'd grown up with, but things between us were far from settled, and nothing good would come of that during our search for my father.

"Well, this is cozy," Hemming said, looking around at the

firs and spruces and elms that seemed less than pleased with their uninvited guests.

"If you leave them alone, they'll do the same," I said, scanning the woods. "At least the trees will. The rest of what dwells here…well, let's just hope we don't run into any of those creatures along the way."

That sentiment did little to assuage his concerns.

"Tell me where my father is," he said, narrowed eyes turning to me.

"First we find mine, then we find yours. That's the deal. If you don't like it, feel free to head back to Daglaar and the mob awaiting your return."

He took a deep breath—the kind he took to calm himself. "Let's go."

I squeezed the blessing stone, and its magic pulsed through me. "This way," I said, heading toward a tiny path through the trees. "But let me make something clear first. You may have saved me in the woods, and I did the same for you in return, but we are not friends. I don't trust you. You make one wrong move, and I won't think twice about burying an obsidian blade in you, got it?"

He stood silent for a moment, assessing me. "Afraid I'm going to stab you in the back as you lead the way?" His tone was cold and mocking.

"You've done it before," I replied, heading for the break in the tree line. "I'd be a fool to think otherwise."

He said nothing in response and fell into step behind me. As we wound our way through the Black Forest, following the shiny beacon in my hand, I tried to focus on what lay in front of me and not what followed behind. If having Hemming with me could help me get to my father before the traitor—or traitors—did, then it was a risk I was willing to take.

ARIEL

"**A**re you sure you know where you're headed?" he asked an hour later. We'd maneuvered in relative silence until then, sharing little more than hostility and a water pouch.

"The Black Forest isn't easy to navigate—nothing in the Midlands is. The whole country is an ever-changing landscape that has kept the fae safe from outsiders. It's their greatest defense."

He let those words sink in before replying. "Fine, but your father's crew can't have had that much of a head start on us."

He was right—they couldn't have. That point was hardly lost on me.

"The stone will lead us to my father," I said with more conviction than I felt. When he didn't respond, I looked over my shoulder to find his jaw clenched tightly. "Something you want to say, *Hemmy*?"

"Want to say? No. But you know that trusting a fae talisman is foolish. It could be leading you into a trap—"

"It hasn't yet."

"How do you know it's even leading you to him?"

"Because I can feel it. My father is alive and this will take us to him," I argued. My words were a lie, but a convincing one. I had no idea if my father was alive, but I saw no point in letting Hemming know that.

He stopped for a moment and stared at me. I turned and tried to keep from pulling my staff free.

"It's Hemming now. Not *Hemmy*," he said. "Nobody's called me that since you...since you left."

"You mean since the night you held a knife to my throat?"

The fire in his eyes dulled. "I had no choice—"

I barked out a laugh. "There is always a choice, *Hemming*. You chose betrayal."

I started to walk away, but he shot in front of me to cut me off. "If we're going to work together to find your father, then we need to get a few things straightened out first, starting with the fact that I didn't betray you. I saved your life."

His words slapped me silent for a moment. "Saved my life? You tried to kill me!" I yelled, shoving him back a step. Four years of unanswered questions bubbled within me, coming out in an angry mess of emotions.

"I barely left a mark!" he argued. "Do you think you could have said the same if I hadn't pushed Tycho aside? If I'd let him do what he wanted to do?"

"I think you could have stopped him."

"That's what I did!" he roared. The trees shook and bent away. "I did the only thing I could have back then—I put myself in charge of the deed. I knew your father would show up eventually. I just bought him time." He began pacing in front of me, his frustration plain. "And then, when I went to check on you later that night—to *explain*, because I could see in your eyes when I held that knife to your throat that you thought I'd forsaken you—you were both gone. There was nothing of you left, just a palpable absence that I've felt from that day on."

His words stunned me, and it took a moment to gather myself after their revelation.

Maybe Hemming hadn't tried to kill me—maybe he had, in some bizarre way, saved me—but his actions hadn't been without consequence, and the sting I'd felt in their wake was still as raw and angry as I was.

"What did you want me to do?" I cried, frustration leaking into my voice. "Stop and say goodbye to the person who'd just tried to kill me right before my father ripped me from my home, only to dump me in a new one, in a strange land, with a new father figure?" Hemming flinched at my words, my verbal blow landing hard. "What you did—it *did* kill me. A part of me, anyway. I'd already been torn from one home in my lifetime, and you forced me from the other. Your actions stole the only two people in this world who cared about me. Even if one of them didn't really care anymore."

For the first time since I'd returned, I saw something other than anger or emptiness in Hemming's eyes. I saw endless sadness.

"I didn't think he'd take you away," he said softly. "Not so quickly, at least. I thought he would bring you home and come up with a plan—that I could talk to him, and maybe we could figure something out together—"

"Well, that didn't happen," I said, dragging my arm across my face to wipe away the angry tears that spilled down my cheeks.

"I know. I just—" He cut himself off and ran his hand through his hair. "I was *seventeen*, Ariel. Old enough to see what was going on, but not wise enough to know what to do.

That night…it happened so fast. All I could do was react. I didn't have time to think everything through. I knew there would be consequences. I just didn't think you disappearing overnight would be one of them." I wrapped my arms around my waist, clutching it like a lifeline. I feared that, if I let go, I would lose myself in my conflicting emotions. "And then, out of nowhere, you returned," he continued. "You walked back into Daglaar as though you hadn't been gone for four years. As if you'd never left—"

"And you looked at me like you hated me," I said, my tone harsh.

His cold grey eyes met mine. "Because I did hate you for returning. For coming back to a place that despises you."

"*Did*…or *do*?"

He hesitated for a moment. "Don't ask questions you don't want the answers to, Ariel."

Even with my scaly armor intact, I felt the full impact of that blow.

"How can you hate me for wanting to come back to my home? For wanting to make sure my father was okay after I got a note from him demanding I flee the Midlands? For doing what I thought I'd been ordered to do?"

"Why did he order you to leave—"

"*How*, Hemming? *How* can you hate me for that?"

"I don't," he exhaled in frustration.

"But you just said—"

"Did your father ever tell you what happened after you left?" he asked, cutting me off. "What happened in the camp?" I shook my head, my anger slowly giving way to the fear growing in my belly. Fear of where his story was headed. "Your father punished me for months after you were gone. He had no choice, really. Law is law, and I broke it. He couldn't make an exception for me, even though I explained how it had all gone down—that it had all been a ruse to save your life. He had to do what he did. He'd have been seen as weak otherwise. So I faced the consequences."

"What did they do?" I asked, daring a step closer. In truth, I already knew the answer. To attempt to kill a fellow warrior was one of the highest crimes among our kind, and it came with one of the most severe punishments.

I slowly walked over to him and reached for one of his wings. He pulled it in tighter behind him and let loose a warning rumble that should have stopped me, but it didn't. Instead, my hand drifted toward the sharp tip at the end and gently pulled it until his massive black wing stretched wide enough for me to confirm my suspicions. The light of the torch illuminated massive scarring along the semi-translucent surface. It was marred with opaque slashes from one end to the other.

I gasped at the sight, and he whipped his wing from my grasp, slicing my finger with its sharpened edge. I put the tip of it in my mouth and licked it, sealing the wound.

"I'm so sorry, Hemm—"

"I said I knew there would be consequences when I stole Tycho's dagger and put it to your throat, Ariel. I don't need your apology."

I took a step back. "If you knew the consequences, then why are you so angry at me about them?"

Hate me for them…

He stared at me across that narrow divide, sadness in his eyes once again. "I never blamed you for the destruction of my wings—for rendering me earthbound for two years." He took a step toward me, and I stood my ground. A part of me —something deep inside—begged me to draw my weapon. Another part begged me to close the distance between us and embrace him. "But the longer you were gone, the more I resented you for leaving me alone in that camp—for forcing me to become someone who could survive there without you —even if it was best for you."

I looked him up and down. He was still bigger than the others, which was an impressive feat. He'd grown stronger and faster, out of necessity as much as his lineage. He'd become a warrior that, despite his half-blood status and attempt on my life, was prized. But in that process, he'd become cold and hard, completely unlike the boy I used to play with as a child; the one who'd protected me until I was able to protect myself. My absence had done that to him— hurt him deeply enough to create this being I barely recognized.

His wings had healed over time.

His heart, however, had not.

"You never answered my question," I said softly. He stared at me silently as if daring me to ask it again. "Do you still hate me?"

He didn't break eye contact for an unbearable length of time, and as I stood there weathering his quiet storm, I thought I might jump out of my scales.

"We've wasted enough time," he said, turning away. "We need to get going."

I opened my mouth to argue—to make him answer me— but his dismissal had been answer enough, really.

"Fine," I said, brushing past him into the shaded woods. "Follow me."

I led the way, following the stone's pull as the hours passed, until night began to settle in around us. With no sign of my father, my hope began to wane.

And with every minute spent in silence with Hemming, my childish dream that we could somehow salvage the friendship we'd once had died a little more.

12

ARIEL

By nightfall, the forest was every bit as black as its name implied. Both unwilling and unable to navigate it in the darkness, we set up camp for the night. I started a fire to stave off the shadows while Hemming set a trap for food. When he returned, his eyes were wide and his breathing ragged. A twig snapped somewhere in the distance and he started, his head whipping toward the source of the noise.

I had to stifle a laugh. "Still scared of what lurks in the dark, *Hemmy*?"

He turned and frowned. "I *am* what lurks in the dark."

"So it seems…" I stared across the fire at him, the flames casting an eerie glow on his dark, tanned skin, highlighting the lighter brown shades of his hair. His pale eyes, however, looked as cold and deadly as I'd ever seen them. There was no warmth to be found in their depths. "Care to elaborate on what happened with Tycho and the others back in Daglaar?"

I took a seat by the fire, and he sat on the far side so he could keep his distance.

I made a point to keep my scales in place.

"Care to tell me how you're going to find my father?"

I pulled the blessing stone from my breast pocket and stared at its polished surface, hoping to find the answer to his question there. I had no idea if it could take us to Hemming's father, but I didn't want to tell him that; tell him I'd preyed on that particular weakness to leverage him into leaving. He'd have been killed if he'd stayed behind, especially with my father gone, and I knew it. Regardless of our issues, he'd come to my rescue when I needed him most. I wasn't going to let him commit suicide because he couldn't see past his damned hubris.

I watched him on the other side of the fire, eating some of the dried meat from my pack in silence while I held mine, my stomach in knots. I wondered if maybe he'd tire and fall asleep if I ignored him long enough. Or forget that I hadn't answered him.

He glanced at me through his dark lashes, the fire reflected in his narrowed eyes. "You're not eating."

"I'm not hungry."

His expression soured. "Then give it to me if you're not going to eat it. No sense in wasting it. The gods only know what might come poking around here tonight in search of a meal."

"Whatever does would be far more interested in us as their main course than our scraps."

His lips pressed to a grim line as he got up and walked over. He held out his hand, and I passed him the piece of meat. A grunt was as close to a thank you as he could muster.

While he continued to dine on the meager provisions I'd brought, I lay down on the grass floor of the forest and closed my eyes. My mind soon drifted to a memory of Hemming and me as young children, sitting outside the group home for young Nychteríde soldiers-in-training. It was a crowded place, and mealtimes were especially violent, the near-feral males fighting over every morsel of food, the drive to be the biggest and strongest already present.

After dinner, when my father would meet with his lieutenants and other ranking officers, I would sneak into our kitchen and stuff as much food as I could into a satchel, then fly down to meet Hemming. He was always in the same spot: the center of the bottom step outside the home. The second he saw me coming, he'd slide to the left, making space for me. I'd stay with him until he finished eating, the two of us as silent as we'd been in the Black Forest. But back then, it had been a companionable silence.

In the forest, it was anything but.

"So," Hemming said, pulling me from my memory, "are you done pretending to sleep because you owe me an answer to my question?"

"You didn't answer mine."

"Yours was rhetorical. Mine wasn't."

I sat up and found him glaring at me across the fire. "Mine was certainly not rhetorical. I want to know how you did that…what that *was*."

"A slaughter," he answered, no hint of remorse in his voice. "Your turn."

I wanted to argue, but I knew he could be even more stubborn than I when he wanted to be. And with the dark of the forest pressing in around us, I wasn't so sure I really wanted to know exactly what had killed Tycho and the others—and I certainly didn't want to anger him and meet it face to face.

"I think I can use my stone to track him," I said on an exhale. I hoped that would be explanation enough, but I knew better. That answer would never satisfy him.

"You *think*? You don't *know*?"

"Well, of course I don't *know*, because I haven't actually tried to find him before, but it's supposed to lead me to whatever I desire. If that's your father, then it should take us to him." Hemming's head lolled back, a typical response when he was frustrated. "Let me ask you something," I said. "Are you sure you really want to find him?"

He levelled his gaze on me, and I instantly regretted the question.

"Some of us aren't as lucky as you, Ariel. Some of us weren't orphaned half-bloods rescued by a long-lost father and brought to a new home to be raised like a princess in a castle high in the sky. Some of us were born bastards and treated as such, ripped from our mother's grasp and placed in the settlement to see how long we'd last.

"You want to know if I want to find him? Yeah, I do, because I want to look into the eyes of the monster that screwed my mother, then left her on her own to fend for herself, knowing that she would bring something into her world that would be loathed."

"Hemming—"

"I don't want your pity, Ariel. I want you to make good on your promise. That's all. You get me to my father. Whatever happens after that…I absolve you of any responsibility. Deal?"

I mulled over his words, watching the tension in his shoulders recede slowly. "Will you let him explain first, or will you just kill him?" The wild look in his eyes made me nervous. I'd only ever seen it a handful of times before, and none of those memories ended happily.

"I haven't decided yet," he said under his breath. "I'll worry about that when you get me to him."

Without another word, he lay down on the ground with his back to me and went to sleep, leaving me a bundle of raw emotions, none of which I could discuss with him. Instead, I followed his lead, turning my back to the fire and closing my eyes. I knew one of us should stay up to watch over the camp, but I just wanted to shut down. To be numb. To not think.

Sleep found me minutes later, coaxing me to her with the promise of nothingness.

It was an offer too sweet to pass up.

ARIEL

I awoke in the middle of the night to find the Black Forest staring back at me. The trees had bent closer as I slept, and I immediately regretted not staying up to keep watch. I also regretted not having peed before I'd retired for the night.

As quietly as possible, I stood up and glanced over to find Hemming asleep, his back to the fire and me. *Good,* I thought, since I had no desire for him to escort me on my midnight bathroom excursion—which he undoubtedly would have. He was as stubborn as I was, at best.

In the darkness, I did my best to traverse the unruly underbrush to a space where I could do what I needed to, then quickly return. I was bone tired and in desperate need of more sleep. My vision was blurry from fatigue, and the darkness did little to help. All I wanted to do was lie down and rest.

Then a noise in the distance niggled at my clouded mind. A faint, tiny voice that called out to me.

"Soph?" I said softly, my mind still groggy. "Soph, is that you?"

Not awaiting an answer, I started off toward the sound, forcing a path through the woods' thick underbelly. Even in the inky darkness, I could see flashes of a light blue blur through the trees. I picked up speed as I called her name again, louder this time. Images of the first time we'd met flashed in my mind as I ran toward her.

I'd barely saved her back then.

My stomach roiled at the thought of not getting to her before something else in the woods did.

I felt like I'd been running forever, my legs heavy and tired by the time I came upon a small clearing with a tiny cottage in the middle. It was quaint and kempt and had an air of welcome that was impossible to deny. It practically begged me to walk in and make myself at home. I was nearly halfway through the door when I realized what I was doing.

"Going somewhere?" Sophitiya called from behind me, and I whipped around to find the young fae girl smiling at me.

"Soph! What are in the name of the gods are you doing in the Black Forest?" I asked, rushing over to her. "Delphyne will be worried sick."

"I came to find you," she replied as she threw her tiny arms around my waist and hugged me. "I miss you…"

I let out a sigh as I wrapped my arms around her. "I miss you too, but we need to get you home. The Black Forest isn't safe—"

"You look tired, Ariel," she said, her sweet little voice cutting me off. "Maybe we should go inside first. Have some tea?"

I looked at the cottage, confusion swimming in my mind. "But this isn't our home," I said weakly.

She giggled. "Of course it is, silly."

The weight of her words helped clear the fog clouding my mind.

Of course it is…

I shook my head and looked back at the tiny home. "You're right. I must really be tired."

"Then come inside," she said, taking my hand in hers. "Have some tea."

She led the way inside the cozy cottage and took a seat at the round table in the center of the room. I felt heat emanating from my breast pocket, but I brushed away the sensation. Surely it was nothing to be bothered about. I felt so safe in the cottage…

"One lump or two?" she asked, holding up the sugar bowl.

"Two, please."

She giggled again.

"Does Delphyne know you're here?" I asked, looking around the small home. There were no beds to be seen; only the table, a kitchen, and shelves upon shelves of glass jars filled with things I couldn't see clearly in the dim light of the room.

"No," she replied as the teakettle began to boil, "because I like to be alone sometimes." She smiled over her shoulder at me. "I do get quite a lot of visitors when I come here, though. But never a dragon."

"*Dragon?*" I said, something tugging at the back of my mind. "You've never called me that before, Soph."

She cocked her head at me curiously. "Of course I have. I call you that all the time." The nagging sensation abated instantly.

Of course she has…

"Your wings are different…" she said, setting the cup and saucer down before me.

"Because I'm only half dragon. You know that," I replied,

taking a sip. It was warm and sweet and flowery, and I closed my eyes as it slid down my throat like it was the most amazing sensation I'd ever experienced.

"Of course I know that," she replied with a dismissive laugh.

Of course she knows...

"My mother was Minyade, and you know my father, the general of the Nychteríde army."

"That's right," she said, her voice soft and distant.

I drained the cup and placed it down. Seconds later, Sophitiya had filled it again and stirred in two sugar cubes.

"Why are *you* in the Black Forest?" she asked, leaning her elbows on the table.

"I'm trying to reach my father. He's in trouble."

She leaned in closer. "Does he know you're coming for him?"

I shook my head, the movement making me dizzy. "No..."

She stood up and dragged her chair closer to mine. The scraping sound reminded me of something familiar—something terrible—but my mind couldn't reach it, too sleepy to focus.

"I've always wanted to have tea with a dragon," she said sweetly. "Do you know much about your Minyade side?"

"Not as much as I'd like," I said, my eyes fluttering shut. I forced them open again, but they were just so heavy. Too heavy to fight.

"Do you know of the legend of the Fireheart?" she asked. I mumbled something unintelligible in response. "It tells of the power deep inside each dragon. The power that fuels their fire—their magic. A power that can be taken…"

The thing in my pocket flared to life again, this time searing my flesh through my leather halter. I opened my eyes to find the tiny girl looming above me. She looked taller than

I remembered. Then I realized I was lying on the floor in the center of the room, the table no longer there.

"It was lovely to see you, dragon."

"Soph…I feel funny…"

"Of course you do, silly."

Of course I do…

She knelt down beside me, her hand hovering over my chest. Instinctively, my scales tried to unfurl, starting at my head as they always did, but they were slower than usual—sluggish, like my mind.

Something sharp pierced my chest, and I launched up off the floor. The haze that had settled in my head cleared in a flash. It was then that I could see through the magic—see the enemy at the gates. A wicked and cruel spider-like creature sat before me, its spiky appendage embedded deep inside me, searching for something. I felt it when it hit the target.

The fire inside me surged, then flowed toward it as though the creature were siphoning my life force.

My Fireheart…

I struggled against its hold, but it was crippling, and any movement I made seemed to only worsen things. I screamed as loud as I could, hoping Hemming might hear, but I had no clue how far I'd wandered from our camp, and I doubted he would. I'd been manipulated and had fallen into a beautifully woven fae web. The fae monster draining my life away clicked with delight, its many beady eyes wide. I couldn't help but wonder what it would do with me once I was dead; if there would be anything left for Hemming to find.

Cold like I'd never known seeped into my veins, and I knew the end was near.

14

HEMMING

I woke when Ariel left camp but didn't bother to stir. Following her to the bathroom wasn't likely to improve things between us. At least that was the lie I told myself.

The truth was, I didn't want to see the remnants of the pain our fight had caused in her eyes. It would have undone me in an instant. One tear from her and I would have been at her side, my arms wrapped around her tightly just like when we were younger. But we weren't kids any longer. The shape of her hips and curve of her breasts reminded me of that every time I looked at her.

The four years we'd been separated had done nothing to change how I felt about her—the love I'd felt since I was sixteen and she'd been too young to feel the same in return. Selfishly, I'd always hoped we'd find each other again, but not under these circumstances. Not with fear and betrayal and resentment still between us. It had made our reunion too painful for words.

It had been hard to keep my distance since her return, and even harder to accept that I might never be forgiven for what I did that night. Chasing her into the woods wouldn't fix what was wrong with us. I doubted anything could.

Images of the day I first met Ariel crept into my mind. Standing there, so small in her sodden dress, her wild brown hair streaked with red as bright as the fire in her heart. Her welcome had been reminiscent of my early years with the other children, them attacking the half-blood the second the soldiers turned their backs, tugging her blood-red wings and calling her names. She had been so tiny then—so fragile. The confusion and hurt in her pale green eyes so plain. My six-year-old self couldn't stand the sight of her unable to defend herself. I'd intervened because I knew what it was like to be her—to be born of an unthinkable pairing. In my case, it was Neráida blood that tainted the Nychteríde; in hers, Minyade. I knew she'd be hated forever, if she even lasted more than a few days at the camp.

She would never have survived on her own.

From that day on, she followed me wherever I went, and I let her, taking her hand to guide her through crowds that would have swallowed her. I gave her the protection she needed, and I got something unexpected in return: an ally. A friend. For years, we kept each other company. We trained together. Ate together. We were rarely apart. What had started as a relationship born out of survival became one of choice—of friendship.

My mind flashed to the image of her lying on the floor of the training building, my sword pressed to the scales of her neck, and the necklace hanging in the deep V of her halter. The shock at seeing it there still coursed through my veins. After everything that had happened between us, she still wore the gift I'd given her.

Hope had blossomed for a moment. Maybe not all was

lost between us—maybe there was still a chance to make everything right. But maybe I'd severed that hope when I sliced the cord of her necklace. Why else would she have made a point of returning it to me before she left?

With that harsh reality in mind, I focused on something else to distract myself. I contemplated the possibility of meeting my father, wondering how I'd react when I saw the male who'd impregnated my mother, then sent her away to be shunned by her own people. A part of me wanted to hear what he had to say for himself, but the rest just wanted to slit his throat before he could spew forth excuses.

The snap of a twig in the distance pulled me from my thoughts, and I turned to see what it was. It was then that I realized Ariel still hadn't returned. With her warnings about the Black Forest fresh in my mind, I jumped to my feet.

"Ariel?" I called. The rustle of leaves blowing in the breeze was the only response. I pressed my ear to the earth, straining hard to hear what the bedrock had to tell me—what the stone of the earth could relay. Through it, I felt the sharp reverberation of a scream coming from the east.

In a flash, I was running through the woods, following the echo of the cries still vibrating the rock below.

"Ariel!" I shouted, fearing those screams were hers and might soon be cut short. If they were, I'd lose her trail.

I pushed harder, suddenly thankful for the long uphill runs I'd taken when my wings were shredded to bits. They had made me stronger and faster than the others. Once again, those traits would come in handy.

Just as I was losing hope of finding her, I came upon a collection of boulders. Between the two largest was a blackness darker than the night around it. Blacker than black. Without a thought, I ran into the opening. It penetrated deep into the earth, twisting wildly along the way. I fumbled along the walls, unable to see. But I could hear her in the distance, moaning in pain. She sounded so weak—nothing like the fearsome girl I'd once known.

My chest tightened, and I ran faster.

I saw the light of a fire in the distance, its warm light bouncing off the rock walls. When I reached the end of the tunnel, that light illuminated a cave of sorts. Ariel lay in the middle of the floor with the leg of a creature impaled in her chest. Her skin was so pale, her lips blue. The beast inside me roared with anger, and I knew there would be no stopping him. He wanted vengeance for the one he loved—*we* loved.

Pain shot through me as my skin broke apart, releasing the side of me that I didn't understand—the other reason I longed to meet my father. The spider-like being turned its attention away from its would-be kill to focus on me. It withdrew its arm from Ariel, and it glowed like an ember.

Neither my beast nor I understood what that meant, but it didn't matter. All my inner darkness understood was that death came for anyone that harmed Ariel. Without warning, he charged the massive spider headfirst and smashed it into the rock wall at its back. The ground shuddered, and the fae creature turned to ooze where it had been hit.

On cloven and clawed feet, the beast backed away, ready to strike again, but it was unnecessary. He'd obliterated the enemy with a single blow.

His gaze drifted to where Ariel lay, lifeless. He nudged her with his muzzle and flinched at the icy temperature of her skin. Unable to help her, he lay down beside her and rested his head on her chest.

Then we shifted.

As soon as my limbs were my own again, I shook her wildly, calling her name. I pressed my ear to her chest, listening for any signs of life. The faintest exhale caressed my cheek, and I realized she was still alive.

"Ariel!" I shouted, tapping her face to revive her. Slowly,

as if pulled from the deepest sleep, her eyes fluttered open—barely. "Ariel…I don't know what to do!"

I looked at her chest, the upper part of her breast exposed where her halter had been pulled down. There was no blood marring her skin; no wound to speak of. The only mark was a faint reddish-purple spot where the spider had speared her.

She whispered something, so softly that I couldn't hear her. I lowered my ear to her lips, begging her to say it again.

"Fire…heart…"

"Fireheart?" I repeated. Her eyes closed. "What does that mean? I don't know what you're telling me!"

In a panic, I shook her harder, this time to no avail. A small, glowing stone fell from her pocket, and I picked it up. It flared to life in my palm, the sensation so uncomfortable that I threw it to the ground. It rolled toward the dead creature and bumped the appendage that still harbored that amber glow, though it had faded.

I hurried over and picked up its arm, looking it over for some clue—some sign of what I should do. I held it up in front of me, only inches away. The second I ran my finger over the sharp tip that the spider had used to impale Ariel's chest, it shot forward into my own. Fire ripped through my body, and I choked back the scream it brought forth. *Pain…* so much pain. The pain Tycho must have felt when Ariel nearly burned him alive. His body had still been smoking when my beast ripped the head from it.

As quickly as I'd been stabbed, the limb pulled out and fell away, leaving me with a fire tearing me apart. The Minyades' fire was the weapon the Nychterídes feared most. It had no effect on our skin, but inside, it was deadly. I had to get it out of me and back into her before it caused both of our demises.

I collapsed to the ground and crawled over to Ariel. I placed my hand on her chest, hoping that maybe the fire would want to go to her like it had wanted to leave the spider. That maybe it would somehow solve the riddle that I could not.

But nothing happened.

I took out a small blade and sliced open the mark on her chest. Then I cut my palm and pressed it to the wound. Blood to blood. Life force to life force.

Nothing still.

Frustrated, I let loose a cry that shook the walls around us. Dust and debris fell in response, but something else happened; something most unexpected. The smallest spark of fire escaped my mouth.

I looked down at Ariel's blue lips and wondered...

"Gods above," I said aloud, "please spare her life. Restore her. Make her whole again." I leaned in, lifting her delicate chin to pull her mouth open. "Don't let me fail her again..."

Then, with a roar of terror at the thought of losing her, I locked my mouth to hers and forced the fire out of my body.

ARIEL

"Ariel?" Hemming's voice was distant, begging me to come closer. "Ariel! Say something…"

"Why does my head feel like it's been smashed into a wall?" I asked.

I tried to sit up with my eyes closed and soon realized that was an awful idea. Dizziness and nausea had me flat on my back in a second. Hemming's broad hand caught me and guided me into a seated position. Once everything stopped spinning, I dared to open my eyes.

I had no idea where we were.

"Do I want to know?" I asked, looking around the cave. Then I let my gaze fall upon his face. Though he tried to fight it, terror poked through his barely controlled expression.

"I'm not sure I can really explain," he said. "You up and disappeared in the middle of the night, and this is where I found you."

"I didn't mean to. I heard a friend calling me from the woods."

His eyes narrowed. "And you decided to go searching without getting me first?"

"I didn't even think about that. It was weird—it was like I was dreaming, but not."

"*Magic…*" That word came out on a growl.

"It had to have been, because that thing is not my friend," I said, pointing to the crushed spider.

"What is it?" he asked, disgust in his voice.

"I'm not sure, but I think it might be a Dreamcatcher. I've heard talk of their kind at the manor. They manipulate your dreams to lure you to them."

"Dear gods…"

"Yeah, like I said, the Black Forest is full of creatures. The Neráida magic—the magic blessing these lands—seems to have evolved over time. Some say it has darkened, while others say it has corrupted susceptible fae. Kaplyn seems to think these beings reflect the gods' cruel sense of humor—a reminder that no race can ever be as perfect as they."

Hemming swallowed back his unease. "Are there many things like this here?"

"I don't know, but I am curious to hear how *that* happened," I said, looking at the squished fae creature. "It's far…*flatter* than it was before." My gaze drifted back to Hemming's stoic expression.

"I got mad," was his only reply.

I let his words settle on my addled mind. "Remind me not to make you mad, then," I said. He let out a breath, trailed by a tiny laugh. "I guess this means you came to my aid? Again?"

"That would be correct."

Silence.

"Does that mean you hate me less?"

"I'm not sure," he replied with a smile. "After what I just experienced, I might hate you more now." The way his smile faltered when he spoke made me curl in on myself. His hand was on my back again in a second. "I don't hate you, Ariel," he said softly. "I never truly did."

"Because I'm too lovable to hate?" I forced a grin, and he laughed at my effort.

"Something like that."

He stood up and reached out a hand for me. With a deep breath to steady myself, I took it, and he pulled me to my feet. He didn't let me go until he was sure my legs would hold me. I looked down at his hand clasped to mine and felt a surge of emotion—a warmth in my belly that I didn't fully understand.

I quickly pulled away and focused my attention elsewhere in the creepy cave. To my right, I spotted my blessing stone on the floor. I nearly dove to grab it.

"How'd you get that thing?" Hemming asked as I tried to steady myself once again. I stroked the smooth stone, and it seemed pleased to feel my skin against its surface.

"It was a gift from someone important to me. It's the guide that will see us through these lands safely—or as safely as possible, I guess." I stared at the smooth black stone with reverence as I ran my thumb across its surface. When I looked up at Hemming, his face was a mask of indifference.

"He must care deeply for you to have given you such a talisman."

"*She* does."

Silence again.

Hemming was staring at me, brows pinched together as if waiting for further explanation. But I wasn't ready to tell him about my time in the Midlands just yet—not after what I'd learned had happened to him after I left. "We should probably get back and collect our things."

"I HAVE A NEW RULE," HEMMING ANNOUNCED AS WE trekked through the Black Forest. "No more splitting up."

"You mean no more magical sleepwalking in the woods alone?"

He shot me a sideward glance filled with warning. "I think my rule covers that."

"You sure have gotten bossier in your old age, *Hemmy*."

"And you've gotten careless in your absence."

"Hey! I thought nearly dying—*twice*—would earn me a little sympathy?"

He let out an exasperated sigh. "You're right. It does. Sorry." A shrug. "Old habits."

"I missed you, you know," I said softly. "I might have come home because of my father, but part of me wanted to see you—to talk to you. To make sense of what went so wrong—"

"And all I did was make you feel like you did the night you left." It wasn't a question. It was self-condemnation.

"Not quite that bad, but not too far off, either."

Silence fell between us again. It felt heavy and wrong, and I was desperate to break it. He must have shared my feelings, because he soon saved us both from it. "You never did tell me about the letter your father sent—the one that made you return."

"It said that I couldn't trust my warden anymore—that I needed to escape. So I did. And was nearly eaten by some fae shadow bird in the process."

The muscles in his square jaw flexed as he listened to me tell the tale of the green-eyed raven that had tried to keep me from fleeing—the one I'd assumed Kaplyn had sent after me. But knowing now that the whole thing had been a lie, I wondered if that creature had come after me for a very different reason.

"When I arrived in Daglaar, Father looked shocked to see me, because he hadn't written that letter at all. I'm starting to think it has something to do with Tycho's threat that someone is going to attack him while he's in the Midlands. I just don't understand why."

I looked up at Hemming's profile again to see his features pulled tight.

"I think you're right."

"We need to find him and get him to Kaplyn. The two of them can sort this out—"

"Kaplyn?"

"Yes, Lord Kaplyn Corvallym. He's the one I've been living with for the past four years."

He shot me a sidelong glance. "*Alone*?"

I choked on a laugh. "Hardly. His estate alone houses well over a hundred. His lands beyond his own home…thousands upon thousands, I imagine. We were most definitely not alone." I swore he breathed a sigh of relief. "Where did you think I'd been all this time?"

"I tried not to think about the particulars too much," he replied. "It would have driven me mad."

His heavy expression was in such stark contrast to how I remembered him that I started to question if my memories were accurate—if I hadn't twisted our time growing up into a tale too grand to have ever been reality. But when I glanced at the braids on the side of his head, his confident stride, and the way he flexed his hands when he was agitated, I realized that, though much had changed, much had stayed the same as well.

"You may not have gone mad, but you certainly have a dark and brooding thing going on." He turned to stare at me, his angry, piercing grey eyes not helping to refute my observation. "Don't get me wrong—it looks good on you." Something in their depths flashed at my words, and that strange feeling in my belly stirred yet again. I tried to ignore it. The unfamiliar sensation fluttered until I blurted out the first thought that popped into my head—anything to drown it out. To keep me from assessing its cause. "I bet it attracts a lot of attention from the females when you visit the villages."

His shoulders tensed at my words. "I wouldn't know. I haven't been allowed there since my punishment."

My heart simultaneously sank and cheered. "Oh…"

"Besides, it's not as though they've forgotten that I'm a mixed-blood bastard. They never will, no matter how much I look like them or how much bigger and stronger and faster I am. I will always be lesser in their eyes," he said, looking down at me, "same as you."

The warmth in my gut died quickly, but I took no offense because I knew he'd meant none. My inferiority in the eyes of the Nychterides was a fact I'd come to terms with years earlier. I'd hoped it would be different for Hemming, but that hope had been wasted. Pure blood was too important to the Nychterídes as a people. Any taint to that was a stain that couldn't be washed away with skill or speed or ability.

"Well, maybe that's the greatest gift they could have ever given us," I said. He stopped short. "I mean, if we hadn't had to prove ourselves, we wouldn't be everything we are now—the beings we've become. And I think *I'm* pretty great, so…"

He smiled, shaking his head. "Only you could see what we are as a positive."

"Your ability to do whatever you did to the Dreamcatcher seems pretty damned handy. They can't do that."

"No," he replied, "they can't."

"See? That's the spirit!" I said, punching his arm lightly,

as I'd done when we were younger. "And my father will need us if a coup is brewing."

"If we aren't too late," he said, and I flinched at his reply. The truth in it stung. I prayed we still had time.

"He shouldn't be too far from here," I said, clutching the stone in my hand. "He told me where they were headed, and provided the Midlands hasn't done a massive restructuring, it should be just before the forest's edge."

"And if it's not?"

"Then we let the stone guide us and pray we get there in time."

My chest seized with pain at the thought of arriving too late and finding my father's corpse lying in the sun, a feast of carrion. I stopped, unable to breathe, and pressed my hand to the wound above my heart. Hemming was at my side in a second, his palm against the flat of my back.

"What's wrong?" he asked, bending down to meet my eyes.

"Can't…breathe…"

"Sit here," he said, helping me to a rock. He pulled a canteen of water from my pack and held it out. I waved it off, unable to take a sip. "Ariel, let me see." I lifted my hand from my chest, and he put his in its place. His brows knit together.

The feel of his cold skin against mine helped calm me slightly, enough that I could breathe with some normalcy.

"I think I'm still healing from…from the attack…and thinking about my father…about not reaching him in time. It's just too much."

"Maybe we should rest for a bit—"

"No!" I shouted, grabbing his arm. "No. We need to press on."

"Then let me carry you, or fly you out of here."

"*Carry me*?" I cried as though his words had slapped me.

"You carry the gravely wounded and the dead, Hemming, not the living."

The corner of his mouth twitched with amusement. "You'll slow us down if I don't."

I wanted to argue but couldn't. He was right, though I was loath to admit it.

"If you tell anyone about this, I'll make your life miserable, understand?"

"And that's different from normal in what way?" I went to hit him again, and he caught my arm, saving me from myself. He held onto it and used it to pull me to my feet. I wavered for a moment, crashing into him as I fought to get my balance. His eyes widened as my chest pressed against him, and I quickly staggered back a step, his hand still gripping me tightly. "Are you good?" he asked, unable to meet my gaze.

"I'm *up…*"

"Good enough." He strapped my pack between his wings; then, without warning, he scooped me into his arms before I could protest. "You need rest. This is my compromise. If you want to argue about it, you can do so when yelling at me won't cause your heart to fail."

"Overbearing mule," I muttered under my breath as exhaustion eclipsed my will to argue.

He merely laughed and continued in the direction we'd been headed. I wanted to scream at him to put me down, but I was half asleep in his arms before we'd gone ten yards. Healing was exhausting under the best of circumstances, for both of our kinds. If I was going to be in any shape to defend my father if need be, I would need to regain my strength and my Fireheart's full capacity. If I had to let Hemming carry me to ensure that end, it seemed a small concession.

Though I doubted he'd let me hear the end of it anytime soon.

16

ARIEL

"This doesn't look encouraging," I said, staring down the high wall of once-manicured bushes in front of us that seemed to stretch on forever. It was a topiary maze, much like the one in the garden behind Kaplyn's manor. But unlike his, this one was overgrown and uncared for, like it had been abandoned long ago. I couldn't decide if that was to our advantage or not.

"I'll go first," Hemming said, tucking his wings in tight behind him. There was just enough room for him to squeeze his broad shoulders through the opening. I stepped in line behind him and followed him through the maze. The blessing stone flared in my hand, a warning that we were getting off course, but the shrubs were too high to see over, and flying, even for a moment, was impossible. The forest canopy was so low that it nearly scraped the top of the maze in places.

"Hemming…we're going the wrong way. We need to veer right if the path splits up ahead."

"I think I see a break in the wall not far away," he called back to me. We pressed on toward the opening he thought he'd seen. But as we neared, a distinct shuffling sound stopped us cold.

"What was that?" I breathed, reaching for my dagger.

"I don't know." Without warning, he ran forward. The shuffling sound began again. "Dammit!"

"What? What is it?" I asked, hurrying over to him.

"The path—it doesn't open here. It just keeps going."

"But I thought you said—"

"I did, because I swear I saw a break in the hedge." He shot me a pointed look, then focused that attention on the scraggly-looking shrubs surrounding us. "Come on. We need to keep moving."

With every step, the blessing stone raged in my hand, silently screaming at me. We continued on for what seemed like an eternity before I stopped, trying to figure out a better plan than the one we had. The canopy was still too low to fly, and even if my damaged fire came when called, using it seemed like a great way to trap ourselves in a bonfire rather than escape. Maybe the fire wouldn't burn us, but we still needed to breathe. The smoke would do us in before we could escape.

But navigating the maze at this pace would take forever, and forever we didn't have.

We needed another option.

"Hemming! Come here. I want to try something." He turned to look at me, his silence an invitation to continue. "Maybe if I stand on your shoulders, I can see over this thing and get a sense of where we are—and a way out."

He crouched down in front of me in a flash. "Climb on, *mikros drakos*."

I smiled as I stepped on his bent knee and placed the other

foot on his shoulder. "Call me little dragon all you want, but if you drop me, I *will* make you pay for it."

A low rumble of laughter. "You can try."

"Would you stop that? Your shaking isn't making it easier to balance!"

Once he contained himself, I propped my other foot on his shoulder and slowly stood. He carefully raised me into the air, his large hands encircling my thighs for stability. The feel of his fingers gripping through my thick leather pants sent a rush of blood through my veins, awakening something inside of me —something both foreign and familiar somehow. Something that made my mind spin, nearly making me lose my balance.

I shook my head to clear it of distractions, then stretched as tall as possible to see over the hedge maze.

What I found was not encouraging at all.

"Hemming…"

"What?"

"I think I know what that shuffling sound was…"

I looked out over a solid sea of bushes and shrubs, with no paths cutting through them. We were completely surrounded, even in the direction we'd just come from. The way had just disappeared. The hedges were moving, guiding us to somewhere—or nowhere at all.

Both options were ominous.

"Ariel," Hemming growled, and I realized I hadn't answered any of the many questions he'd been asking.

"I need to get up higher," I said. "I want to see if we can walk over the top of it."

I grabbed a handful of dead branches beside me and attempted to haul myself up onto the top of the maze. As soon as I shifted my weight to them, they began to grow higher, jutting up through the canopy. Hemming gripped my legs tighter, pulling me off the hedge, and I lost my balance. I fell forward, tucking my head and wings in to flip to my feet. It wasn't graceful, but somehow I landed without incident.

I shot Hemming a death stare that almost wiped the amusement my near-fall had provided off his face.

"The path goes nowhere," I said. His smile fell. "We're trapped in here unless we can scale the shrubs up to the trees or force the bushes to take us where we want to go."

"Which way?" he asked.

I squeezed the stone and waited for its pull to tell me the direction.

"East," I said, pointing for good measure. We were so turned around that I wasn't sure he knew where east was.

He turned to face the wall of dying greenery and drew his sword. "We are getting out of here. *Now.*"

I stepped back to give him room to swing his weapon, then drew my blade as well. If his idea worked, two of us could cut through it faster than one. And time was not on our side.

He assessed the hedge for a moment before pulling his arm back to slash through the decaying wall. The second his blade met branch, the forest shuddered, and an unholy shriek rang out. I dropped my dagger to the ground and covered my ears; it felt like my eardrums were being shredded to ribbons.

"Hemming!" I screamed, but my cry couldn't be heard. I looked over to find him covering his ears too, his face twisted with agony.

Then I felt the brush of brittle branches across my skin.

I shot up straight, blade in hand yet again. The hedge wall before me was moving, cocooning itself around me as sharp, lethal barbs extended from the few living limbs it had. The ones Hemming must have cut through.

The shrieking of the forest ceased but was quickly replaced by my own as the wicked thorns started to bite into my skin. I tried to call my scales forward, but they were sluggish and reluctant. Terror shot through my veins. My weapons were useless against this enemy—my training as a warrior was no match for the deadly maze.

"Hemming!" I cried again, trying to slice the barbs threatening to impale me.

"Ariel!"

"I'm trapped…"

The distinct sound of a blade slicing through shrubbery was so close. I tried to turn and face him, but the hedge pinned me in place with its weapons. When I finally maneuvered around, I saw Hemming through a narrow slit in the hedge. The look of horror on his face was plain, even through the dying branches.

"Your scales!" he shouted at me.

"They won't come!"

His hand pierced through the tangled wall of vines and branches and reached for me.

"Hold on!"

With renewed strength, Hemming carved a hole through the hedge so quickly that it didn't have a chance to grow back before he pulled me through the brambles, my skin tearing on the barbs along the way. But once we were reunited, it was clear that we were still in trouble. The hedge had already started to close in around him, too.

"We have to cut our way out, Ariel, and quickly," he said, turning to the east to slash at the hedge. I did the same, swinging my blade wildly at the magical maze attempting to seal us in forever. Maybe that was why it looked half dead. Maybe it hadn't had a meal in too long.

Our progress was slow, but we were able to stay a step ahead of the animated maze, if only for a little while. When I swung my arm back to land another blow, a spindly branch shot forward and caught my wrist. Another wrapped itself around my dagger and yanked it from my hand.

Hemming soon found himself in the same position.

He reached for another blade but was halted by a vine around the other wrist. I lifted the sharp tip of my wing and ripped through his bonds, but his freedom didn't get us very far. The hedges had hemmed us in together and were inching closer by the second. Hemming's skin would stand up to the barbs, his stony underlayer an armor against their sharp tips, but without my scales, I was defenseless, and we both knew it.

"If I can't get out of here, promise me you'll leave me and go find my father," I said, slipping the stone into his hand. His eyes went wide, then narrowed.

But before he could respond, a giant thorn bit into my arm, penetrating far deeper than any of the others. I cried out as I ripped it away, and my blood sprayed the shrubs entombing us. They drank it up like starving animals.

Because that was exactly what they were.

≈

HEMMING

I looked on, paralyzed, as Ariel's blood soaked into the dead branches, giving them life. The knowledge that we were about to be their next meal was too surreal to comprehend. It was unlike any enemy I'd ever faced. One I couldn't beat.

This was not to be how our story ended. It hadn't yet begun.

I grabbed Ariel and pulled her in tight to my body. With effort, I worked my wings around her, wrapping her in whatever protection I could provide. My wings were far tougher than her skin, but even they couldn't stave off the maze forever.

"Ariel," I whispered into her hair.

"I'm so sorry, Hemmy…" She pressed a wet cheek to my chest, and anger blossomed deep beneath it. Thorns pressed against the thick leather of my wings and snapped off the harder they tried to pierce my skin. Ariel cried out as one of them found its way through a breach in my shield and dug into her back. She bucked against it, and I tried to pull her away, but I had nowhere to go. No way to keep her safe.

The beast inside me raged.

Another sound rang out through the woods, an angry, terrifying roar that silenced the forest. I felt the maze hesitate as the echoes of my beast's rage drifted off into nothing.

I gripped Ariel tighter still.

Then, as slowly as they had come, the hedges began to retreat, inching away from us until not even a thorn grazed our flesh.

"What's happening?" Ariel asked.

"It's letting us go," I replied, pulling my wings back. But my arms still held her close.

She looked over her shoulder to see for herself. "*Why*? Why would it stop?"

"I don't know."

She pushed away from me, and I let her go. There was skepticism in her eyes when she looked at me. "That sound… it came from *you*…"

"We need to go." I pressed the blessing stone into her palm and turned to find a clear path leading eastward laid out before us. "I don't intend to stay here any longer in case this thing changes its mind." I collected our weapons from the ground and grabbed her hand. "Let's go."

ARIEL

Exhausted and wounded, we found a place to make camp for the night. Hemming started the fire to save me from further exposing what I'd already confirmed in the maze—my Minyade abilities weren't working right. Whatever had happened to me in the cave with the Dreamcatcher had altered the essence of my being somehow—damaged it. I hoped that all I needed was time for it to heal, but I just couldn't be sure. I rubbed at my chest, hoping that my Fireheart would be all right; that it hadn't been lost forever.

"How is your back?" Hemming asked, turning the rabbit I'd caught and cleaned on the spit above the fire.

"The wound is deep, but it should heal all right."

He frowned at my response. "Let me see," he said, abandoning our dinner to come inspect it. I rose to meet him, and he turned my back to the fire so he could see the wound better.

"I need to pack it with something," he mumbled to

himself. "It's still bleeding."

"I have some clean wraps in my bag," I said. Moments later, he returned with the muslin strips.

"This will hurt," he said. His fingertips grazed the skin around the wound, and I shivered from his cold touch.

"Just do it."

Pain shot through my torso as he packed the wound, and I tried to focus on my breathing as his arms reached around me to bind it. His body pressed against my back as he crossed the bandage in front of me, and my breath caught in my throat.

"What?" he asked, pulling away quickly.

"It's nothing," I replied, uncertain myself what was going on. "I'm fine."

He tied off the binding and backed away from me. "That should work for tonight. We'll have to remove it in the morning so the wound doesn't close around it."

I merely nodded in response, then sat down. He, however, hovered above me, his silhouette surrounded by smoke and fire. He looked like the god of flame and war. The one my father was named after.

"The rabbit will surely burn if you just stand there and stare at me instead of tending to it," I teased. "Or shall I keep watch over it instead?"

At that, he scoffed. "Unless your cooking has improved, I think not."

I laughed, gently leaning back against the large rock behind me. "Kaplyn has a kitchen full of staff at his estate. They don't let me in there unless he orders them to, which is essentially never."

He squatted across the fire from me, slowly turning the spit. "Sounds fancy."

"It is. Kaplyn is a very important fae lord. That title comes with all the means and finery one would expect."

He was quiet for a moment before replying. "Did you like

it there? With Kaplyn?"

"I did. It's beautiful, full of life and beings stranger than I ever could have imagined, but it isn't home." I choked on that final word. "But I guess home isn't home anymore either…"

Hemming hung his head and attempted to rake his fingers through his tangled hair. When they got caught, I stifled a laugh. He tugged harder and harder to free them, and I couldn't hold it in any longer. My laughter rang out, breaking the tension I'd just created.

"Shall I cut you free?" I asked. I pulled my dagger out as I walked over to him, and he frowned.

"Damned hedges," he muttered under his breath.

"Here. Let me help you before you lose a finger in that mess." I grabbed a comb from my pack and sat down on the rock behind him. "Come closer," I said. "I promise I'll be gentle."

"It's the only time you ever are," he said, inching backward until he rested against the rock between my legs. I tried not to notice that warm sensation in my belly as his shoulders pressed gently against the inside of my thighs.

Instead, I turned my focus to working on the knots in his wavy hair.

"These side braids are a disaster! When was the last time you had them done? When I lived in Daglaar?"

He looked over his shoulder at me. "I did them myself."

His incredulous expression made me laugh. "Well, that makes sense—"

"If you want to eat tonight, I suggest you keep your criticisms to yourself," he countered. "Some of us don't have a team of staff to do things like brush and braid our hair."

Though I knew he'd said it in the spirit of teasing me, his words cut through the humor of the moment to expose the truth. I had been spoiled while away at Kaplyn's, and he'd had nothing more than the food provided for the soldiers and a one-room cabin. The same one I used to sneak into at night when Father was away and I didn't want to be alone. When the nightmares came.

My hands stilled in his hair.

After a moment, he reached back and wrapped his hand around my wrist. "It was just a joke, Ariel. I didn't say it to hurt you—"

"But it's true, Hemmy. It hurts for that reason, not because you said it."

Silence.

"Just because it's true doesn't mean you should stop fixing my hair." He looked back at me again, a grin plastered wide across his face. "You can consider this your penance for becoming a spoiled little Midlands dweller."

I yanked the comb through a knot, and he winced. "*Oops. Sorry.*"

His grin turned to a scowl, and I wondered if we'd soon be sparring by the fire while our dinner was reduced to ash. It wouldn't have been the first time. I silently hoped it wouldn't be the last.

"I'm officially taking back my gentle compliment."

I laughed. "As you should. I'm clearly out of practice."

We sat in comfortable silence for a while as Hemming cooked and I combed. We'd always been capable of that—of being happy around each other without speaking at all. His presence had always been enough. But we had things to sort through; years to get caught up on.

The silence couldn't last forever.

"Tell me more about your new home," he said, his voice low and distant as my fingers worked through his hair, dragging along his scalp in a rhythmic motion. "And *Kaplyn.*"

I pulled through the final knot and paused for a moment, trying to think of how best to describe the immortal Neráida lord that had taken me in. "He's surprisingly kind and generous for someone of his station. He's gracious with his staff and those on his lands. He's given me everything I could ever need and then some."

"He's a diplomat, then."

I nodded, staring off into the trees. "He is, which is so different than what I was used to. The fae work very differently than the Nychterídes. They are cunning, sneaky, and willing to wait to enact revenge when we are not. Their methods are insidious, which has taken some getting used to. It's hard to trust people there—I mean *truly* trust them."

"But you trust Kaplyn?"

I smiled as I tipped his head back against me. "I do. He's different than the others—at least to me."

Hemming looked up at me, his grey eyes reflecting the light of the fire as I sectioned off a lock of hair and began braiding. "Do you love him?"

I considered his question for a moment. "Yes, I do."He pulled away to turn the rabbit again. "He's like an uncle to me, or maybe an older brother. I don't really know—I've never had either."

Hemming's body relaxed back against the rock again. "I'm glad you have someone to watch over you there."

"You'll be pleased to know that he makes me train every day. He's merciless about it, too. Unlike many of the other fae lords, he is not afraid to take up arms in his own defense. The others have minions that do it for them, or so I've heard."

I finished braiding, then tied them back with the rest of his hair in a leather cord.

"A capable male unable to defend himself doesn't deserve to live."

"His thoughts precisely," I said, swinging my leg over his head to stand up.

"Then he cannot be all bad."

"He's not…"

113

Hemming watched me walk back over to my spot on the opposite side of the fire. "But?"

"But like I said before, his home is not *my* home. There were elements of being there that I loved—people there that I care for—but I was forced to be there. My freedom was limited. And I missed the mountain and the cold wind whipping my face when I flew up to my father's house. I missed sparring with the others until I bled and ached, then doing it again the next day. I missed sitting around the fire with Father, sipping on tea and talking…"

He leaned forward, folding his arms over his knees to rest his chin upon them. "Anything else?"

I held his gaze for a moment before turning my attention to our dinner. "Your cooking?" I shot him a playful look, and he laughed.

"Hungry, are we?"

"Nearly being impaled to death—twice—takes a lot out of a girl, Hemming. Not that you'd know."

He shook his head, biting his lip to retain whatever rude comment he'd undoubtedly planned to throw back at me. Instead, he pulled the rabbit from the fire and tore off a leg. He placed in on a leaf and brought it to me.

"Your dinner, *Miss Ariel*," he said with a sweeping bow.

"You're a jackass," I replied with a laugh.

"As are you."

"That's us: just a pair of jackasses trapped in the Black Forest, trying to save my father's life."

"We will, Ariel. Nothing is going to happen to him. I won't let it."

Words failed me in that moment, so I took a bite of my dinner instead, letting the smoky, sweet flavor assault my tongue and drown out the doubts creeping into my mind. I wanted to share Hemming's certainty, but I didn't, and it scared me to death.

HEMMING

I watched Ariel's expression fall before she took a bite of her food to mask it. She was worried that we'd fail, that her father would be murdered. Trying to convince her otherwise wouldn't help; I knew that from past experience. She needed a distraction. Something else to focus on while we ate.

"So what did you do all day on Kaplyn's estate, other than get thrown out of the kitchen and train?"

She smiled past the rabbit at her lips and quirked a brow at me. "I entertained young, virile Neráida lords from all across the Midlands." I spit my food out in surprise, and she laughed. "You should see your face right now!" She nearly fell off her rocky perch, clutching her stomach as she carried on her hysterics.

"Perhaps I don't find the thought of you sleeping with multiple fae males quite as amusing as you do."

"You *should* find it amusing because you know I'd never

do it." Her laughter continued for a minute before she managed to compose herself.

"A lot can change in four years." My tone was harsher than I'd planned, and I could see its effect on her. Her smile waned then fell away, and I hated myself for opening my mouth.

"You're right," she said softly. "It can."

"I didn't mean to imply—"

"I know you didn't." She hesitated for a moment before continuing. "This is hard, Hemmy…being here, with you… it's hard. My mind is in a constant battle with itself, memory and present fighting to figure out how to act—how to be around you. There are moments when, despite our surroundings and why we're here, it's like I never left the settlement. Like the night you held that blade to my throat never happened. But then, just when I think things might be normal again, I say something like that, and your reaction is so unexpected that I'm forced to remember that I don't really know you anymore. At least not like I used to." She picked a tiny piece of meat off the bone and chewed it for longer than necessary. "You're right; a lot can change in four years. I just wonder how much."

I lowered my food to the ground. "Ask me anything you want, Ariel. Ask it and you shall have the truth. No games. No lies."

She took a deep breath. "Did any part of you want to do what you did to me that night?"

"Of course not!"

"Do you really not blame me for your punishment?" she asked, her voice low, her eyes averted.

"I told you, I knew the consequences of my actions when I chose them, Ariel. Your life outweighed my wings."

She nodded, her lips tense, fighting back her emotions.

"What about you?" I countered. "Do you hate me for

what I did?" She shook her head, and a rogue tear streaked down her face. The urge to walk over and wipe it from her cheek was hard to curtail, but she was too raw and vulnerable in that moment to confuse things even further. Instead, I balled my hands at my sides and pressed them into the ground to anchor me. "Are you mad at me for beating you in the arena? For trying to scare you away?"

"No."

"You understand now why I did it? Why I said what I said to you?"

"Yes. You knew I was in danger being there." She met my gaze again. "You knew Tycho would make a move on me at some point, didn't you?"

I let out a sigh. "I did, but I wasn't sure exactly when. It seems I was a little late at the cellar. I had no intention of making that mistake twice, but I did, and I'm sorry for that, Ariel. I should have been there for you in the woods. It never should have gone that far—"

"It's all right, Hemming." When I didn't respond, she bit her lip and peered through her lashes at me. The depths of her light green eyes had my chest tightening. "Do you think I've changed since I left?"

I pressed my hands harder into the rocks beneath them. Their sharp bite wouldn't penetrate my skin, but the pressure felt good. Distracting.

"*Yes.*"

"How so?" she asked, the vulnerability in her stare plain.

"You're taller...smarter." *More beautiful than I could have imagined you'd become...* "But you're the same, too." When she said nothing, I turned the question on her. "What about me? Do you really think I've changed that much?" I asked. She merely nodded. "In what way?"

She wrapped her hands around her waist as though she

were cold and stared into the fire. "You're braver, which I would have thought impossible."

"Perhaps what you perceive as bravery is really just stupidity cloaked in valor."

"No. It's not."

Silence stretched out between us again, and I hated every second of it. Whenever Ariel retreated into her mind, it was hard to pry her out. "Do you have friends at the manor?" I asked, hoping to force the conversation in a happier direction. When her eyes met mine and sparkled, I knew I'd succeeded.

"A few. Delphyne is the manor's seamstress. The one who gave me this." She pulled the black stone from her pocket and lifted it for me to see. "She watches out for me—gives me inside information on all the others. She has a niece she cares for that I adore. Sophitiya is the light of my life there."

Given how she smiled just saying the child's name, I knew her words weren't an exaggeration. "She's the one you saw in your dream?" I asked. She nodded. "Tell me about her —about Sophitiya."

Her smile widened. "I imagine she's a lot like I was at her age. Curious to a fault. Afraid of nothing." Her smile slowly turned to a scowl as she got lost in her memories again.

"Something happened..." I said, reading her reaction.

She took a deep breath. "It was not long after I arrived at Kaplyn's. Delphyne was away, leaving Sophitiya, who was maybe three or four at the time, in the care of the staff at the manor. I doubt she thought anything of it; all who worked there had done so for decades. They were Kaplyn's trusted employees, and Sophitiya treated them as such.

"I was wandering the property when I saw a male walking toward the stables, holding a little girl's hand. I remember smiling at the image, wondering if Kade and I had once looked like that. There was a radiance to her that all but beckoned me to follow, so I did. But once she disap-

118

peared into the building, something in me roiled—a sick feeling that I couldn't shake. Before I knew it, I was sprinting toward the stables, staff drawn." She closed her eyes, squinting like she was trying to purge what she was seeing from her mind.

"Ariel…?"

"I saw him pull her up into the hay loft. Her eyes met mine, and she reached her little hands for me…" She pulled her staff off the ground and gripped it so hard her knuckles turned white. "I knew what would have happened if I hadn't gone after her that day. I still see her disappearing into that loft, my mind playing over a million different scenarios that could have been."

"What did you do?" I asked, anger driving me to my feet.

Her malice-filled eyes met mine, and I thought I saw a spark of her Fireheart alight inside them. "I grabbed her away and told her to run back to the house—to tell Kaplyn to come."

"Then you waited for him?" I asked, knowing full well she hadn't. The Ariel I knew was too hot-tempered to await justice. She'd take it for herself instead.

"No. I bashed his head in with the end of my staff until blood rained down into the stalls below and Kaplyn hauled me away from the bludgeoned corpse." There was steel in her gaze as she looked across the fire at me. She'd raze the world down for those she loved.

It was one of the qualities I loved most about her.

"Good," I said, meeting her stare. "I wish I could have been there to help you."

The corner of her mouth curled—a smirk or a sneer, I couldn't be sure. "I didn't need it."

I mimicked her expression. "Of course you didn't."

She took a deep breath and released her staff. It fell to the ground with a soft thud. "From that moment on, Sophitiya has been by my side, and Delphyne has watched over me in turn. They're like family."

"I'm glad you have loved ones in the Midlands," I said, walking over to her.

She glanced up at me, then down at the ground at her side. "Sit," she said, picking up her dinner. "I hate it when you hover."

"You don't like how short I make you feel," I said with a laugh, dropping down at her side.

"I'm as tall as any of the Nychteríde women," she argued.

"Which still makes you tiny in comparison."

"Ooooh, such a terrifying male Nychteríde warrior you are. So intimidating…" She shook her head and took a bite of her food. I threw a rabbit bone at her and she batted it away, feigning anger. "If it's a fight you want, Hemming, keep it up and you shall have it."

"It might be good for you," I countered. "You could work off some of that pent-up anger you have brewing just below the surface." She shot me an incredulous look, then took another bite. "What's this? Afraid of a challenge, *mikros drakos*? Worried you might lose to me—*again*?"

"No," she said flatly, "I'm worried that your fragile male ego will crumble if *you* lose to *me*." She pinned sharp eyes on me. "Never underestimate a woman's rage, Hemming. It has been the undoing of your sex for centuries."

I rose and took a step back, inviting her to try. After a moment, she stood and grabbed her staff off the ground.

"Don't beg for mercy when you're at the end of my blade again," I said with a smile.

It earned me one in return. "I don't beg. *Ever*."

"We'll see about that." I pulled a sword from my back and raised it with both hands. She twirled her staff around herself a few times, and some of the scratches along her skin opened up and began to bleed with her efforts. "Are you well enough for this?" I asked, no hint of mocking in my tone.

She looked offended by the question. "You can either beat me or baby me, Hemmy. You cannot do both simultaneously." She swung the staff at my head with lightning speed, and I blocked the blow just before it landed on my temple. "I'm not a little girl anymore."

Blood surged through my body at her words as I stared at the fearsome woman she'd become. Fearsome and beautiful.

"I know."

≈

AN HOUR LATER, WE WERE BOTH WINDED, NEITHER WILLING to call a truce.

"You've gotten slow with your follow-through," she said, grinning at me while sweat rolled down her face, mixing with the blood from her cuts.

"And you haven't been running like you should. You're tired. *Too* tired."

"Says the one barely able to hold his sword up any longer."

I threw it aside. "Hand-to-hand combat, then. Let's see if you've been practicing."

I could see from the set of her jaw that she had not, but like the stubborn girl she'd always been, she cast her staff down and steadied herself for the first blow.

"Don't forget that I'm faster than you," she mocked.

"How could I when you insist upon pointing it out all the time?" I replied. She merely shrugged, then winced and rolled her shoulder. "You're hurt—"

She sacked me to the ground, falling on top of me. Her

dagger was out of its sheath and at my throat in a flash. "Do not treat me as your lesser," she said, still breathing hard, "and never mistake my injury for weakness."

Her lips were only inches from mine as we stared at one another, the irony of the situation plain to us both. She shifted her weight closer, and the pressure of her chest heaving against mine was more than I could bear. I bucked her off with my hips, then pounced on top of her, stealing her blade. I pressed the tip of it to the notch above her sternum, where the necklace she'd returned to me should have been, and leaned in close.

The beast inside me stirred.

"Do not treat me as your enemy," I said, staring down at her wide eyes, "and never mistake my kindness for charity. I never have, nor ever will think you're weak. But you are not invincible, Ariel. Thinking otherwise will get you killed."

She struggled beneath me like a wild animal in a trap. I climbed off of her carefully, just in case she decided a counterattack was warranted—her way of having the last word. But she didn't move; instead, she just lay there, staring up at the canopy while she tried to calm her breathing.

"I don't think I'm invincible," she said softly. I sat down by the fire and waited for her to continue. When she didn't, I walked back over and reached my hand out to help her up. Grudgingly, she took it. "You have no idea what it's like to be seen as smaller, weaker—a woman only good for one thing. I've seen it from the men around me my entire life, but never from you."

"I don't look at you like you're only good for one thing—"

"But you did look at me like a wounded animal who needed to be nursed back to health. I know why you did last night, because that was what I needed. But I can't have you looking at me like that again—not unless I'm dying at your feet. If you want to coddle me then, I'll allow it."

The beast growled at the thought. "You won't be dying anytime soon if I can help it." Her eyes narrowed at me, and I threw up my hands in defense. "I won't either…or your father, for that matter. I'll fight to keep us *all* alive, and I expect no less from you."

She considered my words for a moment, then nodded. "We have each other's backs…"

"*Always.*"

The smile she gave me was full of mischief. "Good. Now, since you have my back, you can keep first watch while I have a quick nap to sleep off the throbbing pain in my shoulder from that kick you landed." She rolled it around a few times before shaking her arms out.

"You do that. But maybe try not to snore so loudly that you keep the forest awake tonight. I don't want to have to fight off whatever monster you draw to us with that gods-awful noise while you sleep like a baby."

"I do not snore!" she yelled in protest.

I laughed. "Like a little pig."

She threw her staff at me but it fell short, her arms too tired to put any force behind the gesture. With a feigned pout, she dropped to the ground next to the fire and rested her head against her pack. Seconds later, her eyes were closed, and she began mumbling. "Tell me a story, Hemmy," she said. It was the request she'd made every night she came to me when we were kids.

Something deep inside my chest tightened once again.

"You want a story?" I asked. She said nothing, but I swore I saw her nod. I made my way over to her and perched on the rock at her side. She was breathing deeply, already taken by sleep, but I told her one anyway. The story of a young boy and girl, bound together by fate, destined to become two of the greatest warriors the world had ever known. The kind of legend. Occasionally, she'd mutter something and grow restless until I smoothed her hair and continued the tale. But she was too far gone by the time I reached the end.

She never heard how the warriors were fated for more than battle.

That they were fated for each other as well.

19

ARIEL

I awoke after a short sleep to crusted blood and sweat all over my body and realized that a bath was in order. Hemming, not much cleaner than I was, didn't argue. It wasn't long after we broke camp that we came upon a small lake, and we decided to take a quick bath before continuing our search. The scent of my blood would only serve to attract the darker fae creatures lurking in the forest, and we had no time for any more of those.

I stripped off my leathers on the shore while Hemming lurked in the forest to keep watch and give me privacy. We'd been in myriad scenarios in our time together, but none of them had ever involved being naked. It would be a first for us, when there were few firsts left to share. When thoughts of us naked together rushed into my mind, I jumped into the cold water, and it shocked me back to my senses.

The warmth of the rising sun on my skin felt glorious when I surfaced, and I leaned back to float atop the water,

125

soaking it in. It seemed like only moments later that I realized I'd drifted too far from shore. The birds had grown quiet, and I suddenly felt very exposed out in the open water. Kaplyn had never warned me about what lurked below the placid surface, but I had little doubt that something ancient and hungry might be hiding down there in the darkness.

Because it was the Midlands, and nothing was ever as it seemed.

I swam toward the shore, feeling more secure when my feet could touch the ground. I dipped below the water one last time to scrub my skin and rinse my hair. When I resurfaced, I found Hemming standing by the water's edge, half naked, scanning the lake for me. His eyes went wide when they met my bare skin.

My breasts were hidden behind my cascading hair and the water still sheltered my lower half, but with the way he was staring, I felt like I was standing before him totally naked. But I didn't move. And his gaze never faltered.

"You were taking too long. I got worried," he said, finally turning his back to me. "Sorry…"

I tried to ignore how his eyes on my skin made me feel— as well as their absence. "Sorry for what? Seeing my bare stomach?" I teased to distract myself.

"You know what I meant—"

"How very scandalous, Hemmy." I could hear that he was flustered by the situation, and I couldn't help but prod him in that state. Hemming was many things, but off-kilter was rarely one of them. I realized I liked that I'd shaken him, though I tried not to analyze whether or not I liked the reason why.

"Can you pass me that dry shirt?" I asked, walking up behind him.

He snatched it off the ground and thrust it toward me without turning. "Here."

"Thanks." I stood only feet behind him and dried myself as I examined his naked back in the sunlight. The breadth of his shoulders and cording of his muscles were beautifully sculpted, the perfect balance of size and strength. I clutched the fabric closer to me to keep from touching him. "Can you pass me my clothes, too, please?" My leathers came flying over his shoulder into my chest. "Thanks," I said with a grunt. "You know, you don't need to stay here and supervise me while I dress."

"I'm not supervising you," he replied. "I'm not looking at you at all. I'm making sure nothing happens to you while you get dressed."

"A very important distinction, no doubt."

"It would be to your father."

Wasn't that the truth. "And who will keep you safe while you bathe?"

He dared a glance over his shoulder. "I will."

"Ah, yes, the famous Nychteríde male pride. I wondered when that might make an appearance."

I fastened the ties of my halter at the nape of my neck, then secured it around my waist. My pants proved harder to get on, my legs still damp, but I managed to wriggle into the tight leather. Once they were up, I told Hemming he could turn around. His eyes darted to where I was tying the leather cording of my pants, then looked past me to the lake beyond.

"We should hurry. Are you going in now?" I asked. He nodded. "So…should I hang out here where you can keep an eye on me, or am I free to gather our things?" Sarcasm laced my tone, and he merely exhaled hard in response. "I'm just messing with you. I'll stay here to keep *you* safe, but don't worry—I won't peek."

I walked past him to give him some privacy as he stripped off his pants and got into the water. When I heard the splash, I turned to find him swimming out into the center of the lake where I'd just been, his deeply tanned skin covered in water and reflecting the sun. He dropped below the surface, and I waited for him to emerge. When he didn't, I felt my heart speed up.

"Hemming?" I called. No response. "Hemming! This isn't funny!"

The water was calm. No ripples where he'd submerged. No bubbles erupting at the surface. No signs of life at all. Without a thought, I ran to the edge and dove into the water, swimming beneath the surface, searching for him.

I found nothing.

My wings helped propel me deeper into the lake, but with the depth came darkness, making it harder to see anything at all. My chest tightened with fear and lack of air, and I soon found myself propelling to the surface. I shot into the air, gasping for breath in preparation for another dive. Right before I dipped below again, a hand on my shoulder spun me around.

Hemming was there, smiling like the impish boy I'd once known.

I damn near punched that smile from his face.

"I'm going to *KILL YOU*!" I shouted, reaching for his head. I grabbed hold of his hair and shoved him below the surface. His hands wrapped around my waist, and I soon found myself face to face with him underwater.

His smile faltered slightly as I hung there in the water only inches away. Cool fingertips dug into my hips as the pressure of the air in my lungs tightened my chest. And all the while, those grey eyes bore into mine.

Suddenly needing space—and air—I flashed him a crude gesture, then wiggled my way free. I popped up out of the water just before he did. "You're such a jackass!" I yelled, splashing water in his face.

"And you still spook too easily."

"You disappeared, Hemming! I don't know what's in this water, and neither do you. Would you rather I'd just left you to be eaten by some nightmarish fae?"

His expression sobered for a moment, his grey eyes bluer than normal, reflecting the water. "Yes. I would."

I felt my nose scrunch with confusion. "You'd want me to just stand by and let some water beastie eat you?"

"And if I did?" he countered, irritation creeping into his tone.

I pressed the palm of my hand to his forehead. "Are you feeling all right?"

He batted it away. "Asks the girl who got stabbed by a Fireheart-stealing spider—"

"If you feel fine, then why would you say something like that?" I couldn't hide the hurt in my question, so I didn't bother trying. I bit down on my tongue to keep the tears stinging the backs of my eyes from betraying me.

Tears at the thought of his death.

"I said it because I wouldn't want you to perish beside me. I'd want to die knowing that you got away."

Blood welled on my tongue. "Hemmy—"

"I'm not suicidal, Ariel. Don't worry. I'm not trying to find creative ways to die." He forced a small smile just as a tear I couldn't withhold rolled down my cheek. "I'm sorry I scared you." He held my gaze for a second, then reached for my face as if to wipe that damned tear away. But he never got the chance.

In a flash, he was dragged under the water.

And this time, it wasn't a game.

20

ARIEL

There was no time to think.

I dove under the water to see Hemming being dragged away by a bright yellow sea serpent ten times his size. With only a small dagger strapped to my leg and my broken Fireheart as weapons, I chased the beast as it swam deeper and deeper. Hemming fought against its hold to no avail, the snake's scaly body coiling tighter and tighter around him.

He let loose a silent scream, bubbles rushing from his mouth, and I wondered if it was a cry of pain or one of warning, telling me to turn back. To save myself. But Hemming knew me; he knew I'd never leave him to his death, despite what he'd just told me. We'd been a team for as long as I could remember. We survived together, or we died together. To me, it was just that simple.

I closed the distance as the serpent began to slow and

used that opportunity to grab its tail to get its attention. Hemming was still conscious, but barely, and I was running out of air. Neither one of us had long. Underwater breathing wasn't one of our gifts.

The snake whipped its black-tipped head to face me and lunged. I dodged its strike, its massive fangs just missing my wing. The force of its wake spun me around, and I plunged my dagger just below the base of its head. It bucked and twisted, trying to shake the blade loose, but I held on tight, twisting it as deep as it could go. The serpent released Hemming in its attempt to get away from me, and Hemming started to sink lower in the water. Deeper into the darkness.

I hooked my hand into the beast's nostril and wrapped my legs around its neck as best I could. Then I pulled the blade from its head and reached around, torquing on its nose to pull its head back. With a vicious slice, I ripped my dagger through its neck. I felt the snake shake two more times before it went limp, the fight bleeding from it along with its life. Then I let go.

Ink-black blood surrounded me, blinding me temporarily. I couldn't see my own hand, let alone Hemming. Panic crept in as I swirled around in the water, trying to get my bearings as my lungs screamed for air. But I knew if I resurfaced, Hemming would be lost forever.

I turned my body toward the bottom of the lake and started swimming into the abyss. Once I was clear of the serpent's blood, I couldn't see much better. But I could feel. The second my hand grazed silken hair, I grabbed hold of it for the second time that day and used every ounce of strength and breath I had left to propel us to safety.

I broke through the surface, hauling Hemming behind me, and gasped for air. He did not do the same. Fear rising within me, I started toward the shore. We were far from where we'd undressed, but it didn't take long to reach another sandy bank. I dragged Hemming onto it and shook him while I screamed his name.

"Don't you die on me!" I yelled, pounding on his chest in anger. "You are not allowed to die on me!" I could feel my resolve breaking as he lay there unresponsive. My anger could only remain for so long until my other emotions won out and my heart broke again. "Hemmy, please. Please don't go. I need you…"

With one last strike to his torso, water spewed from his mouth. He rolled to his side, coughing and hacking between greedy breaths. I backed up enough to give him space, but the second he opened his eyes and leveled them on me, I launched myself at him. He fell onto his back again while I hugged him tightly, my body sprawled on top of his.

"You're okay!" I yelled, hugging him tighter. "Thank the gods you're all right."

His arms wrapped around the small of my back. "Thanks to you being the stubborn mule you are."

I pushed up onto my hands to stare down at him. "What was I supposed to do? Just let you drown?"

"I feel like we just finished talking about this—"

"Hemmy! I'm serious!"

"So am I!" he yelled at me. "It was only a matter of time before that thing dropped me and captured you. I didn't want that to be the last thing I ever saw!"

I tried to calm my breathing, my body still full of adren-aline from the fight. "Well then, I guess it's good that the last thing you saw was me kicking that thing's ass."

He let loose a laugh that quickly became a cough. I rolled off of him to let him breathe and then realized just how naked he was. My eyes raked over his body before I quickly turned away. I thought I heard Hemming laugh, but I couldn't tell. It could have been the coughing.

"We need to pack up and go," I said, extending my wings.

"I'll be right back with our stuff—and your *clothes*. Try not to die while I'm gone."

As he lobbed a sharp retort at me, I took to the skies, the flap of my wings drowning out his words.

HEMMING

T*hat damned girl...*

Ariel would surely be the death of me one way or another.

I pushed myself off the dirt-lined shore and tried to catch my breath. Tried to shake the memory of her swimming into the depths of that lake after me. How she'd survived, let alone saved me, was a mystery. Or was it? She'd grown strong in our years apart, and I couldn't help but feel a pang of emptiness knowing that. Knowing that she hadn't needed me in that time.

I flopped onto my back and let the sun dry me as I watched her fly away. There was an elegance to her flight that hadn't been there before, a deftness she'd lacked growing up. Visions of her twelfth birthday, when Kade took us above the wards high up the mountain, assaulted my mind.

We stood at the peak, the three of us staring at the barely visible camp below. Then, without warning, he pushed her off.

She screamed on the way down, her tiny wings barely strong enough to carry her at first. I struggled against the iron grip that held me at his side—the one that kept me from going to her aid.

"She must learn, or she will die," he said, sadness in his tone that contrasted the harsh nature of his actions. "You know this is the way of the Nychterides."

With my heart in my throat, I watched as she mastered the high winds, soaring gracefully across the sky. Once Kade was satisfied, he let me go, and I shot straight for her, the cold air whipping my face until my eyes watered.

"Ariel!" I called. She looked back at me and smiled with childish delight.

"Chase me, Hemmy!"

For hours we flew up and down and around the mountain, until our bodies ached and our lungs burned. That night, she sneaked over to my cabin. I'd told her I had a present for her, but I didn't want anyone else to see it. She came without question.

In the dark of my room, I pulled out a rough-cut crystal I'd bartered for in the village south of the settlement and held it out to her. It was the color of her wings, as red and dark as dried blood. She held it in her hands, the leather cord I'd strung it on dangling between her fingers.

"It's beautiful," she said, staring at it.

"It made me think of you when I saw it." I took it from her and reached around her neck to tie the cord so that the stone sat comfortably in the notch at the base of her throat. She dropped her head and brushed her hair aside. Once I'd secured it, she hugged me tightly.

The memory made me smile.

Then my clothes fell from the sky, landing perfectly in my lap, snapping me back to reality. I coughed out a breath at the impact. Laughter echoed around me.

"Damn, my aim is good," she said, landing at my side.

"I would sleep with my eyes open if I were you," I replied, pulling on my pants.

She glanced back over her shoulder. "I already do."

A pang of guilt washed over me as I strapped on her pack. Once it was secure, I spread my wings. Pain shot through the right one, and I sucked in a breath through my teeth.

"What is it?" she asked, following my gaze to the tip of my wing. At the end was a small puncture wound; not enough to keep me from flying, but enough to be a problem should the wind pick up. The sea serpent's tail had wrapped around me to pull me under. Apparently, it had been barbed with obsidian.

I was lucky my wing was the only place I was wounded.

Ariel walked over and gently took it in her hands. "I can't seal this with fire, not that it's even working," she said. "This part is too thin. It would burn and break."

"It'll be fine," I replied. I lifted it from her grasp and tested it out a few times. Only if I had to beat it with force could I feel the flesh start to give.

"You can't fly with that, Hemming. You'll only make it worse."

"I've had worse and flown. It'll be fine."

"Give me my pack," she said, reaching for the straps.

"What are you doing?"

"Fixing your wound."

"You're being ridiculous." I snapped my wings closed.

"Stop being such a baby and let me put some salve on that wound and wrap it," she said, rifling through her bag.

Knowing an argument would get me nowhere, I complied, and in a matter of minutes, she had it dressed. The salve was already starting to take the pain away. I quirked my brow at her and she shrugged. "Kaplyn has some talented healers. I may have befriended a few—and stolen a few

137

provisions before I left. Not sure they'll be so friendly when I return…"

"Probably not, but thanks for that," I said, stretching my wing. "It feels better already."

"Would you stop moving that around and let it rest, please? We need to get going." She ran her hand across her shoulder and rolled her neck. "This place makes me feel *off*."

Without another word, she started for the trees. I followed close behind her, not wanting too much distance between us. After all we'd been through already, I didn't trust the forest. I feared there would be more nefarious obstacles in our way.

22

ARIEL

We were deep in the woods but getting closer to our destination. With every step, the blessing stone came alive, flaring and vibrating with proximity to my father. It had only been about thirty minutes, but we'd covered much distance. Soon, he would be safe.

Soon, we could kill anyone seeking to harm him.

As we pressed on, a strange feeling grew inside me. It wasn't unpleasant per se, but it made my mind fuzzy, like I'd had one too many glasses of wine without enough food. I wondered if it was exhaustion from fighting the sea snake or the stress of the hunt for my father—or possibly my healing Fireheart.

Or maybe it was something else entirely.

I wiped the back of my neck and rolled my shoulders, trying to will the sensation away.

"Why do you keep doing that?" Hemming asked from behind me.

"It's nothing. Just a kink."

"Let me see." Before I could argue, his cool hand was on my bare skin, searching for an ailment I couldn't define. My skin flared to life with the contact, and every rational thought in my mind disappeared. Consumed by the sensation of his flesh against mine, I leaned back into his touch, my head lolling to the side to afford him greater access. "It doesn't seem that tight to me," he said, broadening his search to the bare muscles of my upper back.

I bit back my moan—or at least I tried to.

His hands suddenly went still. "Ariel…are you sure you're well?"

"Keep doing that and I will be." My voice sounded lower and huskier than normal, even to my clouded mind.

His hand gripped me harder, and he spun me around to face him. "Ariel? Ariel, look at me!"

I lifted my heavy head and peered up at him through my lashes. "Oh, I'm looking." I leaned into his grip. "And I like what I see…"

He muttered something that sounded like a curse under his breath. "Ariel, I need you to listen to me, all right?"

"I can listen to you," I said, leaning against his hold, "but I can think of much more fun things to do to you than that…*naked* things…" My hands drifted up to his bare chest and slid down the hard planes of his abs until they reached the waistband of his leathers. He grabbed my wrists as I attempted to unfasten the button and trapped them behind my back. His body pressed against mine as he held me captive, and all I could feel was the strong beat of his heart pulsing through my body and the leather of my halter keeping his bare skin from mine.

"Ariel…" He said my name like a warning as he stared me down, eyes searching mine for something.

"Hemminnnnnnnnng…"

"You need to sit down," he said, whirling me around and marching me over to a nearby stump.

"On your lap?"

Ignoring me, he placed me on that damned stump and, with some effort, disentangled my arms from him. The second he walked away, I was on my feet.

Another mumbled curse. "Ariel, in the lake—with the serpent—did it bite you?"

"Noooooo," I said, sneaking up behind him, "but my blade bit it. Sliced its throat clean through."

He whipped around and grabbed my chin. When he leaned in closer, his face only inches away, a moan of anticipation escaped me. "Did you get any blood on you? In your cuts?" he asked, staring into my eyes.

"It was everywhere," I said with a laugh, running my hands through his dark hair. It fell out of its leather cord into his face. "I couldn't see where you'd gone through it. It was so dark…"

"Dammit—"

"But I saved you," I said, brushing a stray braid from his face. His sharp gaze softened ever so slightly.

"Yes, you did. And now I need to return the favor."

≈

HEMMING

POISON…

Serpents' blood had that effect on the Nychterídes. I'd

heard stories from Kade about how it had been used as a weapon against captured warriors. They'd say anything while it coursed through their veins—*do* anything. It affected everyone differently, but one thing was always certain; it banished inhibitions in a matter of minutes once it took hold. And given the life of rules and consequences and minimal freedom Ariel had lived, her reaction was understandable.

"I need you to sit down for me while I find something," I said softly, loosening my grip on her. "Can you wait for me?"

Her bottom lip thrust out. "But I don't want to wait…"

"I know," I replied to placate her, "but I have to find something to make this better."

She leaned into me and inhaled. "Nothing can make this better," she whispered, her breath on my skin sending my blood roaring through my veins again. "Nothing but *you*."

The desire to grab her and kiss her right then was overwhelming.

"It will. I promise, Ariel. But I need you to let me go for a minute."

Her hands grabbed the waist of my pants and she yanked me toward her. "I'm never letting you go."

Gods help me…

With some effort, I got her to comply. Once she was sitting down again, I immediately scanned the ground for winter sage. I'd seen it along the way—recognized its tiny red blossoms. If I didn't get some of that into her quickly, her mind would be irreparably damaged.

I spotted some not far from where we were and ripped it from the earth. I ground it up in my bare hands as I made my way back to Ariel, who'd undone the bottom of her halter in my absence. She was working on the top when I reached down to stop her. With a lightning-fast move, she threw me to the ground and straddled my waist.

"Where is it?" she asked, dropping her head to my chest.

The tickle of her hair against my skin made me shudder as she trailed her nose lightly along my neck to my ear. "Where's my present that will make this better?"

Her teeth grazed my earlobe, and I fought to keep control. "I have it here," I replied through clenched teeth.

"Your skin…" she said, her voice trailing off. "Does it taste as good as it looks?" Her tongue was warm against my ear, and I bit back a growl as she nipped it.

"Eat this," I said, trying to push her back far enough for me to sit.

But she barely budged. "I'll eat something…"Her hand trailed down my side until it found the waist of my pants again, and I sucked in a breath as it breached the barrier. Blood pounded in my ears as my body strained against the leather, every fiber of my being wanting her to do what she had planned. But not like that. Not when her mind had been poisoned.

"No, Ariel," I said, catching her hand just before it could reach its target. I pushed her back and quickly sat before she could find another way to get what she wanted. "Here…open your mouth."

"Mmmm," she moaned. "Now we're getting somewhere…"

The way she looked up at me through the damp curls hanging in her face nearly undid me.

The second she did as I bade her, I took the blossoms I'd crushed up from my hand and placed them in her mouth. Her narrowed eyes closed as she chewed the sweet flowers, a look of sheer ecstasy on her face. I wanted so badly to lean in and kiss her—to lay her down and finish what she'd tried to start. But if I did, neither of us would ever forgive me when she finally came to her senses.

Her mouth drew taut as she swallowed the winter sage. Kade had warned of how its sweetness turned bitter when it slid down your throat. How it began to burn in your stomach until you writhed in pain and begged for death. How'd you'd vomit until you could no longer lift your head.

That was Ariel's fate.

She scrambled off my lap, clutching her stomach. "What have you done to me?" she asked just before black vomit shot from her mouth. I crawled over to her side, but she flailed her arm blindly until it smacked mine. "Get away!" she screamed between bouts of spewing the poison from her body. Because that was what winter sage was, too—*poison*. One poison to cancel another. I hoped she'd believe me later when I explained. "You're trying to kill me! I knew it!" she said, her pale, sweating form crawling away from me. "You'll take the stone and hunt my father—"

"Ariel—"

"I knew it," she said again before collapsing to the ground. I watched from a distance as her anger and suspicion slowly faded, the worst of the sage's poison already over. By then, she was face down on the ground, whimpering, her words no longer her own. Twice in that time, she asked me to kill her, to put her out of her agony.

Instead, I pulled her limp, sweat-covered body into my lap and cradled her as tears ran down her face.

"I'm afraid I can't do that," I whispered in her ear as I rocked her to sleep, "even if you don't believe me. Because I made a promise to you: I have to help you find your father. And you have to help me find mine." She mumbled something I couldn't understand before sleep took her, but several words stood out from her incoherent mutterings.

I wondered if my mind had twisted them into something I wanted to hear; something to assuage the guilt I felt. Or maybe I'd heard true.

Maybe she'd just told me she was sorry.

And that she'd always loved me.

23

ARIEL

My eyes felt like they'd been rubbed with sand when I opened them. I winced against the light of the sun, shielding my face with my arm. I tried to sit up, but my body was useless, my appendages leaden weights. Panic surged through me as I looked around, trying desperately to remember where I was and how I'd gotten there.

"Easy, Ariel. Take it easy." Hemming's voice at my ear eased my fears in a second. I turned to find him lying behind me, propped up on an elbow. "You were poisoned by the serpent's blood."

"Uggh," I groaned as I tried again to sit up. "How bad was it?" With cautious hands, he aided me in the process, which was far from graceful.

"Do you want me to tell you or just let you remember for yourself?" I cringed at the thought. Father had told us long ago about its bizarre effects on the Nychterídes. "You were…

acting crazy. I had to give you something to counter its effects. It made you pretty sick."

"By sick, do you mean dead? Because I feel like death had its way with me, then spat me out."

He choked on a laugh, and it made me wonder just how accurate my description had been. His smile belied his true feelings; I could see the concern buried deep in those grey eyes.

The ground rustled under his feet as he walked over to my pack and started rummaging through it. I tried to remember anything that had happened as we walked through the woods. I recalled an odd sensation growing inside me.

The rest was complete darkness.

"Do you really not remember?" His shoulders tightened, like he was bracing for my response.

"Do I want to?"

He shook his head. "It might be best to leave it alone if you can."

"I'm not sure that's possible." That was the painful truth. If I didn't know, my mind would run wild, spinning tales of words and actions that all led to either embarrassment or shame. But knowing could lead down that same road, and I knew it. "Just give me the gist so I can put it to rest."

With his back still to me, he explained how the poison worked, how it lowered your defenses. He told me that I'd raged at him for everything he'd ever done to me. That I'd told him how hurt I was. Then I'd punched him in the face when he fed me the poison.

"I'm sorry I yelled at you," I said, crawling over to him, "and I shouldn't have hit you." He looked back at me and smiled. Once again, it didn't reach his eyes.

"I'll forgive you if you keep that flying fist of yours to yourself from now on."

"Deal." I sat down at his feet, still feeling weak. His wing brushed up against me, and I noticed the bandage on it. "How's your wound?" I asked, peeling the dressing away. The puncture had fully closed, a small, pale scar the only sign it had been there at all.

"It's fine. I'm good to fly if we need to."

"Fly? I'm not even sure I can stand right now."

"Then I'll carry you while you bark directions at me," he said. I opened my mouth to argue, then stopped. His amusement was plain in the set of his smile and mischief in his eyes. He grabbed our things, then picked me up and held me to his bare chest. His cool skin against mine stirred something deep inside me, and I leaned into his strength and rested my head on his shoulder. "Which way?" he asked.

I gripped the blessing stone in my hand and focused on its pull. It was weaker than I remembered, and fear spiked through me, erasing whatever comfort I'd just found in his arms.

"That way—and hurry!" I pointed northeast, and Hemming took off at a sprint.

He barreled through the trees, weaving as gracefully as possible with me in his arms. The stone warmed only slightly even though we'd covered a lot of ground. I could see that we were nearing the edge of the forest, which made me anxious.

"Ariel," Hemming said, drawing my attention. He ground to a halt and put me down before racing toward a makeshift camp, complete with a canvas tent covered with branches for camouflage. But there was no camouflaging the fact that it was a Nychteríde tent.

And it was spattered with blood.

I ran past Hemming on wobbly legs, screaming my father's name. Hemming drew his weapons and ripped the canvas door open to reveal two corpses inside. I moved to check them, but Hemming stepped in my way.

"I'll do it," he said, crouching down to enter.

He rolled the bodies over to expose their faces. Neither was my father, and I let loose a breath of relief, but it was short lived. Erwan and Kolm looked up at the sky with dead eyes, their skin blue and pale. I knelt down beside them and rested my hands on their legs. I whispered a prayer to the war gods to take them—to ferry their souls to the great lands where all warriors went in death. Then I reached over and closed their eyes.

"They were loyal to your father," Hemming said. "I don't understand…"

"They were attacked in their sleep and killed because of that loyalty." I felt a burning in my veins, a slowly growing fire coursing through me at the thought of a coward dispatching my father's lieutenants this way. They were brutal, but had always been kind to me. I felt their loss deeply.

I would avenge them as soon as we found the traitor.

And my father.

"We must go, Ariel," Hemming said, rushing out of the tent. "What does the stone say?"

I closed my eyes and tried to focus on its pulse in my hand. It was stronger than before, and it pulled me toward the forest's edge. "That way," I said, pointing to a distant break in the trees.

"Then let's go."

Hemming scooped me up and bolted through the woods. Once he broke through the tree line, he had us high above the ground to scan the land. The wind whipped my hair around us, and I tried to keep it from my face to no avail. It was unnerving to fly this way—with no control. With total trust in the one holding you. It made me appreciate my wings even more than I thought possible. It made me wonder how those without them could stand to be carried this way.

"Veer right," I told Hemming, and he gently banked in

that direction. A vast meadow opened beneath us, a wide river meandering through the lush grounds like a lazy traveler. The stone began to warm in my hand, every beat of Hemming's wings driving us closer to my father. I frantically searched the ground below for any sign of my father or the other Nychterídes.

In the distance, along the riverbank, I spotted another corpse. We stopped long enough to identify Caelum. His bludgeoned body was splayed across the shore in a gory display. My heart seized tighter in my chest, the thought that my father could have met the same fate impossible to ignore.

Hemming dragged me back into his arms and shot into the sky, following the stone's call. I gripped it tighter and prayed to the gods that Delphyne had been right—that the stone would indeed lead me to what I sought. That it wasn't all a lie—a trick of the fae. Because with every one of my father's fallen soldiers we encountered, my hope waned; I feared my father would be the next. From what I could recall, only five had embarked on the journey to meet Kaplyn in the Black Forest—the journey that had turned into an assassination attempt on my father. If correct, that left only the traitor and my father as potential survivors.

The odds were not in his favor.

"We'll find him," Hemming said to reassure me, but his words fell flat. Neither of us could guarantee that we would. Or that he'd be alive if we did.

I focused on the ground below as we flew toward an uncertain future. Tears I tried to convince myself were a result of the wind rolled down my cheeks, and I wiped them away. I needed my vision sharp—my senses keen. I couldn't afford to let emotions cloud them.

After some time, the landscape started to look familiar. I squinted to see if I could spot Kaplyn's manor in the distance. I hadn't recognized the river as the one that bordered his property, having been turned around too many times in the Black Forest. If the stone was taking me to Kaplyn, then it was likely that my father had escaped and gone to his ally in his time of need.

Or my father was dead, and the stone was returning me home.

"There!" I screamed, spotting the estate on the hill miles away. Without hesitation, Hemming used every bit of energy he had left to fly us there in a flash. We touched down outside the gates surrounding the home, the perimeter of the estate too heavily warded against both ground and aerial attacks to drop in. The only entry was through the gate itself—and only if you possessed the key.

We ran to the wrought-iron bars, and I pressed the stone against the lock. The gate creaked as it swung open for me.

"Thank you," I whispered to it.

"Hurry," Hemming urged, and we took off at a sprint.

The groundskeepers gave us wide-eyed looks as we sped past them toward the stairs, taking three or four at a time. We were soon at the main entrance, and I burst through the doors without an ounce of decorum, Hemming right on my heels. Jahyndra, the housemaid, screamed when she saw me. She chased after us, flustered and stuttering as I stormed toward Kaplyn's study. It was almost dinnertime, and he was a creature of habit. I knew he'd be there.

I threw the study door open and barged in unannounced. "Kaplyn! Have you seen my—"

"Ariel!" my father cried, jumping across the room to grab me. He snatched me into a hug before my mind could catch up. My father was safe. We'd found him. "Where have you been? We were just planning to come and find you!"

He pushed me away to take me in, parental fear and anger in his tight features. Then his eyes fell upon Hemming, and everything fell apart. "*You!*" he shouted, lunging for

Hemming. I barely intercepted him before his hands could wrap around my friend's neck. "I thought I told you to stay away—"

"Baba! He *saved* me. Hemming is the only reason I'm standing here right now. Please…you need to listen to me."

Though he still looked murderous, breathing hard and clenching his fists, he took a step back, giving us all a bit more room. "Hemming and I will discuss this later."

"It's good to see you again, Ariel." I turned to find Kaplyn, standing in his tailored midnight blue finery, his fair hair pulled back from his face. He smiled warmly, then strode toward me, arms wide to embrace me. My body stiffened slightly at his approach, and he halted when he saw my apprehension. "Ariel…did you really think I would be angry with you for leaving? That you would not be welcome here again?"

"That thought had crossed my mind a time or two…"

He did his best not to look wounded by my response, but the tension at the corners of his eyes said otherwise. He looked down at my closed fist—the one holding the blessing stone—and resumed his approach. As if asking permission, his gaze fell to my hand again, then back to me. "May I?" he asked, pointing to my clenched fist.

I raised my hand and opened it to expose the blessing stone. "Delphyne gave me this before I left, to keep me safe. Please don't be angry with her; she was just worried."

"I cannot be angry with her for doing what I once asked her to do," he said, smiling at me.

It took a moment for his words to fully register. "You wanted me to have this?"

He nodded. "I knew you well enough to know that one day you might decide to go against your father's wishes and return home. I also knew you wouldn't come to me with such an ill-conceived plan, so I blessed the stone and gave it to

Delphyne. I knew you would trust her." His green eyes beseeched mine. "Delphyne is not the only one here who loves you, Ariel, which is why your father and I were coordinating a search effort for you—though it no longer seems pertinent."

"For me?" I asked, confusion in my tone.

"Ariel, your father did not show at our designated meeting place, then stormed into my home, covered in blood and demanding to see you, and my heart sank to my shoes. When I told him I hadn't seen you since you escaped for Daglaar, he damn near tore my house down." He flashed me a smile that helped take the edge off the tension in the room, then wrapped his arms around me. He held me tightly for longer than I would have expected. "Once I calmed him down, we started planning."

I'd somehow forgotten about the fact that I was supposed to have arrived at the manor with Adrik while my father met with Kaplyn. Their concern suddenly made much more sense.

"Tycho killed Adrik," I said, my voice distant as I began to relay the events of my escape. "I fought the others and nearly escaped, but they caught me and pinned me to a tree." I remembered the feel of steel sliding between my ribs and shuddered. Hemming put his hand on my shoulder and gave a squeeze. My father's gaze drifted to that hand; he looked as though he might rip it from Hemming's body any second.

"I found them just as he was about to slide a blade into her heart, General. Seconds more and she would have been lost."

"I'm only here because of Hemming, Baba, so whatever you think of him, you need to remember that."

"What did you do to them?" my father asked him, ignoring me entirely.

Hemming hesitated for only a moment. "What needed to be done."

"They were traitors, Baba. That's how we knew you were in trouble. We came to warn you. We've been all over the Midlands trying to get to you." I turned my attention to Kaplyn. "I think your little stone is broken. It sent us through some rather unfriendly places."

"The stone sent you where you needed to go," he answered, not a hint of apology in his tone. Hemming scoffed at his reply, and the fae lord's sharp green eyes turned to him. "You think the magic failed you?"

"I think it nearly got us killed on more than one occasion."

"And yet here you are, standing before me unscathed."

"Not unscathed," I corrected, "but yeah, we're here. Now tell me what happened to you, Baba."

"We arrived early at the meeting place, so we set up camp. Erwan and Kolm were resting when Omar killed them." The disgust in his eyes was visceral. "I had been on watch with Caelum. We returned when we heard the shouting. At first, we assumed they'd been attacked by a fae creature. Omar met us halfway to camp, covered in blood, and claimed he had slain the beast and that it was a trap—that Kaplyn was trying to kill us. That we needed to leave the woods. Omar struck Caelum as we flew off. I wouldn't have even noticed had his blood not hit my wings. I turned to find Omar covered in blood, smiling back at me. But instead of attacking, he retreated. I chased him back to the Black Forest, but he disappeared not long after landing there. Rather than risk an ambush, I came here—to Kaplyn—for aid." He paused for a moment. "Then I found out you had not returned and lost my mind…"

"Do you think Omar's gone back to Daglaar?" I asked, ignoring his final remark.

"I'm sure that's his plan, though whether it's to claim my spot as general or to help someone else claim it, I can't be certain. What I do know is that he couldn't have done this without the support of others."

"We have to stop him!" I yelled.

My father pinned dark eyes on mine. "We will."

Sadness overtook me as the silence in the room stretched out. "Tell me what we're going to do about those trying to usurp my father."

"We hadn't gotten to that just yet," Kaplyn said, walking over to the seat behind his desk. "We were too busy amassing an army to come for you."

"An army?" I asked. I did nothing to hide the incredulity I felt.

"We could only assume that someone was after you as well. Just as you searched for your father, we planned to search for you, provided the traitors hadn't already succeeded in getting rid of you."

"Not for lack of trying," I muttered under my breath.

Kaplyn smiled. "I'll take that as a thank-you for all those daily training sessions we had. The ones you lamented *every single time…*"

I shrugged in response, and he laughed. My father, however, seemed far less amused. "We will talk about this more at dinner," he said, and I could hear the dismissal in his tone. "Until then, Kaplyn and I still have matters to discuss."

"That we do, but first, could someone please introduce me to Ariel's quiet friend? The one you were ready to choke to death in my study only moments ago?"

"This is Hemming," I said, stepping aside so they could formally shake hands. "Hemming, this is Lord Kaplyn Corvallym—the one I told you about."

Kaplyn's gaze drifted up to Hemming, and his expression tensed. Surprise filled his eyes for a moment when they fell on Hemming's ears, though he recovered quickly.

"You are Neráida…*fae*…"

"*Half* fae," Hemming corrected.

"If it were not for your ears, one would never know it."

Hemming's body went rigid. "The Nychterídes know all too well what I am."

Kaplyn's mouth pressed to a thin line as he nodded, then turned to me. "Find Jahyndra and let her know you'll be dining with us," Kaplyn said. "I must apologize that I don't have any extra rooms for you, Hemming. I called in all the surrounding fae lords and their military advisors to aid in Kade's efforts. They're all staying here until further notice."

"He can sleep with me," I said without a thought. The three males in the room stared at me, my poorly chosen words evoking a mix of emotions. Hemming looked shocked, Kaplyn looked amused, and my father looked homicidal yet again. "I meant on the *floor*. He can sleep in my room on the floor. If that's okay—"

"It most certainly is not," my father said, heading toward us.

Kaplyn elegantly slipped into his path. "They've just endured a harrowing experience in the Black Forest together. Ariel may find comfort in having her friend at her side should nightmares strike."

"She can stay in my room if that's a likelihood," my father seethed.

"I think being in a familiar place would be good for her," Kaplyn said, his tone civil but firm. "I'm certain Hemming knows your feelings on the matter and would not wish to incur your wrath any further." Kaplyn glanced at Hemming, silently demanding his agreement. Hemming merely nodded. "Then it is settled for now. As soon as a room is available, I shall have Hemming set up there."

My father looked less than pleased with this plan but said nothing else. Before he decided to change his mind, I led the way out of the room, Hemming falling in behind me. We were well into the grand hall before he said anything.

"I'm pretty sure your father is plotting my death at the moment." He tried to sound amused, but there was too much potential truth in his words for the humor to ring true. It was a valid concern, and we both knew it.

"He'll be fine. Now that he knows I'm alive, he can focus on what really matters; flushing out the traitors, killing them, and regaining his command."

"You are what really matters to him," Hemming said. His words stopped me cold.

"He loves me, but he would not give up his position for me, and we both know it. He's proven that already. But I understand why and accept it. He was born to lead them."

Before Hemming could argue, a voice rang out through the hall.

"Ariel!" I turned to find a familiar man heading our way. "Thank the gods you're back!"

Shayfer, Kaplyn's liaison—and spy—to the other fae lords, and the son of one himself, rushed toward me, arms outstretched. His short black hair fell into his honey brown eyes as he bent down to hug me without hesitation or formality. He'd long since abandoned any shred of pretense around me. It was pointless wasting his fine manners on someone raised by Nychteríde warriors. "I have been combing the Midlands for you."

I pulled away from his embrace to look him over. He did seem a bit worse for wear. Besides his hair looking uncharacteristically unkempt, his clothes were just a touch disheveled, like he'd slept in them, and the dark circles under his eyes hinted that he'd been up all night. Perhaps searching for me.

As though he knew what I was thinking, he smiled wide, mischief in his eyes as always. "You don't look so put-together yourself," he said, that smile never faltering, "and you've smelled better, too."

"Such a gentleman. You sure know how to speak to a lady."

That damned smile widened. "*Lady*? I see no lady here."

I punched him in the arm, and he flinched—that wasn't an act. "It's good to see you, Shayfer."

"I can't say I've missed your violent temper, Ariel, but temper aside, it's good to see you as well. You had us all worried sick."

"Trust me, that was not the plan."

"I'm sure this will make for an interesting story later…" It was only then that he seemed to notice Hemming hovering behind me like a Nychteríde bodyguard. Shayfer's keen, narrowed eyes assessed him, taking in everything he could in an instant. Then he stepped forward, hand outstretched. "Where are my manners? Allow me to introduce myself, since this young *lady* has neglected to do so." He cut me a sideward glance and winked. "Shayfer Tryndall of the East-side Marsh and Meadow."

Hemming looked at Shayfer's well-manicured hand for a moment before taking it. "Hemming."

"*Hemming*? Just Hemming?" Shayfer asked, his eyes darting to the points of Hemming's ears for a fraction of a second. I instantly knew what he was thinking, and I cringed. "No fae surname?"

"I'm sure I have one. I just don't know it."

The ice in Hemming's words sent a shiver through me. Shayfer had meant no offense, but Hemming had taken it all the same.

"Hemming doesn't need a surname," I said, stepping closer. "Notorious warriors never do."

Shayfer's expression didn't falter, but I knew him well enough to know he wasn't quite sure what to make of the situation. We'd been friends from the day I arrived at Kaplyn's. I'd called him a spoiled little fairy for ignoring me at lunch, and he'd spit out his tea in a fit of laughter. He'd never ignored me again.

"We were just about to go get cleaned up," I said, drawing attention to my bloodstained leathers. "Apparently, we're not properly attired for dinner." I smiled up at him, and he laughed.

"Somehow I think Kaplyn might make an exception for you, but yes, please do go see to that. I'll find you later." He took my hand in his and bowed low enough to press it to his forehead, then his lips. "I'm glad you're safe, Ariel," he said before shifting his gaze to Hemming. "A pleasure to meet you, *Just Hemming*." With a respectful nod, he headed toward Kaplyn's study.

"Friend of yours?" Hemming asked, watching him disappear into the room.

"He's rich and entitled, but pretty fun once you get him to drop a lifetime of grooming. And he's sneaky as can be—great at pilfering wine from the cellar."

"And in a fight?" he asked, turning to look at me.

"I'd wipe the floor with him."

At that, he smiled. "Good. Now, care to show me this room we'll be sharing?"

"Right this way, sir," I said with a sweeping bow that would have made the house staff proud.

Hemming's laughter escorted us all the way down the hall.

HEMMING

I tried not to notice the opulence of Ariel's room when we entered, but I failed. It was larger than at least four Nychteríde cabins combined and filled with expensive furniture and fabrics. The bathroom was not only indoors, but attached to her room—no sharing necessary.

She caught me taking it all in, and her shoulders slumped. "It's a pretty cage, Hemmy. That's all."

"A cage with an indoor bathroom," I replied, trying to lighten the mood. My attempt fell flat, judging by her frown.

"It has that and so much more, but does it really matter if it's still a prison of sorts—somewhere you can't leave without consequences?"

"You couldn't leave your room without permission?" I asked, my anger spiking.

"No, no, I'm speaking in metaphors—and poorly, apparently. My point is that this was not where I wanted to be, yet I couldn't leave. In a sense, that made it a prison."

Her conflicted emotions were plain in her eyes. It was then that I realized how complicated her situation had been. I'd mocked her for becoming soft and spoiled in her time away, but in reality, it had been torture for her in many ways. Any joy she'd found in the Midlands had been tainted by the knowledge that she was trapped there.

"Do you want to get cleaned up first? I can wait out here in your pretty prison cell." I flashed her the grin she never could resist to cheer her up, and she smiled. Then she threw a lace-trimmed pillow at my head.

"You can go first. I need to pick out something to wear to dinner and find something for you to wear, too." Before I could defend my filthy leathers, Ariel opened the door to the bathroom and started filling the massive white tub in the center. I'd never seen one before—not like that. It looked as though I could disappear in it. "Try not to drown," she said as she brushed past me. Then she closed the door behind her, leaving me alone in her Midlands home.

≈

ARIEL

I HURRIED THROUGH THE HOUSE IN SEARCH OF DELPHYNE. IF anyone would know where I could find adequate clothing for Hemming while his was tended to, it was her. I found her in her fabric room at the end of the east wing, running her hands over a black silk that seemed to shine with every color of the rainbow when it moved.

"Ariel!" she cried, dropping the bolt of silk as she ran to me. Her frail arms wrapped around me and held me tightly. "Lord Kaplyn said you'd be all right, but with your father's arrival and the fae lords and their advisors, I didn't know what to believe."

"I'm fine, Delphyne. I just had a bit of a rough journey back to the Midlands."

She pulled away from me to see for herself that I was in one piece. Her eyes roamed over my body; she even spun me around to make sure she hadn't missed a cut or abrasion. "Well, your leathers are in rough shape, but you seem to be all right."

"About those," I said, looking down at my clothes, "any chance you have anything that would fit a Nychteríde warrior —one taller than my father?"

She let out a low whistle. "That's a lot of man, Ariel."

"He is indeed. And he's currently naked in my bathroom getting cleaned up with nothing to wear once he's done." Her gaze turned motherly at the mention of a naked man in my room. I shut down her suspicions before the interrogation could begin. "We've been friends since I was four, Delphyne, and Kaplyn said there were no spare rooms in the manor, hence the need to share mine."

"As long as he keeps his hands and other bits to himself, I'll allow it. Now, about something for him to cover those bits with…" She searched her walls of fabric until she squeaked with delight as her eyes landed on a pile of weathered black leather so high up on the wall that even I'd have needed a ladder to reach it. Poor Delphyne, with her petite frame, barely stood as high as my chest, but she was fierce and fear-less and could dress down a man three times her size with her sharp tongue and death stare. "Give me an hour," she said, sliding the ladder over. "I'll have something for him by then."

"Thank you, Delphyne."

"No thanks needed. Just tell him to keep his leathers on while he's sleeping so I don't have to kill him."

I laughed at her threat, knowing full well she meant it, and headed back to my room and the cleaner—but still naked —warrior waiting there for me.

≈

ARIEL

"THERE YOU ARE!" SHAYFER CALLED AS I TURNED DOWN THE hall that housed my room. "I'm glad I found you."

"A questionable accomplishment in my own hallway." I flashed him a grin, and he shook his head at me in mock irritation.

"I'm pleased to see they didn't dull that sharp wit of yours over there by the mountain."

I rolled my eyes and started to walk away. "You're such a snob, Shayfer. They're not mindless brutes," I said, then realized that some of them were exactly that. But he didn't need to know that fact; my father and Hemming spoke to the contrary. I thought it best to let them represent the Nychterídes, especially to a fae spy. "What do you want so badly that you're stalking me near my bedroom?"

"I want to know what happened. Kaplyn wouldn't say, and your father didn't speak more than two words with me in the room."

The corner of my mouth twitched, unable to contain my amusement. "He's too smart for that."

Shayfer sighed. "Are you going to tell me, or will I have to get you drunk tonight until your wine-loosened lips spill whatever secrets I wish to hear?"

"My lips are a fortress you cannot penetrate," I replied, smiling wickedly. "There isn't enough wine in this manor to make me tell you my secrets."

My challenge, as always, intrigued him, and he leaned in closer. "Are you so sure about that?"

"Very sure."

He put his hand on my arm and bent toward me in conspiratorial fashion, his pouty lips at my ear. "After dinner, then? The usual spot?"

"Only if you wish for me to empty Kaplyn's wine stores and make you look foolish."

A door opened behind me, and I started to turn to see who was there. Shayfer stopped me and pressed a chaste kiss to my cheek before he pulled away, smiling. "After dinner it is, then." He walked away and disappeared around the corner. I turned to find Hemming scowling at the spot where Shayfer had just been standing.

"Good news," I said, heading toward Hemming as he peeked out from my room. "You should have something clean and decent to wear in about an hour."

I pushed the door open to find a sheet wrapped around his waist, the thin white fabric slung low across his hips. The memory of him naked beside the lake flashed through my mind, and heat warmed my cheeks. I hurried into the bathroom and kept my head down as I began refilling the tub.

"What did Shayfer want?" he asked. I dared a sideward glance to find him leaning against the doorframe, arms crossed. The wet fabric clung to his legs and hips and…

I quickly refocused my attention on drawing my bath.

"When it comes to Shayfer," I said, running my hand through the warm water, "it's hard to know." Hemming didn't respond, indicating that my answer didn't suffice. "He wants to know what happened to us on our journey, okay?"

"You mean he wants to know what happened to *you*."

"Same thing. Information is Shayfer's currency," I explained. "He's just fishing for gossip and drama to fill his time here. Kaplyn and my father are so wrapped up in how to proceed that Shayfer is in limbo until they have a strategy that requires his particular talents."

"So you're his entertainment?"

I shrugged. "Maybe. He does like to try to get me drunk…"

"I bet," Hemming replied. I looked up from the tub to give him the evil eye but got waylaid when I saw his arms stretched above him, his fingers hooked on the top of the doorframe. The sharp cut of his muscles was far more distracting than I cared to admit, and I tried not to stare. Unfortunately, I failed miserably. "Do me a favor, Ariel. Be careful around him, okay? I don't trust him."

"You barely trust anyone, Hemming."

"True, but for good reason."

"I'm aware of the kind of guy Shayfer is. I'm not blind, and I'm not stupid. His tricks don't work on me. But under that puffed-up peacock façade is a decent being who was fun to hang around with."

I let the implied "when I didn't have you" hang in the air between us. Saying it wouldn't improve our conversation.

Steam started to billow through the room, bringing my attention back to the task at hand; the task I'd been side-tracked from by Hemming's questions and naked torso. "I should get cleaned up," I said, turning the water off. He loomed in the doorway for a beat before stepping back and closing the door.

I let out a harsh breath, then stripped off my dirty clothes. The water was too hot, but it felt amazing on my weary body.

I slid down deep until it covered the lower half of my face. I lay there until my skin started to wrinkle and the water started to cool. I could hear Hemming pacing outside the door.

Waiting had never been his favorite pastime.

When I pulled the drain in the tub to get out, I stood up to find I had nothing to dry off with. "Of course…" I sighed. "Hemming?" I called. "Can you bring me a towel?"

The door swung open and he stepped through, still wearing that damned sheet. I crouched down in the tub and tried to cover myself.

"Sweet gods!" he shouted, shielding his eyes with my towel. "What are you doing?"

"What are *you* doing?" I countered. "I asked you to bring me something to dry off with, not barge in like the room was on fire!"

"I thought you'd be under the water!"

"Surprise! I'm not!"

"Here," he said, blindly reaching the towel toward me. I wrapped it around my body so I could climb out of the tub. Once I was covered, he dared to look at me again.

"Does this make us even now?" I asked, flustered by the situation.

"I didn't know we weren't—"

"Because I saw you naked?"

"You did?" he asked, feigning shock. "When? I feel so violated…" I shoved him out of my way, and he followed me out of the room. "It was an honest mistake, Ariel. You know I would never—"

He cut himself short, not wanting to say it out loud. Of all the men I'd known in my lifetime, my father included, I'd never met one kinder to the opposite sex. Maybe that was just who Hemming was, or maybe it was because he had convinced himself that he was the product of rape, but either way, his respect for females was unparalleled in our world.

He would never have done something untoward intentionally.

Because I knew that, he didn't take a blow from my staff to his precious bits.

"I know, Hemming. It's not like that with us," I said, an ache in my chest growing as I spoke those words. Maybe it had never been like that between us, but I was starting to question whether I wanted it to stay that way.

He clenched his jaw, the muscles working hard to contain something he clearly wanted to say. "I can leave if you want to get dressed," he said, sitting down on the edge of the bed.

"Just turn around. And no laughing when you see what I'm wearing, okay?"

"No laughing? Why would I laugh?"

I pulled a silk gown from my closet and sighed. Dinner always required a certain level of attire—attire like I'd never worn before my time at Kaplyn's estate.

"You'll see," I muttered under my breath as I wrestled the gown into place. I held the bodice against me and walked around the bed, the swish of the fabric against the floor announcing my approach. When I stopped in front of him, he just stared in silence. "You're not laughing. Why aren't you laughing?"

"You told me not to," he replied, staring at the midnight blue dress.

"Can you lace this up for me?" I asked. I turned to expose where the gown lay open all the way down to the small of my back. "You have to start at the bottom and work your way up to my wings."

He stood and stepped closer. I could feel his breath rustle my hair as he took the laces of my corset and began to cinch me into my dress with deft fingers. When he reached the top, he tied it off, and his hand grazed the sensitive spot between my wings. I stifled a shiver.

"All done," he said, his voice low and husky.

"Could you fasten the choker for me, too, please? I can barely lift my arms with this thing on. It's so restrictive." He did as I asked, clasping the beaded neckpiece before walking around me slowly. "Still no laughing," I warned as his eyes moved from my head to my toes, then back again.

"You look…you look like…"

"A fool?" I asked.

He shook his head. "No. A *lady*."

At his words, it was I who burst out laughing. "I may look like one, but you and I know better. This lady could kill someone five different ways before they could cry out for help."

A wicked look crept across Hemming's face. "Perhaps that makes you the best weapon ever. A lion dressed as a lamb."

His stare lingered on my dress for a moment longer, the silence in the room suddenly too heavy—too thick. A knock on the door was a welcome interruption, and I rushed to open it. I found Delphyne standing on the other side, arms full of black leather piled all the way up to her nose. Her eyes narrowed when her gaze drifted past me to Hemming in all his half-naked glory.

"Might I suggest that you put these on now, *warrior*, before her father finds you in here dressed in only a sheet and flays you alive—assuming that I don't first."

"Thank you, Delphyne," I said, reaching for the clothes. "I'll see that he puts them on immediately."

"No, you most certainly will not," she said, tossing the leathers to Hemming and grabbing my hand to drag me out. "He'll see to that himself." The slam of the door punctuated her sentiment perfectly. "You, girl, are playing with fire," she said, walking me down the hall. "He's the one, isn't he?" she asked, having pieced together who my nameless friend was.

The one I'd told her had tried to kill me.

"It was a misunderstanding, Delphyne. We've hashed everything out. It's just like old times—when we were friends."

Except, back then, I didn't ogle him when he was nearly naked...

She turned, pinning her beady blue eyes on me, her child-like features twisted into a snarl.

"That man—boy—whatever you want to call him, is *not* your friend, Ariel. I don't care if you two have made amends, or if you believe his intentions were honorable—"

"Which they were—"

"Once you come of age, Ariel, *no* man is your friend."

"You don't know Hemming."

"I know men," she replied, her expression sharp. "He may have been your childhood companion, but neither of you is a child anymore."

"So are you mad at him because you're holding a grudge against him or because he's male?" I asked, sounding every bit as irritated as I felt. "I'm confused—"

"Why are you confused?" a voice asked from around the corner. Kaplyn appeared a moment later, his expression as pleasant as ever.

"My lord," Delphyne said, inclining her head. "I was just imparting some wisdom upon Ariel, and she seems to be having trouble following along."

"Wisdom about what?"

She hesitated. "The opposite sex."

"Oh," Kaplyn said, mischief in his smile. "She doesn't seem very impressed by it."

"The truth is not always as palatable as we'd like it to be, sir. Especially about that."

Kaplyn's eyebrows shot up in surprise. "Well, I'm sorry to interrupt this conversation, but I must steal Miss Ariel."

"Of course," Delphyne replied with a smile before turning to me. "Remember what I told you." Just then, my bedroom door opened, and Hemming stepped out, his new leathers stretched tight across his body like a second skin. Delphyne caught me looking and pinched my arm. "You are *no longer children…*"

She disappeared down the hall just as Hemming arrived. "I don't think she likes me much," he said. I couldn't help but laugh, his observation breaking the tension.

"Shall we?" Kaplyn said, gesturing toward the dining room. He offered me his arm, and I took it out of habit. "I wouldn't worry about Delphyne, Hemming. She has a soft spot for Ariel. I'm sure she'll like you just fine, provided you do nothing to offend her favorite guest."

"Then I am in trouble," he muttered under his breath.

I looked over my shoulder to find him grinning at me. "Your favorite place to be."

HEMMING

I shouldn't have been surprised by the size of the dining room—everything else in Kaplyn's home was lavish and gaudy—yet somehow, when I walked through the massive double doors with Ariel at my side, I found myself in awe, staring from the polished wooden floors to the mural on the ceiling depicting the fall of The Three. It was so real that I wondered if I'd soon find three naked women on the floor.

"This way, please," a young male server said, ushering me toward my seat across from Ariel. Enough room had been left on either side of our places to allow for our wings. I was thankful for that space when I looked over to find Shayfer headed for the seat to Ariel's right.

"You look stunning this evening," he said to her, waiting for the servant to pull his chair out. Once seated, he leaned in and kissed Ariel on the cheek for the second time that evening. I looked down at the silver knife in my place setting and wondered how much damage I could inflict with it before someone stopped me.

Not coming to dinner fully armed was an oversight I wouldn't repeat.

"You say that to all the ladies in the house," she replied with a playful laugh. "Is that how you manage to get them into bed with you?"

"Them and half of the men, too," he replied with a wink. "But they don't play hard to get as well as you do."

"Hard or impossible?"

"Nothing is impossible, Ariel dear." The heavy weight of his gaze on her bare skin had me gripping my chair so hard the wood groaned in protest.

"I fear you may find that you're wrong about that," she said, arranging her wings around her chair.

"We shall see," was his only response.

Kaplyn sat at the head of the table, with Kade at the opposite end. Fae lords began to join us, taking seats around the table. Our dinner would serve as both a meal and a tactical meeting. Though the goal might have changed, military intervention would still be required if Kade were to have his rule restored and the peace between the fae and Nychterídes were to be upheld.

As wine was poured, Kaplyn stood and addressed the room.

"Again, I thank you all for coming. As you can see, Ariel has returned unharmed, and for this I am extremely grateful, but I am still in need of your assistance. You will want to hear me out on this matter," he said, his host voice lowering to one of business and strategy—one that made me realize why Kade and he were allies. "Our peace is in jeopardy. An attempt on the life of General Kade has been made."

A collective gasp broke out among the fae lords. Ariel looked at me with fear in her eyes. I wanted to reach across the table and take her hand in mine, but it was not the place for that, and I knew it. As if reading my thoughts, she straightened her back and lifted her chin, every bit the warrior her father had trained her to be.

"One of the traitors may still be in our lands. He must be found and dealt with, and I am requesting your aid in this matter. I need you to employ whatever means are at your disposal to bring this Nychteríde to me. If he escapes, the consequences could be dire." Kaplyn shot my father a serious look. "Kade and I have worked hard to maintain the truce between our people. If he is usurped, I cannot see anything but war in our future."

"And what if this is all an elaborate ploy by the general?" a redheaded fae lord asked.

"To what end?" Kade asked. "If I wanted to attack the Midlands, I would not come here first and warn you of the trouble ahead."

"This sounds like a matter for the Nychterídes to settle, not us," another chimed in. Others dressed in finery not built for war—most likely because they'd never stared down the blades of their enemies—echoed his sentiments. That a potential coup was not their problem. That they wanted no part of hunting the traitor.

I looked across to Ariel, the heat in her eyes plain as the entitled lords of the fae gorged themselves on food and wine without concern, as though what happened to the Nychterídes had no impact on them—on their people. I knew her anger wouldn't be contained forever. Her father's life hung in the balance.

Moments later, she shot up from her seat, her chair dragging across the floor loudly enough to garner the attention of everyone in the room. "Let me speak plainly," she said, meeting each of their gazes. "If my father's leadership falls and there is discord in our lands, are you truly foolish enough to think that strife will not befall you?"

"Ariel," Shayfer said, placing his hand on her arm. She pulled it away without pause.

"If war were to break out—even a civil war in Daglaar—where do you think the women and children will escape to? They'll come to the Midlands in droves—warriors, too—in search of food and shelter. Your resources will be strained in every way possible."

"And who is to say that we wouldn't just eliminate the trespassers?" the redhead asked.

"You wouldn't have the manpower needed to do so, Lord Teigan." Her words were a thinly-veiled insult, and the fae lord's face went as red as the tomato soup in front of him. "It would cost you a fortune to deal with the fallout."

"How dare you—"

"Oh, shut up, Teigan," Shayfer said, swirling the wine in his glass. "No need to get yourself worked up when she only speaks the truth."

"You expect me to sit here and be insulted by this...by this *half-breed*?"

Ariel stiffened at his insult, and it was all I could do not to walk over to Lord Teigan and drive a sword through his throat—had I one to use.

"You will," I said, my tone a threat all its own, "if you'd like to walk out of this room with all your body parts intact." I slid my gaze to him. The shock he felt was clear in his expression. "Say half-breed again and you'll wish you'd never laid eyes on one."

"Enough!" Kade roared, silencing the room. "Like it or not, Lord Teigan, my daughter is right." He placed his hands on the table and leaned toward the fae lord dumb enough to speak ill of Ariel. "And if you ever talk about her that way again, you won't have to worry about a war. Your corpse will have long cooled by then."

I didn't bother to hide my smile.

"I would prefer to keep the threats of death to a minimum during dinner, if possible," Kaplyn said. "First, I need to know which of you are willing to hunt this warrior down or lend your resources to the search. If you are not, leave now." He leveled his gaze on each of them. None of them moved— not even Lord Teigan. "Good. Now that that's settled, let us work out the logistics."

He spent the bulk of the first two courses listing off who would be doing what. The others made suggestions based on their particular gifts and magic and those of their house members. By the end, everyone at the table had been assigned tasks except for Ariel and me.

"Excellent," Kaplyn said, looking pleased with how things had gone. "We leave just after sunrise. There is no time to waste."

Ariel looked at me from across the table, frustration evident in the set of her jaw as she clenched her teeth. For the second time that evening, I feared what she was about to do. "What about us?" she asked, looking back and forth from Kaplyn to Kade. Both men tensed under her scrutiny.

"You will remain here," Kaplyn said. "Someone must watch over the manor in my absence. Who better to keep those here safe than you and Hemming?"

"He is not staying here alone with her," Kade all but growled. He turned his pitch-black eyes to me and silently dared me to challenge him.

"Baba, we've been over this already—"

"We have been over nothing," he said, turning those cold eyes to his daughter. "Have you forgotten what he did?"

"I have already explained this to you. Hemming saved my

life and risked his own to help me find you. Isn't that enough?"

"NO!" he yelled, slamming his fists on the massive table. "Your time away has clearly erased the memory of why you had to leave. And upon your return, you chose to accept him at his word? Let his lies indulge your fantasy that all is as it once was?" The anger behind his words was palpable, and she shrunk under its weight. "Has it not even once crossed your mind that he could somehow be involved in all of this?"

"You already know why I did what I did that night," I said, turning to my general. "I told you then. You just chose not to believe me." The room was so silent that I could hear Kade's ragged breaths from where I sat.

"Be silent," he said.

I stood up. He did the same.

"I knew you were blind to what was going on in the camp. To how things were changing. To how they all looked at her—"

"Shut. Your. Mouth," he seethed, knocking his chair back.

"It was only a matter of time before something happened…"

Kade slowly drew a blade from the sheath strapped to his chest.

"Hemming, don't," Ariel pleaded.

I stared Kade down and kept going. "I did what you could not. I sacrificed myself to keep her safe."

With a roar that shook the crystal on the table, Kade launched himself at me, blade pulled back to strike.

ARIEL

I couldn't believe what I was seeing.

My father's battle cry and drawn blade startled me into action, and I flew across the table to land in front of Hemming just before he did. I spread my wings wide, knocking flatware from the table in an attempt to create a shield. If my father wanted to get to Hemming, he would have to go through me.

"Ariel, move—"

"No, Baba. You're wrong about him, and I know it."

"You know nothing," he all but growled in response. "I had one of my men look into Hemming's story to see if there was any truth to it. He reported back that he could not confirm Hemming's account."

"Was it Omar?" I asked, letting my anger seep into my tone.

"*No*," was his only response.

"Maybe you couldn't confirm his story, but I can confirm

that everything Hemming has ever done since the day I set foot in Daglaar was to protect me. On our journey through the Black Forest alone, he saved me from a Dreamcatcher and a bloodthirsty hedge maze. And I saved him from nearly being drowned by a sea serpent. He and I have always looked out for one another since we were little. I will not let you hurt him again—you've punished him enough already."

The serrated edge of his blade glistened in the firelight as he held it only inches away from me. If I had somehow over-played my hand, I'd have no way to stop him.

"I gave him an *order* to stay away from you, and he disobeyed it. There are consequences for that—"

"Just like there were consequences for what he did that night? Hemming *knew* what would be done to his wings when he faked his attack on me, Baba, and he did it anyway. For *me*. To keep *me* safe because he knew Tycho would kill me if he didn't."

My father's eyes drifted up to Hemming for a moment, assessing him, then returned to me. "If it is true—that it was a ruse—what kind of fool plan was that?" he asked, trying to puzzle out why he'd done it. "Why not just come to me? Tell me what was happening?"

"She wouldn't have survived long enough for you to intervene," Hemming said plainly. "They caught her off guard and unarmed. There were too many for even me to stop them all."

The blade before me lowered. "And when she returned?" he asked. "Explain your actions."

"She'd been gone for four years. I knew what Tycho was capable of, and I didn't know if she could handle him in a fight, so I stepped in to try and scare her off. To make her see her mistake in returning." I looked back at Hemming—at the strain in his features. He avoided my eyes altogether, his focus solely on my father. "Her leaving was the worst thing

178

that has ever happened to me, but I would do it again—I *will* do it again when this is all over—if it's what's best for her."

My heart sank to my shoes at the thought. "Baba—"

He silenced me with a raised hand. "You will stay here with Hemming, and that is final. The two of you have been through enough. You need rest for what is yet to come."

"Your father is right, Ariel," Kaplyn added. "Now please, sit. Eat. Let us enjoy what is left of this dinner before tomorrow comes."

Hemming's hand fell on the small of my back, urging me to return to my seat. Again, I glanced back at him, but this time, he met my stare. The sadness in his eyes made my heart ache. "Go," he said softly. After a moment's pause, I did as he asked. I passed my father and continued to where Shayfer waited with a rueful look.

"I fear your family might be even more dysfunctional than mine…"

I ignored him and picked at my food, avoiding eye contact with everyone at the table. As the shame of challenging my father in front of the others crept in, all I wanted to do was sleep until I forgot that night had ever happened. But it had.

And there would be no taking it back.

27

ARIEL

As Kaplyn's guests filed out of the dining room, whispering to one another, Shayfer took my arm and escorted me to the door. "Meet me by the willow tree in twenty minutes," he said in my ear. "I have to procure some refreshments for us." The moment we stepped into the hall, he broke away, headed toward the kitchen and, beyond that, the storage room. I shook my head and laughed.

"Did the spy say something funny?" Hemming asked. He fell into step beside me, and we made our way to my bedroom.

"Not intentionally."

"Mmm…"

"So," I said, wanting to change the subject, "what do you think of this plan?"

"You mean the part about us being left behind?" he asked, eyebrow quirked.

"No. The rest of it."

He looked thoughtful for a moment. "I think if we can capture and torture Omar, we might learn how bad this situation is—what we're up against."

"And if we can't?"

The hard angle of his jaw grew harsher. "Then we face the unknown…"

Nothing about that sounded good.

"Well, *we* won't be facing anything from here," I said.

I could feel Hemming's gaze on the side of my face, boring holes through it with the intensity of his stare. "What are you planning?" he asked.

Before I could reply, a squeaky female voice rang out through the hall. I turned to find a golden-haired girl running toward me, arms spread wide. "Ariel!"

"Soph!"

She took a flying leap at me, and I caught her in midair, pulling her in close. Her legs wrapped around my waist, careful not to kick my wings. She squeezed my neck so tightly I had to pry her away a bit in order to breathe.

"Auntie said you would be okay, but I heard Kaplyn talking to the big scary warrior with the black wings. They were yelling about you—saying that you were missing."

"That big scary warrior is my father, Soph," I said, suppressing a laugh.

She pulled away to capture my face with her hands. "He is? Has he come to make you stay here for good this time? No more leaving?"

"I may have to leave for a little while again, but I could never leave you forever. You know that." She hugged me again, burying her face against my shoulder. "Shouldn't you be in bed right now?" I asked. "Does Delphyne know that you're roaming the manor at this hour?" She shook her head. "Wicked little girl," I teased, tickling her.

She threw her head back, laughing wildly, until she realized Hemming was standing behind me, an oversight she'd made in her excitement. She leaned back to take him in, assessing the Nychteríde warrior at my back. If she thought my father was terrifying, her opinion of Hemming would likely be no better.

"Sophitiya, I'd like you to meet a very good friend of mine. This is Hemming. We grew up together in Daglaar." I looked back over my shoulder to find Hemming grinning at the girl in my arms. "Hemming, this is Sophitiya, the one I told you about."

To his credit, his smile never faltered at the memory of what had almost happened to her; the grim circumstances surrounding Sophitiya's entrance into my life. "It's nice to meet you, Sophitiya," he said, using the kindest tone he could.

She said nothing for a moment, and I turned to find her beaming up at him. She giggled when I caught her staring. "He's *handsome*." More giggling, and I knew we were in trouble.

"He is *very* handsome," I agreed, stepping away from Hemming, "and bossy and arrogant…it's best not to compliment him too much for fear his head will grow so big and heavy that he can no longer fly."

Her giggling turned to laughter at the thought. "He would have to drag it along the ground!"

"Yes!" I agreed. "And then he'd be of no use to my father anymore. You wouldn't want him to get kicked out of the Nychteríde army, would you?"

She stopped laughing and considered my question. Her brows knit together as she contemplated his fate. She looked every bit the high fae woman her mother had once been— before she was cast out by her lord and left for dead.

Sophitiya had found her way to Delphyne.

Her mother had found her way to her grave.

"He has our ears," she noted thoughtfully. "Would he come to the Midlands if he was kicked out of the Nychteríde army?"

"I…I don't…"

"I would come here and watch over you," he said, stepping closer. "I would be your personal guardian. Would you like that?"

Her giggling began again, accompanied by blushing cheeks. "Yes, but that's Ariel's job."

"Ah, then I would not want to take away her duties."

Sophitiya's laughter stopped. "But you would still come here, right? For me…and Ariel?"

He put his fist to his chest and bowed his head. Her smile returned in an instant. "There is no place I would rather be."

The young girl climbed down and ran to Hemming. She clung to his leg, hugging it tightly. "Then I hope you lose your position with the Nychterídes."

I watched as he patted her head and wondered if that fate might be in his future, because my plan to hunt down the traitor had been forming from the moment I sat back down in my chair at dinner. There was no way I would be left behind —pushed aside. I had been through hell and back to find my father, all because of Omar. He would pay for his part in the attempt on my father's life and the deaths of his loyal soldiers. I would make sure of it.

When I pulled myself from my musings, I found Hemming staring and quickly forced a smile. "Soph," I said, pulling her away from Hemming's leg, "I have to be somewhere soon, and you should be in bed."

Her bottom lip thrust out, and she folded her arms across her chest. "Fine, but will I see you in the morning for breakfast?"

I dared a glance up at Hemming and instantly regretted it. His narrowed eyes told me he knew I had no intention of being there. "I don't think I'll be at breakfast, but I'll find you as soon as I can, okay?"

The clever girl mocked Hemming's expression; her awareness of my evasion was uncanny for someone her age. Her mother must have been a force to be reckoned with. "Promise me I will see you again," she said.

I swallowed hard. "I promise."

After a moment's hesitation, she ran over and hugged me, then took off down the hall. Hemming watched her go, a mix of emotions in his eyes. Then they fell upon me, filled with suspicion, and he started toward my room.

"I need to get out of this dress," I said, arching my back away from where the bodice dug in below my wings. "Delphyne usually works magic on her creations, but this one was made for someone without these." I twitched my wings for effect. "It's sad that she wasted such a beautiful gown on me."

Hemming stopped just shy of my door and turned to face me. "It's a shame that some young woman in need of such beauty could not have it," he said, unable to meet my eyes. "But that isn't you." Without another word, he opened the door and stepped into my room, leaving me in the hall in that ill-fitting gown weighing his words very carefully.

"You're just not used to seeing women dressed this way," I said, deflecting what I assumed had been a compliment.

"*True.*"

"Maybe once all this is over and we find *your* father—if you give him a chance to explain and you accept it—you might one day find yourself at dinners like the one tonight. At parties with women in lavish dresses." I said, hesitating slightly. "Maybe then you'll see the appeal."

He turned to face me as he strapped his blades across his chest. "First, that will never happen because my father is a dead man. And second, the appeal of this dress is not lost on me, Ariel. It accentuates all that makes a woman a woman—tapered waist, low neckline meant to show just enough to tempt but not enough to taste. A full skirt meant to leave a man to wonder what lies beneath all that silk. For one like Shayfer, who revels in games—the chase—costumes like these are perfect. But not for me." His eyes narrowed as he stared at the dress in question. "I prefer simplicity. The tight line of leather across the hips. The exposed back of a halter. The cross of a harness between the breasts. That, to me, is beautiful—is *real*. The rest is all pretend."

I stood there, mouth agape, staring at my friend as he put on weapons as if he were going to war instead of bed. The shame I felt in that moment seeped into my every pore. He was a Nychteríde soldier—at his core, he knew that. That dress represented everything he disliked about the other half of his lineage and the world they embraced.

I'd never wanted to disrobe so badly in all my life.

I reached behind me, arching to grab the ribbon that tied the back closed. When I couldn't find it, I let out a breath of frustration.

"Need some help?" Hemming asked. He walked up behind me, the distinct sound of a blade being pulled from its sheath echoing through the room. He grabbed the top of the dress and tugged me backward. With a pass of his blade, he sliced the ribbon free, and the bodice fell forward. I caught it just before it dropped too far. "That dress is just another pretty cage," he whispered in my ear. "Never forget who you are, Ariel. Who you were raised to be."

He walked into the bathroom and closed the door behind him.

I dropped the dress to the ground and put on my leathers as quickly as I could.

≈

HEMMING

Ariel didn't tell me where we were going, but given Shayfer's behavior both before and after dinner, I was pretty sure he was involved. There was no way I was staying behind so they could have their clandestine meeting. I didn't trust the spy at all.

We made our way out to the yard, headed for a massive tree on the east side of the property. I smiled at the sight of Ariel in her leathers—especially the blade she'd strapped to her leg. I wondered if she trusted Shayfer as little as I did.

I didn't see him waiting for us until we were only yards away. He jumped down from high in the tree branches. Disappointment flashed through his eyes when he saw me, but he recovered quickly. Ariel probably didn't even notice.

"Kaplyn has an excellent selection to pilfer from," he said, gesturing to the wine bottles at the base of the willow. "Ladies first."

"You know I don't care," Ariel said with a laugh. "You pick."

He smiled at her, then grabbed a bottle of red wine from the stash. "I think this one suits you best. Not too sweet. Not too dry. The perfect balance of both."

"Thanks," she said, uncorking the bottle.

Shayfer reached for a glass, but Ariel merely put the bottle to her lips and began to drink. Shayfer shook his head at her.

I burst out laughing. "She's a wild one, *friend*. She'll never be tamed."

He looked up at me with fire in his eyes. "I do love a challenge..."

"Would you two stop yapping and start drinking? It's been a long day. One I'd like to forget ever happened."

"Then forget you shall," Shayfer said, tossing me a bottle and grabbing one for himself. Much to Ariel's amusement, he opened it and drank directly from it, just as she had. She nearly spit out her wine at the sight.

"Such a savage," she teased him. "Whatever would your father say?"

"My father isn't here," he replied with a wink. "Can I trust you not to tell him?"

"That depends. Can I trust you to find the traitor that tried to kill my father?" Liquid flew from Shayfer's mouth, and Ariel erupted in a fit of laughter. "Shall I take that as a no, then?"

"Forgive me," he said, dabbing the corners of his mouth with a handkerchief. "You surprised me with that question."

"Apparently," I said, leaning against the tree. Shayfer shot me a look over his shoulder that was anything but friendly. I smiled in return.

"I leave tomorrow to use my particular skill set to track him down," he said, taking another sip of wine.

"I know," she said, stepping closer to him, "and I want to come with you."

"Ariel—" I started before she cut me off with a raised hand.

"I want to help find him, Hemming. I want to be the one to bring him to my father. And I have the blessing stone—maybe it can help."

"Ariel..." Shayfer said her name like a warning. "You heard what your father said. And besides, I'm not so certain your stone will work."

"Why not?"

"Have you tried it?' he asked, his sharp stare cast at her.

"I did, but nothing happened. I thought maybe it was because I was in the manor—"

"Or perhaps someone is helping the traitor through the Midlands," he replied, his expression dark. I felt my hackles rise at the thought, valid though it was. "Otherwise, he'll certainly be dead by now, and we'll be chasing a corpse."

"Fine," she replied, trying to pull herself together after Shayfer's blow. "Maybe the stone won't work, but I'm going with you anyway—"

"Kaplyn and the others were very clear about how our mission is to be carried out."

"What's the matter, Shayfer? Afraid to break the rules?" She waggled her bottle at him before taking a long drink. The way she let it linger near her mouth when she was done seemed intentional. Shayfer's eyes widened as she slowly lowered it and licked her lips.

My skin crawled and I fought to keep it from showing, knowing what she was doing. Because, like her, I wanted to be there too. Omar's treason had nearly cost us both our lives. He would pay for that before he answered for his assassination attempt. He'd answer to Ariel and me both.

"I never was much for rules," he replied, mimicking her long sip of wine, "but I do love my skin attached to my body. I'll surely be flayed if we get caught."

She shrugged. "Then we won't get caught."

Shayfer frowned. "No offense, Ariel dear, but I think your father and Kaplyn will surely notice you've gone against their wishes if we arrive with the traitor in tow—"

"I will not stay behind in this gilded cage while they go after the usurper," she replied. Her green eyes turned to me and held my gaze for what seemed like an eternity. "I'm a warrior of the Nychterídes. I will act like one as long as there is breath in my lungs."

"And fire in your heart," I added, still staring at her. She gave a tight but worried nod.

Shayfer's eyes darted from her to me, then back to her again. He let out a put-upon sigh before draining the bottle. "You two are way too intense for me tonight. I need you to drink faster."

"Does that mean yes?" Ariel pressed.

"No."

"Does that mean no?"

Shayfer exhaled hard and looked at the dwindling stash of wine. "I should have brought more…"

I bent down and grabbed another bottle, then tossed it to him. "I'm sure you can steal some more if need be."

≈

ARIEL

TWO HOURS AFTER WE ARRIVED AT THE WILLOW TREE, THE three of us were on our backs, laughing up at the sky.

"You did *what*?" Shayfer asked. I could barely make out his words through his fit of laughter.

"She walked up to him in the middle of training and drove her staff into his balls so hard I thought one of them burst," Hemming replied, wiping the tears that were streaming down his face at the memory. "I heard this loud popping sound…I was certain she'd ruptured one."

Shayfer rolled on the ground, holding his manly bits while wincing at the thought.

"You guys are so precious about your genitals. At least a blade to yours won't kill you."

Hemming's laughter ceased immediately. Shayfer rolled to his side and looked at me, curiosity in the tomcat's eyes. "Has that happened to you?" he asked.

I emptied the second to last bottle of wine and threw it across the yard. "No," I said before a burp that would have made the Nychterídes proud escaped me. "Because I'd be dead, silly." I ruffled Shayfer's hair, much to his dismay.

"Thank you for that important distinction," he said, smoothing his hair to perfection. "What I meant was, have you found yourself in that situation before?"

"Sure," I said, flopping back onto the grass between the two of them, "but only once."

"I find that hard to believe, given where you were raised," Shayfer said. There was a note of contempt in his voice that I hadn't heard before. An uncharacteristic slip.

"I was lucky. I was well protected as a child." I reached over and laced my fingers through Hemming's. "I had this guy to watch over me. Nobody there was dumb enough to mess with him. Not for a long time, anyway."

Shayfer looked over at our interlocked hands and frowned. "You kept her safe?" he asked.

Hemming nodded. "As best I could for as long as I could."

"And if I were to oblige Ariel's request to let her hunt Omar, should I assume you would come along too?"

"I go where she goes." Hemming's hand squeezed mine lightly. My cheeks warmed and my head felt funny, so I let go and stood up. The two of them looked at me, a mess of emotions swirling in their combined stares. On shaky legs, I walked over to the willow tree, circling it slowly as the light of the moon highlighted the texture of its bark. I came upon a spot that was smoother than the rest, a vertical column a few inches wide and several feet tall.

"Strange," I said, fingering the willow's scar. "I've never noticed this before."

"What is it?" Hemming asked, curiosity in his eyes.

"I don't know…"

"You do know," Shayfer said, coming to stand beside me. "You just don't realize you do."

"What does that even mean?" I asked, my head swimming from the wine.

"Look at it," he said, guiding me back a few steps. "Does its size remind you of anything?"

I cocked my head at the tree. "It's the size of my staff."

"Well done, Ariel dear."

"Wait…*this* is the magical tree it was cut from?" I asked. Shayfer merely nodded. "*Kaplyn* gave it to my father?"

"He did indeed."

"How did I not know this?"

"How could you?"

"Wait—how do *you* know?"

He splayed his arms in an elegant gesture that said everything and nothing. "I'm a creature of details, Ariel. You know this."

I reached for the final bottle of wine and uncorked it. I'd drained almost half of it when Shayfer pulled it from my grasp. "I think perhaps you should call it a night," he said.

"Just me?"

"No. All of us. It's late, and I have rather important business to attend to early tomorrow. You have guard duty." He winked at me, then scooped up the empty bottles from the lawn.

I wanted to argue—to try again to persuade him to take us with him—but didn't. Instead, I wrapped my arms around his neck and hugged him goodnight and goodbye and good luck all at once. "Rest well, Shayfer."

"Keep hugging me like this and I won't be getting any

rest at all," he said, pulling away to flash me a wicked smile. "And neither will you." With a kiss on my cheek, he walked off, disappearing into the darkness.

Hemming watched him leave, tracking every movement the fae spy made.

"Do you think he'll find him?" I asked.

"I think he's capable of it," was his only response. He looked back at me, shadows carving harsh lines in his expression. "We should go to bed, Ariel. Tomorrow will be a long day of waiting, and neither of us will handle that well."

"Yeah…"

The reality in his words reached through the haze in my mind and struck me hard. Waiting to hear how the search went was going to undo me slowly. Being tired wouldn't help at all. I needed water and sleep and a massive distraction— one that could keep my mind off the traitor the others hunted and the truth that would come to light once he was caught.

If he was found at all.

28

ARIEL

Hemming tumbled onto my bed as soon as we entered the room, his wings spread out wide beneath him. He looked so peaceful—so serene—so unlike the boy-turned-man I knew. I stared at him as I leaned against the bedpost for stability. I still felt too strange to trust my legs.

A soft snore escaped him, and I covered my mouth to stifle a laugh. It was apparent that I would be the one to sleep on the floor that night. I untucked the edges of the blanket and wrapped it around his body as best I could with his wings pinning most of it down.

I leaned in to push the hair from his face, and his head turned toward me, eyes still closed. His lips were stained red from the wine, and with my mind addled by alcohol, I thought about licking the stain away. With a shake of my head to knock that thought away, I bent down and kissed his cheek instead. "Goodnight, Hemmy," I whispered, my mouth at his ear.

As I pulled away, a vision flashed through my mind. It was fast and fleeting, but clear enough to see an image of my face buried in his neck. I staggered away from him, my stomach rolling, but not from wine. I gripped the bedpost and closed my eyes, trying to escape what I'd seen. Unable to steady myself, I lurched forward, landing on top of Hemming. His eyes shot open, and his hands wrapped around my arms, pushing me back.

The two of us lay there, both confused and breathing hard. I knew my mind wasn't playing tricks on me; the sinking feeling in my gut was testament to that. But still, I couldn't make sense of what I was seeing, and it scared me.

"What's wrong?" he asked, loosening his grip.

"I saw something—*remembered* something," I said, scrambling off of him. "I saw my tongue on your ear...my body pressed against yours..."

His eyes went wide with fear. "Ariel—"

"I don't understand, Hemming. I don't remember—"

"I need you to calm down," he said, sitting up.

"Why can't I remember?"

"When you were poisoned..." he said, the terror in his eyes so real that paralyzing numbness coursed through me.

"What did I do?" I asked, my voice low and shaky. "What did I do when I was poisoned?"

"Ariel," he said, staying as still as a statue, "nothing happened. I swear on my ancestors' graves."

"Then why do I feel this way?" I asked, tears rolling down my face. "Why am I panicking at the tiny memory I saw?"

His hands balled into fists at his sides. "I lied to you about what happened, but I did it to save you from what you're feeling now. I didn't want you to be ashamed—"

"Ashamed of *what*, Hemming? Tell me what happened. Now!"

"You—" he cut himself off, struggling to find the words that would set things right. In that moment, I wasn't sure they existed. "It's true that the poison removed your inhibitions, Ariel. I didn't lie about that. What I lied about was what that meant for you—for your behavior." He took a deep breath before climbing off the bed. "You didn't yell at me and hit me. You were flirting with me—trying to undo my pants. Kiss me. Maybe more…" Ice ran down my spine as more memories came to me, clearer than the first. "I managed to get you to eat some winter sage. It neutralized the poison and made you sick. I held you until you stopped crying, then laid you down when you finally passed out."

Embarrassment flushed my cheeks because of what I'd done.

"I'm so sorry, Hemmy," I whispered, crawling backward off the bed. I tripped on the rug and barely managed to stay upright. Then I staggered to the bathroom and locked myself in.

"Ariel," Hemming called, rapping gently on the door, "please talk to me."

'I'm sorry' were the only words I seemed capable of uttering. I said it over and over again until he stopped knocking and I fell asleep on the cold stone floor of the bathroom, wondering which was worse: the fact that I'd done what I'd done to him and he'd been forced to lie to me to save me from embarrassment; or the fact that I'd done what I'd done because some poison drew my inner desires to the forefront, and the object of those desires had been forced to stave off my advances. Because he didn't want them. Because he didn't feel the same.

The former made me feel like a fool.

The latter broke a piece of my heart.

29

HEMMING

I awoke to a rapping at Ariel's door. Though my body was stiff and sore from sleeping on the floor next to the bathroom, I shot to my feet, weapon drawn. Shayfer stuck his head in seconds later. One look at my blade, and the mischief in his eyes died.

"I've been out most of the night in search of information on the traitor," he said, looking at the empty bed. "Where is Ariel?"

I jerked my head toward the bathroom door. "In there."

"She's up, then? Good. I'll be back in a few minutes."

"Whatever you need to tell her, you can tell me."

He assessed me for a moment, like he wanted to argue, then thought better of it. "Fine. Tell her to get ready. You, too."

"For what?"

The mischief in his eyes returned. "To retrieve the one

who betrayed her father." Without another word, he slinked back into the hall and closed the door.

I moved to knock on the bathroom door but hesitated. I'd hoped that Ariel would be woken by our conversation, but she hadn't. She was exhausted from crying herself to sleep alone, with only her shame to keep her warm. If she'd hadn't been so fragile and raw, I'd have ripped the door off its hinges and gone to her. But I knew better.

I understood her too well to do that.

"Ariel," I called softly, "Shayfer was here. He thinks he's found Omar. We have to prepare..."

The light shuffling sound of her feet dragging across the floor came from the bathroom. She unlocked the door and stepped out. Her eyes were red and swollen at the edges, her hair a tangled mess. "I just need my weapons," she said as she walked past me, giving me a wide berth.

"Ariel, we don't have long, but I think we should talk about—"

"I said I'm sorry, Hemming. What else is there to say?"

Hemming, not Hemmy. For once, I wished she'd used the name she'd called me growing up.

"I don't want you to apologize, Ariel. I want you to *talk* to me."

"And say what? That I'm mortified for more reasons than I could even begin to count? That I hate that I did that to you? That I wish I could take it all back?" she asked, staring me down in the dim light of the room. "None of that will change it."

"I just...I just want things to go back to how they were." That was the truth laid bare for her; the one thing I'd prayed for until I fell asleep against her bathroom door.

She barked out a laugh as she strapped her staff to her back. "Me too. But what's done can't be undone. Just know that I won't ever do anything like that again, okay? That I can guarantee."

I tried not to flinch at her words.

Before I could tell her that I wanted her to—tell her that it wasn't her advance that was unwanted, but rather the circumstances—Shayfer knocked lightly on the door, then walked in uninvited. He took one look at the two of us and froze. "Am I interrupting something?"

"No," she replied. "Hemming says you found Omar?"

"It seems so. He could be on the move, though, so we shouldn't delay any further," he said, sneaking into the hall. He waved us out, and together, we crept toward the servants' staircase and, ultimately, an exit through the storeroom below the kitchen. Outside, the barest hint of morning sun cut through the darkness.

"I figured you two would prefer to fly, but we'll be taking an easier way," he said. "I got word in the wee hours of the morning that there was a Nychteríde wounded and wandering the valley near the border. If we can get there in time—before he gets himself eaten by one of the many nasties that dwell there—you will have your traitor."

"Good," Ariel replied, anger thick in her tone.

Shayfer looked over his shoulder, his vicious smile a slash of white across his face. "I'll do my best to get us there and back in one piece, but there are no guarantees—not in the Midlands." He walked ahead to the gates, his laughter drifting back to us on the wind.

Ariel stopped to tighten her harness, then stood there for a moment, hesitating.

"Have you changed your mind?" I asked her. "Do you not want to go?"

"I want to find the one that made a mess of everything," she said under her breath, "and bring him to his knees."

Without another word, she took off to catch up with

Shayfer. There was such anger in her—such contempt—that I knew our journey couldn't end well. She needed an outlet for her self-loathing, and the assassin would provide just that. If I didn't keep her in check, there would be nothing left to interrogate when she was done.

But she'd turn that hatred on me if I didn't let her exorcise those emotions, and I feared that would be the point of no return for us. The line that could not be uncrossed.

30

ARIEL

Shayfer didn't tell us much about how we'd be travelling, but in hindsight, that had likely been for the best. If I'd known how awful it would make me feel, I wouldn't have agreed. One minute, the three of us were standing by the gates to Kaplyn's manor as dawn settled in, and the next, we were by a cave somewhere in the Midlands, the sun already risen. In a blink, we'd gone from one place to the other. Suddenly, Kaplyn's use of Shayfer as a spy made far more sense.

"What in the name of the gods was that?" I asked, hands on my knees to steady myself. I looked over to find Hemming in the same position.

"We all have our gifts, Ariel dear. That's mine. But as with all things, it comes at a cost. Crossing that distance with the two of you in tow takes a toll. I won't be able to repeat it for a bit, which means you might have to fly your traitor back to the manor or wait for me to move you one at a time."

"Fly," Hemming said. "I'm never doing that again."

Shayfer laughed. "You get used to it eventually, Just Hemming."

One look at Hemming's face told me he was neither convinced nor interested in testing that theory.

"We should get moving," Shayfer said. "Time is not our friend at the moment."

He started into the cave, and my anxiety spiked. I wasn't happy about being in one again—not after the Dreamcatcher incident—but Shayfer assured me as we entered that it wouldn't take long. That it would be fine. And like a fool, I believed him. In fairness, it *was* fine until we walked out the far end into a gory scene. There, tied to a tree mere yards from the mouth of the tunnel, was Omar, his body covered in blood.

He was alive, but barely.

The stench of rotting flesh assaulted my nose as we rushed toward him. He opened his eyes, having heard our approach, and he struggled to get loose—or to tell us to let him loose. I couldn't tell, and neither could he. His tongue had been cut out. A fate befitting a traitor.

"Gods above," Hemming breathed, looking at his former lieutenant. "What happened to him?"

"The better question, Just Hemming, is *who* happened to him. And not to spoil the suspense, but I'm quite sure you won't like the answer."

I pulled my dagger from its sheath on my leg and began cutting the vines that tethered Omar to the tree trunk. But with every cut I made, more vines wrapped around his arms. Hemming took out a longsword and slashed at them to no avail. Even with a clean slice, new vines shot forth to capture the already captured.

It reminded me of the hedge maze, and I shuddered at the thought.

"How are we going to get him out of here?" I asked.

"Do you think you can try your fire? Maybe burn them off?" Hemming asked, stepping away.

The sad truth was that I didn't know. I hadn't used my fire since it had been taken from me. I didn't even know if it still worked.

Without answering, I put my mouth near the vines that bound Omar and channeled all my anger and rage at him, throwing in my embarrassment from the previous night for good measure. I could feel the fire stir in my veins, but coaxing it out would take a lot of energy; energy I wasn't sure I had.

I closed my eyes and focused until sweat rolled down my temples and my legs began to shake.

"Is she all ri—"

"Shh!" Hemming snarled at Shayfer. "Leave her be. This isn't easy."

I exhaled slowly, a plume of smoke escaping along with a spark of fire. I tried again, this time able to shoot a solid flame at the vines. They withered as the fire drained their magic. I repeated it on the others until Omar collapsed to the ground. Hemming moved to pick him up, but I stopped him with a look.

"Can you write?" I asked the traitor. He looked up at me, fear in his eyes, and nodded. I bent down before Omar and put my blade under his chin. "You tried to kill my father, and you murdered the others. Tried to have *me* killed—a poor life choice, my friend. If you weren't already half dead, I'd show you just how poor a choice it was."

"We should take him and be gone," Shayfer said, looking around. Suspicion creased his brow, which was an ominous sign indeed. Hemming bent down and hefted Omar over his shoulder. Omar groaned in pain, the gaping hole in his stomach undoubtedly jostled in the process. *Good*, I thought. Let him suffer for his sins.

Shayfer started for the cave's opening, Hemming and me right behind him. I nearly ran into him when he stopped short of the darkness within and muttered something unbecoming of a fae lord's son. When I saw the shadows beyond begin to move, I repeated his words.

"They're stealing our food, Sister One," a scratchy female voice called out. It echoed for a moment before an identical voice replied.

"What shall we do with them, Sister Two?"

"We should make them food as well, should we not, Sister Three?"

"Yesssssss," they all hissed in unison.

Shayfer looked over his shoulder at me, eyes wide. "I cannot take us all at once."

His words dawned on me like a slowly rising sun; his magic was still too weak to whisk us all out of there. Hemming might be able to carry Shayfer and Omar, but after the energy I'd just expended to burn through the vines, I wasn't sure I could make it over the mountain.

Just as Shayfer had said, time was not our friend.

Hemming, reading Shayfer's expression and then mine, came to the same conclusion. Whatever was headed our way, we'd have to face it long enough for us all to escape at once.

"Show yourselves," I yelled at them, wanting to see the enemy. When they obliged, I instantly wished they'd stayed where they were.

Dressed in shredded robes with equally shredded hoods to shroud their faces were three *Magisses*—fae witches—the kind from the nightmarish stories I was told as a child. The kind that ate flesh and bone and plucked the wings off Minyades and Nychterídes alike. The kind that could kill you if you gazed upon their terrible faces for too long.

"Don't look at them!" I yelled to the others.

"I'm well aware of that, Ariel dear. But please do make sure Hemming knows. I'd hate to lose him at this particular moment. Another time, perhaps, but not now."

The witches spread out, circling us slowly. I heard Hemming drop Omar to the ground with a thud so he could draw his sword. He handed me another, and I took it. Then, out of habit, I put my back to his. Shayfer closed our ranks, drawing a sword of his own—one I hadn't even seen him carrying.

The witches seemed to grow in height as they moved, doing little to help my unease. Getting eaten was not on my agenda for the day.

"I like the tall one, Sister Three. That warm, tanned skin —he looks *delicious*."

"I will have the Neráida lord, Sister Two. I have a taste for them."

"And I will have the little dragon, Sister One. I bet her blood is so fiery and sweet…"

I pressed my back tighter to Hemming as the witch cocked her head at me, her hood shifting as she did. "You should take Omar to my father," I whispered to him.

"And leave you alone with them?" he replied. "I think not."

"Because I can't handle it?"

"Because we've been over this a million times, you stubborn mule."

"I realize you two still haven't worked out whatever issue it is you're having today, but might I recommend another time for that?" Shayfer bit out his acerbic words through clenched teeth. "Perhaps after certain death is no longer on the table?"

The witches all took a step toward us. "If you leave, we

will find you," they said together. "We have your scent now. There is nowhere to hide."

"Do you have wings under those rags?" I asked, raising my short sword. "I can't tell."

"We don't need them." Their three voices echoing as one was really starting to unnerve me.

"Hemming, get him out of here. Shayfer and I have this under control."

"I beg to differ," Shayfer said as the witches closed in on us even further.

"I'm not leaving." Hemming's tone was as final as my father's; I could only imagine the look on his face when he said those words. "I still want to finish our talk."

I damn near choked on a laugh. "Then might I suggest you start killing these things before they kill us?"

"With pleasure."

I felt the muscles in his back go rigid, preparing to swing his blade at whatever numbered witch was in front of him. Simultaneously, we attacked the shabby-looking beings before us. Shayfer was a beat behind but joined in, the three of us swinging our swords with speed and precision. But no matter how many times our blades met bodies, nothing happened. No blood. No gore. No death.

"Did I forget to mention," Shayfer said, sounding winded, "that the sisters can't be killed? Not by normal weapons, anyway."

"*What?*" I shouted, daring a glance at him before I dodged the clawed hand swiping at my face. "That would have been great to know when they first showed up!"

"I grow tired of their talking, Sister One."

"I grow hungrier by the minute, Sister Two."

"And I want you all to die, Sister Three," I said, slashing my blade at the witch in front of me. It did little to thwart her approach. Instead, she reached a grey, wrinkled hand toward me, her claws reaching for my throat. With some effort, I forced a few scales to emerge. They locked into place just as those sharp tips scraped along my neck.

With weapons that couldn't kill them and no way out, we were in a mess of trouble.

≈

HEMMING

I SAW ARIEL THROWN TO THE GROUND OUT OF THE CORNER of my eye. Shayfer was fighting—and losing. One of the witches had him pinned against the mountain, her jaws snapping at his throat. With a massive kick, I drove the witch in front of me back and dove at the one climbing onto Ariel. I crashed into her with such force that she flew through the air, slamming into the tree the near-dead traitor had been tied to.

Before she could attack again, I snatched Ariel up and shoved her behind me.

"Hemmy!" she screamed, but not soon enough. I felt the witch's teeth penetrate my rock-hard skin and sink into the soft tissue below. My wings snapped back in an attempt to knock her loose, and my beast roared inside, ready to tear the Magisse apart. Ariel was scrambling to help when the witch suddenly released me, stumbling back with wide eyes.

Her sisters stopped moving.

"We didn't know," she said, retreating, her hands up to fend me off. "Please don't hurt us, *Prince*. We had no idea..." She wiped my blood from her face, licking her lips. Horror overtook her expression as she turned to Ariel, as though realization of something I couldn't comprehend had just struck her. "Have mercy on us, please. Please, *Princess*…"

"What are you talking—" I started, but Ariel cut me off, gripping my forearm tightly.

"We will show you mercy if you can restore our prisoner," she said, pointing to Omar. "He has information we need. If he dies, we cannot get it from him. And that will anger the prince and me…"

The witches rushed to Omar's side, turning him over. His eyes were wide and vacant, his skin a shade too pale. Panic overtook the witches' bodies, each one quaking with the realization—and fear of the retribution they perceived was soon to follow.

"He is already dead, Sister One."

"He cannot be saved, Sister Two."

"But can we still give the princess what she wants, Sister Three?" Sister Two asked, looking to the others. They nodded at her, and she pulled Omar's head into her lap. She slid her talon-like nail beside his eye until it hooked behind. With a flick of her wrist, it popped from the socket. She removed the other one the same way, then severed the nerve to free them.

On hands and knees, she crawled to me and presented the dead warrior's eyes. "Take these to the Seer—see what the warrior has seen," she said.

"Will that make amends?" Shayfer asked, his tone more formal than I'd heard it before. I turned to look at him, and he bowed his head. "For what's been taken, Princess. Is her offering enough?"

"No," Ariel said, stepping toward the witch. "You took something from us. It will be enough when we've done the same in return."

"What does she want, Sister One?"

"A sacrifice, Sister Two?"

"*Yes*," Ariel said before the final witch could speak. The

210

sisters gasped and huddled together. They suddenly looked small and weak; not at all like the wicked things that had ambushed us.

"We don't have time for this," I warned Ariel. "We need to return before we are missed."

"We could help you," the three said in unison. They pointed to an opening in the mountain that hadn't been there when we arrived. "For this, will you grant us mercy?"

Ariel looked to me, the need for vengeance still burning in her eyes. But there was a weariness there, too. I feared it was because of her failing Fireheart.

I headed for the opening, Shayfer following my lead. Just as I was about to enter it, I saw Ariel looming over the sisters, weapon still drawn.

"Ariel. We must go." She didn't budge. "*Princess…*" I said, beseeching her. Her head slowly turned to me. "Come." I reached my hand out to her, and she stared at it for a moment, then up at me.

"It's not over," she said before heading toward us.

"I know," was all I could say in response.

31

ARIEL

The portal the sisters opened for us spat us out at Kaplyn's gates—as though they had somehow known that was our destination—then disappeared into thin air.

"Of course," I muttered under my breath. "Only in the Midlands."

"You should be thankful for that," Shayfer said. "I could not have transported us all back at once, and you don't have long." He pointed at the pouch that held Omar's eyes. "The drier they get, the less they can show you."

"Then let's find this Seer," Hemming said, still riled up from our fight with the Magisses.

Shayfer looked around as though he'd heard someone approach. "I cannot go with you," he said, still scanning the area, "but I will tell you how to get there. The Seer lives in the Black Forest." Hemming and I cursed simultaneously. Shayfer turned and smiled a wicked smile. "Not fans of the woods, are we? Well, that's where the Seer resides. If you want answers, that is where you must go."

"She doesn't live in a cave or a massive hedge maze, does she?" I asked, praying the answer was no. We'd killed the dweller of the former and narrowly survived the latter.

"No. *They* live in the tree-that-is-not-a-tree."

Hemming cursed again. "That's it? We go looking for something that looks like a tree but isn't?"

"If you'd let me finish," Shayfer said, shooting Hemming a nasty look. "The tree-that-is-not-a-tree is in the center of the woods. That is a constant that never changes in these ever-evolving lands. Fly until you see a maple that looks to be trapped in eternal autumn. The vibrant red is unmistakable. When you reach its base, bury the eyes amid the roots, then back up."

"Back up?" I asked, surprise in my tone.

Shayfer shrugged. "Unless you would like to become a permanent part of the Seer's home, I would give the tree a wide berth until it finishes its transformation."

"Why aren't you coming with us?" I asked.

"Because, Ariel dear, the Seer and I have history, as it were. I'm not sure my presence would be welcome, and I do not wish to jeopardize your mission." He looked to Hemming and back to me. "Besides, I think you two could do with some alone time—maybe work out some of your issues while you travel." He turned and opened the gate, headed for the manor.

"Shayfer," I called, looking at the half-sun rising in the distance. "The others will be awake by now. Perhaps you should stay away until we return…"

He saw the unease in my expression, driven by the thought of my father and Kaplyn realizing that Hemming and I were gone and finding Shayfer there—the only one with answers about what we'd done. He would be flayed for helping us against their orders and then abandoning us. The potential risk for him was great.

"Perhaps you should hurry before those eyes dry out to useless vestiges and our mission was all for naught." Worry flashed in his expression before his face smoothed to impassive perfection. "Farewell, Ariel dear…Just Hemming…" With a snap of his fingers, Shayfer disappeared from sight.

I stared at the spot he'd just occupied, worried for my friend. Worried for our task ahead.

"We should go," Hemming said softly. "Shayfer will be all right, but we need to hurry."

"I hope so," was my only response before I spread my wings wide and shot up into the air. Hemming was at my side in an instant, and together, we made our way back to the forest of nightmares, where another potentially awaited us. The Seer might be the key to getting the answers we needed, but I couldn't help but wonder what else they would have in store upon our arrival. Shayfer's willingness to stay behind and possibly face my father and Kaplyn, rather than the Seer, made me nervous—suspicious, even.

And as we cut through the sky, my unease rising with every beat of my wings, a dark voice in the back of my mind whispered things to me. It spoke of treachery and deceit and betrayal. It wondered if we hadn't just been sent to our deaths.

≈

HEMMING

THE SILENCE BETWEEN ARIEL AND ME WAS DEAFENING. EVEN the howl of the wind in my ears couldn't fill it.

"How far?" I finally dared to ask.

"I don't know."

The silence returned.

"Ariel, I understand why you're upset—"

"You understand *nothing*," she snapped in response.

I swallowed back my reply and focused on the forest in the distance. Our problem from the previous night might not have been resolved, but she had no intention of doing it then; that much was clear. I struggled to think of a way to breach the wall she'd erected between us. If she wouldn't open the door, I'd find a way to knock it down. I wouldn't allow it to undo all that had been mended.

"What the witches said..." I began, hesitating to see whether she'd cut me off again. When she didn't, I continued. "...calling me 'Prince'. What do you make of it?"

"I think they were clearly drunk on Omar's blood and talking nonsense."

"And yet they stopped trying to eat us because they believed it to be true—"

"Do you want it to be true? To be some long-lost *Neráida* royal—the descendent of a forgotten line?" She choked on a laugh. "That's about as likely as me being a real princess, Hemming, or did you forget that part?"

"No, I did not—"

"What does it even matter?" she continued. "They're fae. It's the Midlands. Neither is to be trusted blindly."

"You trusted Shayfer, and he led us right to them."

"He led us exactly where we wanted to go: to *Omar*—and he nearly died alongside us for his efforts He cannot be held accountable for where that somewhere was and who else dwelled there."

"And now? Do you trust where he's sending us now?" I

pressed, having seen the uncertainty in her eyes as Shayfer disappeared toward the manor. Her hesitation was plain, and her unwillingness to answer me spoke volumes.

"I don't see any other option," she finally said. "If you don't want to risk it, turn back. Tell the others whatever you must to keep them from punishing you. I'm certain Shayfer will go along with it to save his own skin."

The beast inside me raged at the thought of abandoning her. I steadied my breath and hoped he didn't try to make an appearance high above the trees. He, unlike me, could not fly —at least I didn't think so.

"I go where you go," I said. The words came out angrier than I'd intended, but they illustrated how I felt in that moment. If she didn't like it, that was her problem.

"Then you're going to this not-really-a-tree to find the Seer and get our answers."

"Fine with me—"

"And if we die in the process, you can tell me what a fool I was to believe him."

"Nobody is dying, Ariel."

She clenched her fists at her sides and closed her eyes. The wind tossed her hair around her, and the sun caught its red streaks, making them burn like fire. Then she opened those light green eyes and turned them back to me. "They'll all die once I learn who did this to my father. That's all that matters to me right now. All I can think about."

Beyond her, in the distance, I saw a touch of flame amid the dark canopy of the forest. The fiery red of a maple tree before its leaves begin to fall. "There!" I shouted, pointing it out.

"I pray this works," she said just loud enough for me to hear.

"Even if it doesn't, we will find those behind the coup and kill them one by one. They'll taste the death they tried to give your father. By your staff and my sword, it will be done."

She glanced at me once again and nodded. She held my gaze for a moment longer than necessary, then sliced through the air like an arrow, aimed perfectly at her target. I did what I could to keep pace, but her body was so lithe, her wings smaller and more agile than mine. I watched as she dipped low and disappeared into the canopy of trees.

Then I heard her scream.

32

HEMMING

Heart in my throat, I pushed my wings to their limit, racing toward where she'd disappeared.

"Ariel!" I called to no answer.

Branches slapped my flesh as I traced her path through the canopy as closely as possible, hoping I wouldn't be its next victim. I was in a dive, unable to spread my wings until I was only feet from the ground. I slowed myself just enough not to crash, but the landing was hard, and the ground shook with the force of it. I shouted her name again, looking everywhere for a trace of her, but found nothing.

Just before my beast let loose a cry of his own, I heard a faint voice from far above.

"Hemming!" The sound was muffled and distant, but definitely Ariel. I tracked it until I stood below her, her body dangling from an invisible snare. The relief I felt at seeing her alive was immense. "Can I get a little help over here?" she asked, trying to look at me through the veil of brown hair that hung in her face.

"Can you cut through it?" I asked.

When she finally met my gaze, her eyes were murderous. "I've tried that and lost both daggers for my efforts—they just disappeared into thin air," she replied, turning in slow circles overhead. The more she struggled, the more she spun. Knowing that she wasn't in immediate danger, I couldn't help but see the humor in it. I tried hard to stifle my laughter, but it eventually escaped. Her head snapped back to scowl at me. "Are you laughing?"

"No," I said, laughing harder still.

"I will beat you within an inch of your life—"

"Once you get down—"

"—if you don't get up here and help me."

"All right, all right, I'm coming. No need to get your leathers in a knot—"

"I'll get *your* leathers in a knot," she muttered to herself as I flew up toward her carefully. The last thing we needed was for us both to be suspended high in the air with no way down and only an argument to keep us company.

"Where is it caught?"

"Just below my knee."

I slid my hand along her leg until it met resistance; a pulsing, living energy that tethered her to nothing but the air around her. I tried to grab hold of it, but it blasted my hand away.

Perhaps I was lucky it didn't disappear like her daggers.

"I've tried pulling it open," she said. "It doesn't work. I don't think even you can muscle it apart."

I dropped my gaze to her. "Is that a challenge?"

"If it gets me out of this thing, then yes, it is."

"Challenge accepted," I said with a smile. But the snare

didn't budge. Every attempt I made led to the same outcome —my hands blasted away by magic.

"I feel like I'm drunk," she said. "It's as if all my blood is in my head."

"Did you try to call your fire? Maybe it will work on this?"

She bent her head to look up at me. "I did. It doesn't. It's not strong enough. Vines, yes. This thing, no. Whatever this snare is made of, it's formidable."

I went back to work on the invisible rope in silence. Frustration crept in and I found myself growling at it, my beast prowling around inside me like he wanted a turn. If he were capable of flight, I would have let him try, but letting him loose only to have him plummet to the ground below was less than an ideal plan.

He seemed to realize that as well.

But he *was* the expression of my fae half, and we were in the Midlands, with fae magic and fae traps. Maybe the reason neither Ariel nor I was capable of freeing her was our lack of fae-ness. The beast did not share that deficiency.

Perhaps finding a way to use him *was* a viable plan.

"Ariel, I need you to do something for me."

"I can't do much from here," she replied in an acerbic tone.

"Close your eyes and call your scales forward, if you can."

"What are you going to do?" she asked. The concern in her voice was palpable.

"Just do as I ask. *Please*."

She cursed under her breath but closed her eyes. I tried not to notice her lack of scales and the sinking feeling in my stomach that her Fireheart wasn't healing properly.

I made one final effort to grab the tether, only to be met

with a more powerful blast than before. Powerful and painful. Painful enough to anger the beast.

"You'll only have a second," I said under my breath, attempting to work with the beast rather than stave him off or let him loose. He growled as though he understood.

I held Ariel's leg tightly and tried to relax enough to let the wingless beast loose. I felt tingling in my hands, the magic coursing toward them, transforming them—and *only* them. Huge talons shot from my fingers that were no longer mine. I looked at the inky black claws of the beast at the end of my arm.

They slashed at the invisible snare, and the second they struck it, light exploded around us and the tether snapped. The beast's hand clutched Ariel's leg to keep her from falling, careful not to pierce her skin. He'd never forgive himself if he hurt her. My wings beat harder to keep us aloft, and the beast withdrew into his cage inside me. Within seconds, my hands were my own again.

"You did it!" Ariel exclaimed, opening her eyes. I pulled her up to me, and she threw her arms around my neck.

I guided us gently to the ground. "I don't like to lose."

She laughed and straightened her harness that had twisted on the descent. "So what did you do?" she asked. "Why did it work that time? And why did I have to close my eyes?"

"So many questions when all you really need to say is 'thank you, Hemming. You're amazing'."

"Amazing might be an overstatement," she replied. I folded my arms across my chest and stared her down. "But you did well. If we make it through the day, I'll thank you properly."

My body went rigid as she reached toward my pants. I fought to remain still, tracking her movements like a hawk as her hand grew nearer. My breath caught in my throat when she looked up at me through her lashes. Her hand hovered there for a moment before she grabbed the pouch containing the eyeballs off my belt and started toward the red maple.

"Are you coming or are you just going to stand there and stew?"

I let out my breath and shook my head, hoping to regain some blood flow there. Her actions had nearly sent me over the edge, misinterpreted though they were. We may have moved past our fight from the previous night, but we were far from where I wanted to be. And I was starting to think she felt the same. If the serpent's poison had removed her inhibitions, then some part of her desired me—at least physically. But that would never be enough for me, and I knew it. What I felt for her had evolved over time into something far deeper than that. I needed to tell her how I felt sooner than later, before I did something I couldn't take back.

I couldn't lose her again.

I loved her too much.

33

ARIEL

I felt Hemming's heavy stare on my back as I led the way to the Seer's tree-that-is-not-a-tree. Shayfer had said to bury the eyes in the roots, then back up quickly. I prayed he was right about that. If not, the eyes would be ruined.

Crouched down by the tree's trunk, I started digging a hole. Hemming was there a moment later to help, his large hands tearing through the ground with ease. Once the hole seemed deep enough, I pulled the eyes from their leather pouch and dropped them inside. Together, Hemming and I covered them up and stepped back, giving the tree a wide berth.

The ground shook, and the tree before us started to shiver. It looked blurry, its motions growing more jerky and violent by the second. I instinctively reached over my shoulder for my staff, fearing an ambush of some kind.

Suddenly, that blur of motion shot out in all directions, expanding until the tree-that-is-not-a-tree transformed into a small house. I shuddered, thinking of the cottage I'd seen before—the one with the little girl who'd invited me in and then stolen my Fireheart. My aversion to being duped again was only heightened by the similarities in the situation.

Seeing my hesitation, Hemming strode toward the front door, sword drawn at his side. He knocked three times, then backed away, never taking his eyes off the home. It seemed like forever before we heard a sound inside.

The sound of footfalls on a wooden floor.

I edged up beside Hemming just as the door creaked open to reveal an unlikely sight. The Seer, dressed in a fine ebony robe and elegant slippers, stepped out into the forest, their head angled down to the ground. Their thick black hair hung in their eyes, but when the Seer raised their chin to greet us, I realized I was wrong—they didn't have eyes at all. Sunken pits where they should have been stared back at us, and I could feel sweat begin to run down my neck.

"Who has come to visit me this fine day?" they asked, accent thick and melodious. It dripped like honey from their tongue, and I found myself drawn to it. I took a step forward without thought. Only Hemming's hand on my wrist held me still.

"I am Hemming of the Nychterídes. This is Ariel, daughter of General Kade, ward of Lord Kaplyn Corvallym. We seek your help. We've brought you the eyes of a traitor. We need to see what he has seen. To know what he knew."

The Seer turned to Hemming and smiled. "*Hemming…* this is not a Nychteríde name."

"No, it is not."

"Do you know the meaning of it?" they asked, stepping toward Hemming. "Did your mother give you this name?"

"I don't know."

Hemming went tense at the Seer's approach but didn't move. He waited for the Seer to stop mere inches from him, so close it was almost intimate. They reached up and ran a finger along his face, exploring the curves and angles with a delicate touch. Their dark umber skin made Hemming look pale in comparison.

"Hemming is an ancient name of these lands. It means 'to change shape'."

Watching the Seer touch him in that way—like a long-lost lover—made my hand grip my staff tighter. "Can you help us?" I asked, impatience tainting my voice. "I was told visions would be lost the drier the eyes become."

The Seer's face turned to me, the pleasant expression it'd held when speaking to Hemming gone entirely. "Ariel. Your name, too, is not of the Nychterídes. Who gave you this name?"

"My mother."

"Do you know its meaning?" the Seer asked, reaching for my face with far less tenderness than they had Hemming's. They cupped my cheek, then grabbed my chin and jerked my face closer. I nearly fell forward a step. "It means 'lion of the gods'. Is that what you are, Ariel? A lion? Or are you its prey?"

I yanked my face from their grip and drew a blade from Hemming's harness in one smooth motion. I held it to the Seer's throat with every intention of using it should they push me again. "I grew up in a land of lions—of *warriors*. Which do you think I am?"

A serpent's smile spread across the Seer's face, their teeth gleaming in the scant sunlight permeating the canopy above. Then they laughed until the woods seemed to laugh too.

"Come with me." They led the way into the tree-turned-home. "You have woken me and answered my questions. I'm satisfied with your responses, so I shall do what you ask."

The interior of the home was splashed with bright color from floor to ceiling. What should have been gaudy was instead delightful. Silks, beads, and gold adorned the open space, and bright light—the source of which I could not find —only made it more resplendent. The Seer directed us to sit on large pillows in the center of the room. Once we were settled, they sat down across from us, Omar's eyes in hand.

"These are not as fresh as I'd like," they said, rolling them around in their palm, "and they seem to have sustained some damage—"

"He was tortured before they were extracted," I said.

The Seer tilted their face toward me. "A lion indeed, then." I didn't bother to correct the assumption, too focused on getting the information we'd come for to tell them I hadn't been the one to kill Omar.

The eyes went still in the Seer's hand, and they drew a deep breath. They held it for a long time before exhaling slowly.

"Do you know how this works?"

"No," we replied in unison.

"I can only show one of you what I see." Hemming turned to me as if to ask if I wanted him to do it, but before I could tell him no, the Seer made the decision for me. "And that one must have *fae* blood in his veins. The gods' lion shall have to trust this task to the shape-changer. Can she do this, I wonder?"

Hemming shot me a wary glance, and I nodded. "She can and she will. Now get on with it."

The Seer laughed at my brazen reply.

"What do I have to do?" Hemming asked them.

"You must come closer and hold your hand over my eyes."

"But you don't have—" Hemming's words were cut short the second the Seer took Omar's eyes and shoved them into their empty sockets. The stolen eyes bulged out of the Seer's face in a grotesque way, no eyelids to cover them in the expected manner. I was thankful they needed to be covered by Hemming's hand.

Hemming did as he was directed and sat next to the Seer, his hand quickly draping over Omar's eyes. The second it did, Hemming's body went stiff, and his eyes rolled back in his head.

Then he stopped breathing.

I screamed his name and tried to pull his hand away, but neither had any effect. The gods' lion couldn't wake her friend from the throes of death. I realized in an instant that we'd made a terrible mistake.

34

HEMMING

I t was like stepping into a windstorm. Objects flashed past me, too fast to grab hold. I stood in the middle of these swirling images, unsure of where to start.

"Think of what you want to see." The Seer's voice was gentle in my ear, but when I turned to look for them, only the images were there. I closed my eyes and thought about Kade —about the Nychterídes that had been killed in the Midlands. When I opened them again, the winds had slowed, allowing the visions to become clearer. But still, they never stopped.

Seeing things as Omar would have, I looked into the faces of Kade's soldiers, whispering in the shadows—clandestine meetings under the cover of night. In the woods. Behind buildings. In the storage cellar. There, I saw a room containing Minyade prisoners and heard laughter among the Nychterídes present. I saw Ariel at the solstice celebration, headed off toward the training center. Omar had followed her

—watched her approach Kade and Baran before returning to the others. Then he'd pulled Tycho aside and whispered into his ear. When he moved away, the delight in Tycho's eyes was plain. I tamped down my anger and tried to focus. The visions sped up as I struggled to think of what other answers we needed. I tried demanding to know who was behind it all, but the visions didn't respond. I wondered if that was because it wasn't only one male behind it, or if Omar didn't know.

Then something occurred to me—something I had not yet considered.

I focused on how Omar had survived for so long in the Midlands on his own. Ariel and I had barely made it to Kaplyn's alive with the help of the blessing stone. I knew he couldn't have gotten that far unaided. I wondered if there were traitors among the fae as well.

The images disappeared, leaving only a few blurry and disjointed ones behind. I saw a fae lord, his face out of focus. I squinted hard and silently begged to see him clearly. For the image to grow sharper. Eventually, the silhouette tightened, and the fine lines of his face took shape, the bright red of his hair coming into view. There, smiling back at me, stood Lord Teigan, a pouch of gold in his hand.

Omar had purchased safe passage through his lands. My beast roared, knowing that Teigan had sat at Kaplyn's table, his arrogance thick and infectious, and opposed the search for the murderer. The reason was clear now. He'd had a hand in his escape.

I thought about the other fae lords and anyone else in attendance that night who might have had contact with Omar. I wanted to know if Teigan was an exception. I soon learned he was not.

A dark-haired male with sharp , narrowed eyes stared back at me, his expression full of mischief. He drew Omar in closer to whisper in his ear, and I bellowed in anger at my inability to hear what he'd said. The image disappeared just as Shayfer pulled away, still smiling.

≋

I FELL BACK ON THE FLOOR, GASPING FOR BREATH LIKE A FISH out of water. I coughed and hacked, and my throat burned with every raspy inhale. Ariel was there, her hands on my shoulders—her face in my face—asking me if I was okay. Asking if I'd seen who had helped plan to kill her father.

"He'll need a moment," the Seer said from their perch on the pillow. Unlike me, the Seer seemed utterly unfazed by what we'd just done. I, however, felt like I'd swallowed Ariel's Fireheart again.

"Hemmy? Just tell me it was worth it," she said, hoisting me up to a seated position. The desperation in her eyes was plain; she needed to know that I'd learned something that would help keep her father safe. I nodded, and she let out a breath.

While I tried to compose myself, she surveyed the room until she spotted what she wanted. Moments later, she had a glass of water for me. I drank it down in one gulp. "It's worse than I suspected," I said, voice still hoarse.

She bit out a curse. "How many?"

"I can't be sure. I didn't see everything. I feel like I got stolen moments, but not the full picture."

"You must remember, shape-changer, that not all you have seen is as it seems. Moments out of context can be damning, but not justly so." I nodded, then tried to stand up. Ariel was at my side, her arm wrapped around my waist for support. The Seer led us to the door, their silk robe trailing behind. "However, that isn't to say that some things aren't *exactly* as they seem. It is your job to decipher which are which. Not an enviable task, that, I'm afraid."

The Seer opened the door and stepped back to let us through. With some effort, we made our way outside to a dark forest. The sun was high in the sky, though it barely permeated the canopy. It made me wonder how much time had passed while I was locked in Omar's memories.

"Tell Shayfer I will see him soon," the Seer said before slamming the door. Seconds later, their home magically transformed back into the tree-that-is-not-a-tree, its crimson leaves barely noticeable in the growing darkness.

Ariel and I shared a pointed look—we'd never mentioned Shayfer.

"Are you all right to fly?" Ariel asked. She was nervous and fidgeting, her wings twitching as she scanned the forest.

"Do you plan to carry me if not?"

"If I have to—seems only fair. And besides, we need to get back. We've been gone too long, and I'm worried that Kaplyn and my father will have realized we're gone. If they find Shayfer and interrogate him…"

I opened my mouth to tell her what I'd seen—that Shayfer had met with Omar in private—then snapped it shut, the Seer's warning playing over in my mind. *Not all you have seen is as it seems…* Had Shayfer betrayed us, or was the context of that moment not clear? Had he been working with Omar? And to what end? Teigan I understood, given how he'd bristled at Ariel's remark about his finances, but Shayfer…his motives were far from obvious. He cared for Ariel, and even if I didn't fully trust him, I trusted he did not want her hurt.

"What?" Ariel asked, seeing my hesitation.

"You're right. We need to go. I should be fine…just don't

234

lead me into any traps." I forced a smile, and she rolled her eyes.

"Follow me," she said, heading to where she'd broken through the trees upon our arrival. "And try to keep up this time."

35

ARIEL

I could hear the screams all the way from the front gate. It only took a second to realize who they were coming from. "*Shayfer*," I said under my breath, panic gripping me hard.

Hemming took off before I managed to make my legs move. He was through the front door of the manor just as I hit the bottom step. By the time I caught up, I found him in Kaplyn's study, where a tiny war was about to break out.

Shayfer knelt before my father, his face bloody and bruised. Kaplyn hovered nearby, his features pinched with anger, but angry or not, he did nothing to stop the beating my father was giving his spy.

"Baba, stop!" I yelled as he raised a blade to Shayfer's throat. "NO!"

His rage-filled eyes slowly lifted from the fae at his feet to me. "I will deal with you in a moment." Hemming went stiff beside me.

"Please," I said, stepping closer to my father. "Shayfer didn't do anything wrong. Let him go."

The fae spy's swollen eyes drifted up to me, a tinge of disbelief in them, like he was surprised I'd come to his aid—or maybe that we'd returned at all. Either way, without him, the traitor would be dead and gone, eaten by the sisters, and we'd never have gotten to the Seer. Never would have learned what Hemming had.

"Are you trying to tell me that he didn't take you from this manor to hunt Omar against Kaplyn's and my directive?"

"You know I would have gone without him," I argued, not certain it would help. "Shayfer didn't want us to get hurt. Escorting us was the lesser of evils in his mind."

My father's murderous eyes fell to the fae. "He was told very clearly that you were not to leave this home today. That there would be consequences—"

"We found Omar because of him," I replied, anger creeping into my tone. "You should be thanking him, not punishing him."

"The end does not outweigh the means. I know all about your encounter with the Magisses. He practically fed you to three of the oldest fae in the Midlands, Ariel! For that, he will be punished." Father drew back his sword, and Shayfer lifted his chin to ensure that the blow would be clean; that his death would be quick. As the blade arced toward him, I lunged, whipping my staff from my back. I blocked the general's sword only inches from Shayfer's face.

"I said I would have gone without him," I stated again as I strained hard against the blade. "Killing him for this is madness."

My father's wide eyes narrowed to slits. He let loose a battle cry that shook the crystal chandelier above our heads, then shoved me with such force that I flew halfway across the room. I slammed into the wall and crashed to the floor, my head spinning.

Then another male voice ripped through the room, the roar so loud I covered my ears for fear they'd rupture. When it stopped, I looked up to find a black, leathery beast unlike anything I'd ever seen in my life charging my father. His ox-like form was three times the size of the actual animal. His feet were cloven in the back and clawed in the front, with black, dagger-length talons—black like my obsidian blade—the kind that could slice through skin as thick as the Nychterídes' without effort.

The kind his teeth appeared to be made of as well.

I couldn't move in time to stop him. The beast lowered his head and slammed into my father. His body sailed through the air so fast it was hard to track; if he hadn't spread his wings to slow himself, he would have gone right through the wall. As it was, he put a dent in it deep enough that he was stuck there for a fraction of a second.

The beast scratched the floor—a warning of the next hit to come. It was then that I fully understood what had attacked Tycho and the others in the woods of Daglaar. The beast lurking in the shadows: Hemming, the shape-changer.

Just as he started for my father again, I staggered into his path and threw up my hands. "Hemmy, stop!" I shouted. He skidded to a halt only inches from me. The beast snorted in my face, then looked beyond me to where my father stood.

He scratched the floor again.

"*Hemming*," I said again, hoping his name might coax him from his wild state—the one his other side had never shown. "I'm okay." I reached a shaking hand toward his thick black neck, hoping my trust in him wasn't misplaced. I closed my eyes and pressed my fingertips to his thick hide; it was the same texture as Hemming's wings. When he didn't move or attempt to tear my hand off with his teeth, I dared to look.

Eyes as dark as the night sky stared back and swallowed me whole. For a moment, I was completely lost. There was no impending war. No bleeding Shayfer in Kaplyn's study. No angry father behind me. It was just me and this beast of shadow and leather and stone.

"Hemming," I whispered, stepping closer, "he's my father..." He let loose another roar that blasted my hair from my face and shook the room. I tried to steady myself, but my confidence in the situation was waning by the second. If I couldn't calm the beast, I feared no one could. "He is all the family I have," I said, my voice cracking. "He and *you*." The beast lowered his head to level his gaze on me, and I thought I saw sympathy in the black depths. "Hemmy, *please...*"

He huffed out a breath of frustration or resignation—I couldn't tell—but seconds later, he retreated a step. Then another. Then another. He backed himself all the way across the room until he stood next to where Shayfer had propped himself against the wall.

I heard my father approaching behind me, and I turned to find him scowling. The beast growled in warning, his claws drawing a long line across the golden hardwood floor.

"I'm going to help clean Shayfer up, and then we'll come back down here to tell you and Kaplyn what we learned," I told him, my fear turning once again to anger. "You disappointed me today, Baba. This is not who you are." I turned to leave without another word.

"I did not dismiss you—" he said, reaching for my arm.

The beast launched through the air in response.

"*Hemming!*" Kaplyn shouted. The second Hemming hit the ground in front of my father, he turned and stared down the fae lord as if his call had interfered.

"Hemmy," I said, stepping between him and my father again, "let's go. It's time to go..."

He nudged me out of the way with his massive muzzle, then pressed it into my father's face, growling.

"Ariel is right. It's time for you three to go," Kaplyn said. His voice had an edge to it that I'd never heard before; a tone that demanded compliance. "Take Shayfer to your room and tend to him there, Ariel. I will send for you soon—you and Hemming both—and I expect you to be very forthcoming." I turned to look at him and nodded. "And Ariel?"

"Yes, Kaplyn?"

"I'm glad you're all right."

I walked over to where Shayfer stood and looped my arm around his waist. The beast followed us through the double doors and down the hall, stopping occasionally to make sure we weren't being followed. When we reached my bedroom, I maneuvered Shayfer through the door and into the bathroom.

"Sit here," I told him, lowering him to the edge of the bathtub.

"Are you going to take my clothes off for me next?" he asked, wincing as he shifted onto the white porcelain.

I quirked a brow at him. "Haven't you been waiting for this day for years?"

He barked out a laugh, then clutched his ribs. "Yes, but somehow in that time, I never quite envisioned this to be how it would all play out."

I forced a smile. "I'm so sorry, Shayf—"

He deflected my apology with the palm of his hand. "I knew the risk when I decided to bring you with me," he said. "I could see how important it was to you to find Omar, and I feared you'd run off and get yourself killed trying to hunt him. I thought it better to go with you and pay for it later than to let you go alone."

"But I wouldn't have been alone," I replied, looking at the black beast looming outside my bedroom—the one much too large to fit through the door.

His gaze followed mine, and he let out another painful laugh. "No. It seems you would have had quite the weapon at your disposal."

I stared at the beast's flank until he turned and pressed his head to the doorway, a single eye staring at me. "Have you ever seen anything like it before?" I asked, the words escaping on a breath.

"Only once, Ariel dear. Only once."

≈

HEMMING

MY BEAST PACED THE HALLWAY, SHAKING HIS HEAD AS though he could dislodge the vision of Ariel flying into the wall from his mind; we'd both feared she wouldn't get up. Uncontrollable anger had surged through me at the sight of her father tossing her aside—there was no chance I could have contained the beast. Not that I'd wanted to at the time.

The bathroom door clicked shut, closing Ariel in with Shayfer.

The beast paced faster.

Some time later, he calmed to a manageable level, and I shifted back. Just as I walked through the bedroom door, Ariel emerged from the bathroom. We both stopped and stared, hundreds of unanswered questions filling the space between us.

"How is Shayfer?" I finally asked.

"A bit broken, but healing. It seems he's hardier than I thought. Maybe he has more abilities I never knew about."

She brushed the stray hairs from her face and tucked them behind her ear. "Speaking of abilities…"

"I'm sorry that I scared you. He—the beast—he'd never hurt you. I need you to understand that." I left *because he loves you as much as I do* unspoken.

"Why didn't you ever tell me about…*him*?"

I hesitated, not really knowing how to explain. "I never intended to keep it from you. It's just that, by the time I realized I had this other side, growing stronger and more fearsome every day, I was terrified he would hurt you somehow. That you would fear me because of him. So I never told you, and I forced him back as best I could. It wasn't until after you left that his power became fully realized," I said, the image of her wounded expression staring back at me as I held a knife to her throat plaguing my mind. "By then, it was too late to help you."

"Did you tell anyone?" she asked gently. I shook my head. "You've been hiding him all this time? Keeping him secret?"

The look of pain and disbelief in her eyes was too much. I turned away from her and sat on the edge of the bed, the frame creaking under my weight. "I didn't want to—I just thought it would be safer if I did. You know how the Nychterídes see our differences—"

"Yes," she said under her breath, "I do." She grew quiet for so long that my heart started to run wild in my chest. It beat so loud that I feared she could hear it. Finally, she spoke, ending my suffering. "And I'm sorry, too." She crept two steps closer, her footfalls light on the floor." "About last night…" My heart raced faster still. I didn't dare move or speak. "I wasn't mad at you. I was just so embarrassed…"

I dared a glance in her direction. "Which is why I didn't tell you the truth in the first place. You woke up with no memory of the event, so I thought it best to keep it that way —for both our sakes."

More soft footsteps toward the bed. "I handled the whole thing poorly, Hemmy, and I'm sorry." The bed shifted slightly as she sat down beside me. Close, but not touching. The inches that separated us felt like miles.

"And I should have told you."

Silence.

"On our journey to the Seer, when you asked about what the witches said…about you being a prince…" I could feel the weight of her gaze on my profile. "Tell me honestly, do you think their words were in earnest? That you really are one?"

"I don't know." That was the truth.

"Do you think she tasted something in your blood? Something that made her think this?"

"Maybe." I glanced down at her hands in her lap as she picked at the leather cording of her pants.

"If they did, though…and they didn't bite me..." She spoke so softly that I could barely hear her. "Why would they call me Princess?"

"I don't know, Ariel," I sighed. "I really don't. None of it makes any sense."

Her hand reached over and rested atop mine. I spread my fingers to interlace them with hers, my heart in my throat.

"About what you told me last night…" Her eyes drifted up to meet mine, holding me in place with her pale green stare. "About protecting me from myself after the serpent's poison…" She cut herself off. Her cheeks reddened, and she started to turn away, but I followed her, leveling my face with hers.

"Yes?"

"Was I hard…I mean, was it hard to…"

My heart thundered in my chest so hard I feared it might break free. "Hard to what, Ariel?"

She looked at me with eyes so full of emotion that I couldn't begin to decipher what was going on in that mind of hers. Then she squeezed my hand tighter, and for the first time since she'd returned, I had hope. Hope that she felt for me what I did for her.

She opened her mouth to reply, and the bathroom door crashed open, startling us both. Shayfer staggered into the room, a towel wrapped around his waist. One look at us sitting on the bed, hands clasped, and mischief overtook his bruised and sallow face. "Oh, for the love of the gods, will you two just have a quick romp and get it out of your systems, already? Kaplyn will be coming for you soon," he said, leaning toward us as he clutched the bedpost for balance. "You don't have much time."

He winked before making his way to the bedroom door. He faltered once, and I shot up to catch him, but Shayfer batted me away. "Perhaps you should reserve your groping for the lady, Just Hemming." He stepped through the door and frowned when he looked down the hall. "It seems the groping shall have to wait a little longer," he said under his breath. "Kaplyn is coming."

Shayfer disappeared, closing the door behind him.

"I should change," Ariel said, hurrying to the closet. She pulled a dress from the bunch and rushed to the bathroom to change. I tried not to notice the lock clicking into place. Moments later, she emerged in a plain black dress—one made for utilitarian purposes, not luxury. She rushed past, unwilling to look at me, and opened the door just as Kaplyn arrived.

His eyes darted from her to me and back again. "Your father is waiting for us in the dining hall," he said, stepping aside. "Are you both feeling better now?"

Ariel nodded.

"We're fine," I said.

"Good. Now, I will say this once and only once, so listen carefully. Kade is still on edge after all that has happened. You would both be wise to tell us everything you know as plainly as possible without being prompted any further, is that clear?" He pinned us with narrowed green eyes, and we agreed. "You both challenged his authority at a time when it hangs in the balance. That, in and of itself, is a betrayal of sorts, and though I appreciate why you both did it—as I'm sure Shayfer does, too—you cannot show that level of insubordination again. I can assure you it will not be tolerated a second time." Kaplyn's gaze shifted to Ariel, and her shoulders slumped. "Not even from you, Ariel."

He turned and walked down the hall, an unspoken command for us to follow. Ariel hesitated for a second, and I waited at her side. "Your father still loves you, Ariel," I said, placing my hand on the small of her back.

"I know he does," she whispered. "Somehow, that makes it all so much worse."

Before I could reply, she hurried after Kaplyn, the crisp fabric of her dress dragging along the ground behind her. Ariel had always been strong but sensitive—a contradiction, much like her mixed heritage. But her sensitivity was beginning to override her strength, and I feared for what that would mean in the days to come—what would happen when she faced the consequences of this fight.

The beast inside me raged at that thought.

We will never let her fall…

36

ARIEL

I sat in a plush chair listening to Hemming relay all that he'd seen while in the Seer's thrall. When he was done, he turned to join me, but there was something in his eyes. He looked unsettled, and it didn't go unnoticed by any of us in the room.

"Is there something else?" Kaplyn asked, his voice gentle but filled with authority.

Hemming froze. "I don't know…"

"It is a simple question," my father said, heading for him. I shot out of my seat to stand by Hemming. The general stopped his approach and frowned.

"Where is Shayfer?" Hemming asked.

Kaplyn and Father shared a curious look before answering. "He is with the healer," Kaplyn replied. "He will join us as soon as he's done."

"Then perhaps I should wait to tell you until he arrives."

"Hemmy?" I grabbed his arm to draw his attention. He

looked at me with eyes full of regret. Full of sympathy. "What did you see? Tell me…"

He took a deep breath and let it out slowly. "Shayfer met with Omar, somewhere near the border, as far as I could tell. It looked very much like the encounter Omar had with Lord Teigan, though I saw no money exchanged."

"*Shayfer?*" Kaplyn asked, genuine surprise in his voice. "Are you certain?"

"Yes, Lord Kaplyn. There was no mistaking his identity."

Kaplyn cursed under his breath. My father raged. "I should have killed him earlier—it would have been a mercy compared to what he faces now—"

"The Seer said that not all is always as it seems," I explained, fear rising within me. "Perhaps Shayfer did this as part of his spy work?"

"Or he was conspiring with those determined to usurp me," my father countered. I couldn't refute his point. However, as I dissected the information, it didn't look good for Shayfer.

While I mulled over any rational possibility that could clear Shayfer's name, the fae in question strolled into the room like he hadn't almost died earlier—like his life didn't still hang in the balance.

"Why did you meet with the Nychteríde traitor?" Kaplyn asked, his casual tone contradicting his fighting stance.

Shayfer stopped dead in his tracks. His eyes drifted over to me, an apology buried in their brown depths. "I met with him at his request. I agreed because I could not understand what a ranking officer in the Nychteríde army might want from me, though I suspected it wouldn't be good. When we met, I did not know the nature of our meeting."

"What did he want?" my father asked, sword in hand.

"He wanted a guide through the Midlands. When I

demanded to know why, he would not provide me with an acceptable answer, so I declined."

"And why have I not heard of this until now?" Kaplyn asked, his temper rising.

"Because it seemed unimportant. It isn't as if such requests haven't been made before by Nychteríde women and warriors alike. It wasn't until we found him with the witches that I realized the greater meaning behind his request, and at that point, it was too late. Teigan had already done what I would not."

"Why didn't you admit it then?" Hemming asked, his body coiled for a fight.

Shayfer turned to him, a wry smile on his face. "Because the traitor could not out me without a tongue. I saw no reason to endanger myself or my position by admitting to something that had no bearing on the situation at hand."

"But you knew the Seer would use Omar's eyes—that we might still find out," I said, working through his rationale.

His smile fell, and he looked at me with sad eyes. "That is partly why I did not come with you, Ariel. I feared what you might see—what you would assume it meant. I couldn't bear the thought of you looking at me as though I'd betrayed you —the way you're looking at me now."

"Since Lord Teigan was willing to do what you would not," Kaplyn said, "he will pay for his treachery."

"I'm sorry I have disappointed you, Lord Kaplyn," Shayfer said with a low bow. "You know where my loyalty lies—to whom I have pledged my fealty."

"I do know, which is why you are still breathing at the moment. Were it up to Kade, we'd be standing over your corpse having this conversation."

"There is still time to make that happen," Father replied.

"Shayfer risked being implicated to help us, Baba," I argued. "Surely that speaks to his character. And if you cannot believe him, then believe me. He has been my closest friend since I arrived here, aside from Delphyne and Sophitiya, and Kaplyn, of course. His sneaky nature makes it difficult to trust him, but it is what makes him an asset to his lord and his house. And, though I may have doubted him at times, he has always done right by me in the end."

That wry smile returned to Shayfer's face—the one that promised all kinds of trouble. "How you flatter me, Ariel dear. And in front of Just Hemming, no less—I'm touched. Truly. But let's not make him jealous. I'd hate to see the beast return."

"You're dismissed," Kaplyn announced with a wave of his hand. Shayfer bowed low once again, then retreated from the room. I could only imagine the sigh of relief he let out in the hallway. "Now that we have that matter settled, we need to formulate a plan to return Kade to his position of power. Thus far, it appears that Omar was not acting alone." His eyes cut to my father. "We need to know who else is behind this—if someone else is in charge."

"There's no way Omar was behind it himself," Hemming agreed. "From his visions, he seemed more like a spy. The one who got things done behind the scenes."

Just like he was for my father…

"Then we can only assume that someone is wondering where Omar is. When he doesn't return, will they think that he was killed upon his retreat through the Midlands, or that he was unsuccessful?"

My father's brow furrowed as he considered the question. "I do not think they can afford to assume he was successful. I think they will dispatch someone—perhaps a small search party—to confirm my death...or his."

"Unless they only need it to *look* as though you were killed," I said, trying to work through the traitor's possible motives.

"What are you implying, Ariel?" Kaplyn asked.

"I'm suggesting that, judging by what Hemming saw, there are many involved in this plan, not just a single individual making a bid for power. If Father returned, I'm wondering if it would even matter. If maybe they would have somehow turned the others against him by then."

"But how?" Hemming asked. "Why? Why wouldn't they believe General Kade?"

"I don't know," I said, pacing the room. "But if they could discredit him somehow—dishonor him—then they would have the leverage they needed. Whether Omar was successful or not would no longer matter."

"I understand what you're saying," Kaplyn said, "but unless there is such information in existence, your theory is just that. Pure speculation."

I nodded, knowing he was right, but I still couldn't shake the feeling that my theory had merit. I turned to my father, who was uncharacteristically silent, and wondered…

"Baba, those Minyades in the cellar—the prisoners—could they have something to do with this?"

My father went rigid. "*No.*"

I wasn't convinced. "But Baba, if they know something that could—"

"It is not them, Ariel!" he shouted over me. "And any Nychteríde warrior who puts their trust in a Minyade soldier over me deserves death!"

His words felt like a blow to the gut. "Even me, Baba? Would I deserve death if I believed them…?"

My father never answered that question. Instead, he turned his attention to Kaplyn and started discussing a counterstrike. While my heart broke a little, they weighed their options and decided on a medium-sized army to march into Daglaar. If there was to be a conflict, they would have the element of surprise if they did it soon.

"The eclipse is tomorrow night," Kaplyn pointed out. "I cannot be away."

My father's lips pressed to a grim line, and he nodded. "We will leave the morning after, then. We will use that time to prepare for whatever awaits us in Daglaar."

The two of them shook on it, then began drafting letters to the lords who had helped in the search for Omar and begun the search for Teigan, who had, not surprisingly, gone missing. Whether or not they were willing to go to war to maintain the truce remained to be seen. I didn't have high hopes.

Hemming took my arm and gestured to the door. The two of us exited the room without so much as a word from either Kaplyn or my father.

"Are you all right?" he asked, undoubtedly having seen the hurt I'd felt at my father's words.

"I'm fine." I knew he didn't believe me, but he didn't press the issue further. Instead, he changed the subject altogether.

"Tell me about these Minyades," Hemming whispered in my ear. "The prisoners I saw in Omar's visions." We hurried to my room, and I locked the door behind us. I filled him in on our brief encounter, and he stared at me in silence, mulling it over. "You think they came for you—to *rescue* you?"

I nodded. "That's how it sounded. My father said they are not to be trusted, though, and it's entirely possible that he's right. I mean, why would they come to collect me after all this time? How did they even know I was there? From what I remember of the attack on my home, the entire place was destroyed. I was the sole survivor."

"Maybe it was a trick to convince you to free them."

"I considered that, and given my father's reaction when I asked why they were being held prisoner, it made sense, but now I'm not so sure."

"But what could they possibly know about your father

252

that would cause the others to turn on him? He'd have killed the Minyades if they had something on him. Why keep prisoners that could endanger your position?"

"Exactly! Father is far too smart for that."

"Maybe it has nothing to do with them at all," Hemming said, flopping down on the bed. He stared up at the ornate ceiling as if the answers were hidden in the golden embellishments that adorned it. His leather shirt pulled up as he stretched his arms high above his head, exposing the sharp V-shape carved into the plane of his abs. That warm sensation spread through my stomach—and lower. I sucked in a breath just as he began speaking again. "Maybe they're distracting us from the real reason this coup is happening."

His words took a moment to settle upon my mind, and I shook my head to help clear it.

"Could you tell from the visions how long this plot has been brewing?"

"It was spring in one image—I could see the trees budding in the background. The rest appeared to be in summer."

"I wonder when the prisoners were captured," I muttered. "Did you know about them?"

Hemming threw an arm over his eyes. "I knew we had captured foreigners and that a cell had been dug inside the cellar. Beyond that, I knew nothing."

"That's not helpful."

"It's still the truth," he countered, propping his elbows behind him. "This is a mess, Ariel. This whole thing."

"I know," I said, leaning my head against the bedpost. "I'm really worried that this shift in power doesn't hinge upon Father's death. That maybe it was just a convenient way to be rid of him, but not actually pertinent."

"Yeah," Hemming said, his mind a million miles away. "There's no way to know until we go back there."

"And by then, it might be too late."

His silence was agreement enough.

Both of us knew that the plan to restore my father's rule was shaky at best; at worst, it was a suicide mission. Even with some of the fae behind us, I wasn't convinced it would be enough. The Minyades were somehow the key to it all—I just knew it. But how and why, I couldn't fathom. Either way, we would soon be walking into battle against the very warriors we had grown up with. And the only certainty in war was death.

I looked at Hemming lying on my bed and prayed that fate would not befall him. He'd sacrificed so much for my father and me already, but I wondered if even his beast would be enough to ensure his survival against a legion of Nychterídes. I needed it to be, for his sake as well as my own.

ARIEL

Later that day, my father and Kaplyn were scarce. I'd been put in charge of helping organize the feast for the eclipse, which would have been fine had the cooks let me anywhere near the kitchen. Instead, I lasted all of ten minutes before one diminutive chef escorted me out with a particularly firm grip.

With nothing to do but worry about what was to come, I went outside, hoping the crisp afternoon air would help distract me. I soon found Hemming hanging upside down from a massive oak tree, his wings wrapped around him tightly. Sophitiya squealed with delight from below him as he pretended to be a bat.

I watched as she'd sneak up on him while his eyes were closed. She didn't know how well he could track footsteps—how he'd know exactly where she was. Every time she'd reach out to touch him, his wings would snap open and he'd pretend to bite her hand. She'd scream and run and fall down laughing.

Then they'd do it all over again.

I walked up to them, not wanting to disrupt their game, but the second Hemming saw me, he flipped out of the tree and made his way over. "Any news?" he asked, running his hand through his dark hair to tame it after his upside-down escapade.

"The chefs don't want me in the kitchen. That's all the news I have for you."

"Smart chefs," he muttered under his breath, knowing I'd hear him. I punched his arm, and he feigned injury.

"Ariel!" Sophitiya screamed. She ran and jumped into my arms. It was then that I saw the elaborate harness she had strapped around her chest and shoulders. It held up a pair of oxblood leather wings.

"Where did you get these?" I asked, running my hand along the tip of one. The detail was incredible—they looked just like mine.

"Auntie made them for me...so I could be like you."

My heart melted in an instant. "I think I like yours better than mine. Should we trade?"

She giggled at the thought. "No, silly. You can't take yours off! They're *permanent*. Mine are just for fun." She scrambled down and turned her back to me. "See? I can make them flap, but they don't carry me anywhere."

"That's because you haven't worked them hard enough yet," Hemming said. "The Nychterídes train for years when they're young to develop their muscles. It takes work to be able to fly."

The girl's eyes lit up with determination. "So I just have to practice?" she asked. Hemming nodded. "Will you show me how?"

He scooped her up in his arms to look her straight in the

eyes. "After I return, it will be the first thing I do."

"You really are going to come back, Hemming? Auntie said she didn't think you would—that you would stay by the mountain."

"But I just made you a promise. And a Nychteríde warrior never breaks his promises."

She beamed at him like she was the sun. "Will you return with Ariel?"

His gaze drifted over to me, and he held my stare for a beat longer than necessary. I felt my heart speed up. "If she wishes me to."

The girl turned her most pleading eyes to me. "Pleeeeeease, Ariel? Can you bring him back with you?"

"Hemming is a grown man, capable of making his own choices about where he will go."

"And Ariel is a grown woman," he countered, eyeing me over Sophitiya's head, "capable of freely stating what she does or does not want."

Something flared in the depths of his grey eyes, and my breath caught in my throat. "I want you to do what *you* want to do."

His eyes narrowed. "That's a rather general statement, Ariel." My body tightened under the weight of his stare. "One could take it many ways."

I squared my shoulders and put my hands on my hips. His gaze faltered to my chest where the deep V of my halter led. "*One* can interpret it any way *one* would like."

Hemming slowly placed Sophitiya on the ground and took a step closer. "And if you don't like my interpretation?"

I moved forward a pace to meet him, chin lifted high. "Then I will have to deal with those consequences, won't I?"

We stood there for a moment, inches apart, just staring at one another to see who would flinch first. It was a strange and seemingly dangerous game we were flirting with. One I didn't fully understand but couldn't help but play.

Because the way Hemming was looking at me was all I never knew I wanted.

"What are you two talking about?" Sophitiya whined, breaking our silent battle. "Grownups make no sense sometimes."

The seriousness of the moment was shattered by her statement. I covered my mouth to stifle my laugh. Hemming didn't bother; he let his ring out through the yard. The loud, booming sound sent the birds from the trees.

And a welcome shiver down my spine.

"Come, Sophitiya," he said, taking her hand in his. "Maybe Ariel will be better able to make a sound decision if we steal some food for her from the kitchen. She's been kicked out—again—or so I hear."

The girl let out a sigh. "It's for the best, really. Her cooking is *atrocious*."

Hemming shot a look over his shoulder at me, his eyebrows lifted high with surprise at the girl's comment.

"She has an excellent tutor!" I yelled after him.

I watched as the two walked hand-in-hand toward the manor, his massive frame towering over hers. There was such a gentleness to him when she was around—a tenderness I'd never seen a Nychteríde warrior display. Not even my father. I wondered if it was his fae side shining through, or if it was the effect of being in the Midlands that brought it out of him. Before that day, I'd only ever seen him treat one other so delicately.

It seemed Sophitiya and I had more than just our wings in common.

ARIEL

Early the next day, I found Delphyne where I always did —in her den of fabrics. She smiled at me when I walked in and pushed her chair back from her golden sewing machine.

"Somehow I knew I'd be seeing you today," she teased. "I have a feeling I know what you're about to say."

"Could you make something special for this evening?" I asked, slightly embarrassed by my request. I had a closet full of dresses perfect for the occasion, but for some reason, none of them seemed right. Probably because none of them were really me. "I know it's very last-minute, but—"

"*Special*?" she asked, cutting me off.

"Different…"

Her smile widened. "What were you thinking?"

I described to her what I envisioned in as much detail as possible: the cut of the neck, the cinch at the waist, the low back. She quirked a brow at me when I finished. My idea had her intrigued.

"And what fabric should I make this elaborate creation from?" she asked as though she already knew the answer.

"Leather," I replied. "The same as the wings you made for Sophitiya."

Her mouth tightened. Her expression hardened. "That'll be quite a look."

"That's my hope."

"I can't help but wonder why you're going to such lengths for the eclipse. You've never cared much about it before."

"We will be leaving in the morning to face the Nychterídes. To be blunt, I don't know if we will survive. Maybe…maybe I want to erase that knowledge from my mind for one evening. To have one last night of joy before we go to war."

She walked over to me, face full of worry, and wrapped her tiny arms around my waist. "You, my sweet girl, will be just fine," she said. It wasn't reassurance for me; it was a directive, like she was forbidding me to be otherwise. "You must return…home. To Sophitiya. To me."

I hugged her back. "That is my plan, for what it's worth: restore my father to his position and then come back to live in the Midlands. There's nothing left for me at the mountain—it is no longer my home."

She pulled away and stared up at me. Her sharp eyes read the lies in my expression. The sadness I tried to hide. "I think that all depends," she said.

"On me surviving?"

She pursed her lips in a scolding manner. "Yes, that too, but that's not what I meant. I was referring to a certain Nychteríde warrior—one who I've been told suffered greatly for forcing you out of Daglaar. The one with pointed ears and eyes for only you."

"You mean the one you wanted to kill?"

She smirked at me. "Kill? No, though I'm tempted to throttle him with an iron for making you think he was going to murder you."

"That seems a touch harsh," I replied with a laugh.

She shrugged unapologetically. "Harsh or not, it doesn't make it any less true. Or my assessment of how much he cares for you, Ariel—"

"Hemming is just my friend," I said. The words sounded empty as they left my mouth because I hated the truth in them. I wished there wasn't.

"A friend who looks at you like you hung the very moons that will eclipse tonight."

I sighed heavily. "He watches out for me—"

"Correction: he *watches* you." She took my hand in hers and rubbed her thumb over my knuckles. "He is the reason you want me to make that dress."

"Delphyne—"

"Tell me I'm wrong," she said, propping her hands on her hips, a clear challenge.

"I can't!" I snapped, then regretted it immediately. "I can't tell you that because you're right, Delphyne. But that doesn't change anything." My frustration deflated, leaving me with an overwhelming sense of sadness. "Hemming will go back to my father's army once he regains his position in Daglaar. Because of his loyalty and the loss of almost all my father's most trusted lieutenants, he'll likely be promoted to his inner circle. Even if things change—if we root out all the traitors--it won't change what I am. How everyone from the settlement, and the villages around it, will still look at me. I will never belong there, no matter how hard I try to convince myself otherwise. I couldn't see it when I was younger," I said softly, "and now that I am older, I can't unsee it." I let out a heavy sigh. "Why do you even care? You don't like Hemming."

"My feelings toward him have evolved since Kaplyn told me everything he has done for you. And I've seen him interact with Sophitiya. That child is smitten with him, and he with her. To put it plainly, he is not at all what I expected. He's quite full of surprises." She hesitated for a moment before continuing. "Maybe he would surprise you and come to live in the Midlands if—"

"His life is in Daglaar, Delphyne," I said, cutting her off before she could plant that seed of hope in my brain. I'd only nurture it further, allowing my delusion to grow and flower, and it would be that much more painful when it was trampled by the truth. "And mine is here now. It's that simple."

She cocked her head and stared. "Then why do you need me to make you that dress? One that speaks to your Nychteríde heritage? One that will surely appeal to any man in attendance, but most certainly your *friend*?"

I inhaled deeply. "Maybe you should forget I asked. I'll wear something I already have," I said, headed for the door. "Sorry to have bothered you."

Before she could stop me, I hurried down the hall, headed for my room. Her words seemed to chase me as I tried to outrun their truth. But my words were true as well, which made for a cruel battle in my mind—one between what I wanted and what I could have. Acknowledging my feelings for Hemming would only drive the knife deeper because it would change little—maybe nothing at all. Daglaar would never be my home again, even if he was by my side. I wanted more than that now. I craved a life filled with more than just survival.

I laughed at the irony. I wouldn't have a life at all if we failed.

And neither would Hemming.

ARIEL

A few hours before the festivities began, my father pulled me into his room, a serious look in his eyes. "This is not what I want to do, Ariel, but I see no other choice," he said, unable to meet my eyes.

"What is it?"

He took a deep breath, then forced himself to look at me. "We do not have the numbers Kaplyn and I had hoped for to face the Nychterídes tomorrow. You will need to fight."

"I know that. I had planned to."

"I want you at Kaplyn's side the whole time—"

"But Baba—"

"I am their primary target, so you cannot be near me, understood?"

I wanted to argue but kept my mouth closed. He was right, and though I wanted to be his champion, Hemming was far better suited for that role than I. My father would be safer with him at his side.

"Since you have never seen battle—not like this—I need you to listen to everything Kaplyn tells you." He took my hand in his, his thumb brushing the back of it gently. "It will be dangerous, Ariel."

"I understand. I will be fine."

He squeezed my hand. "We will need your fire to eliminate some of their initial defenses. You will have to get close to them."

I swallowed hard. "Baba—"

"It will be dangerous work, but Kaplyn will keep you safe with his obsidian blades—"

"But Baba—"

"Damage as many as you can. Kaplyn and the others will finish them off—"

"Baba!"

He pulled away. "What?"

"My Fireheart…something's wrong with it. It doesn't come to me as it should anymore; not since Hemming saved it from the fae creature who stole it."

Panic overtook his expression. "We must tell Kaplyn this."

He dragged me down the hall toward Kaplyn's study. We barged in uninvited, and my father quickly informed the fae lord of my problem. Kaplyn's wide eyes stared at me in disbelief. "Why have you not mentioned this before now?"

"I thought at first it just needed to heal. Then I realized something was wrong, but there was so much else going on that I didn't have time to worry about it."

"I'll get the healer," he said, storming from the room. Moments later, he returned with a willowy young male whose pale skin was nearly as white as his short-cropped hair. "Scan her," Kaplyn ordered. The male nodded.

He came to me and rested his hands over my chest. I felt

his energy pulse through me, searching for what was wrong—for the solution to my problem. "It is not settled where it should be," he said, his voice like the soft whisper of the wind.

"Fix it," my father growled, but the mild-mannered fae shook his head, unfazed by the general's anger.

"I am afraid I cannot."

"You're a healer, are you not?" Father asked. The healer nodded. "Then heal her!"

"My apologies, General, but this is beyond my magical ability. I fear that her restoration was not complete. Were her Fireheart merely damaged or depleted, I could be of service, but I cannot recreate what is missing." The pale fae turned his silver-blue eyes to me. "I am sorry, Ariel. I wish I could be of service."

I nodded in reply, unable to find my tongue.

"The creature that attacked you," Kaplyn said, his voice distant, as though working through the problem aloud. "Does it live?"

"No."

Kaplyn frowned. "I fear Hemming wasn't able to withstand all of your power—some of it must have been left behind. And if the Dreamcatcher is dead, there will be no recouping it."

"So I'm a Minyade without Minyade traits?" I asked, finally facing the reality I'd been evading for days.

"Not necessarily," he replied, the crease in his brow disconcerting. "There may be another way."

The healer looked to his lord with wide eyes. "You speak of the Barterer."

Kaplyn nodded. "He may be the only way, but it's risky. I would only call upon him as a last resort, and I'm just not certain we're at that point yet."

"Why not?" my father asked.

"Because the price to pay would be high. I fear what he would ask for in return…"

My father looked from Kaplyn to me, a mix of emotions playing in his expression. "This changes nothing. Fireheart or not, you will still fight at my side. I will amend our plan of attack to account for this new variable. It will be fine, Ariel. I promise."

I forced a smile. "I will serve in whatever capacity you deem fit, Baba."

"Good. We will need you."

With a curt nod, he dismissed me and went over to where Kaplyn stood by his desk to confer with the fae lord. I could tell the two were downplaying how much my admission changed their plan. I tried to tamp down the feeling of disappointment as I headed to my room to prepare for the eclipse.

I didn't feel much like celebrating anymore.

I felt like mourning.

≈

HEMMING WAS NOWHERE TO BE FOUND WHEN I ENTERED MY bedroom, but something else awaited my arrival. Spread across my bed was the creation I'd told Delphyne not to make for me, only with a twist. It was every bit as stunning as I ever could have hoped for and then some. I ran my fingers over the petal-soft leather, smiling despite myself.

Instead of a full skirt, she'd left the front of the dress without any at all, tapering from my hips down into a train in the back. Next to the dress were oxblood leather pants to be worn with the half-dress. It was more amazing than I ever could have imagined.

It was perfection.

I picked it up and held it before me, admiring the detailed stitching that pieced it all together. It truly was a work of art. I rushed to the bathroom to try it on and was half undressed when I heard the bedroom door open.

"Ariel? Are you in here?" Hemming called.

"I'm getting dressed! Don't come in the bathroom!"

I heard the squeak of the bed as he sat down.

"I just spoke to your father." The shame in his voice was palpable through the door. "I'm sorry. I tried to save it, but I guess I failed you. *Again.*"

"It's not your fault, Hemmy. Maybe when all this is done, I can go back to the Black Forest with Kaplyn and the healer and find the Dreamcatcher's remains. Maybe, with their help, it can be fixed."

"*You* can go back? Not *we*?"

I clenched my teeth until I fought back the tears welling in my eyes. "You'll be too busy helping my father restore his army to come with me. Besides, what can you do? You've already done all you can."

His silence stretched out for so long that I wondered if he'd left altogether. "Hemmy? Are you still here?"

"Do you think we're walking into a trap?" he asked. His voice was sharp and distant—the one he used when doing his best to be diplomatic.

"I don't know." I fastened the halter around my neck and smoothed out the leather bodice. "I hope not."

He began outlining all the potential scenarios we might face the next day—strategy and formations and all the things we'd been trained in since we were young. While he continued, I pulled on the tight leather pants and laced them up on the sides where the skirt hid the ties. Once I'd pulled on my knee-high boots, I smoothed the bodice one more time, though there was no need to—the dress fit like a second skin. I let my hand linger on my stomach as I took a deep breath to calm my rising nerves. Then I opened the door and stepped into the bedroom.

Hemming shot up from the bed and stared, mouth open.

My heart started to race in my chest.

"I had Delphyne make this for me…actually, I asked her to make it and then told her *not* to, but she didn't listen because she might be the most headstrong woman I've ever met…"

"You're rambling," he said, eyes pinned on me. He slowly stepped closer, his entire body taut, as if poised for a fight.

"You look like you're going to hit me," I said with a nervous laugh.

He froze in place. "Definitely not."

His eyes tracked over my body—my dress. The intensity of his gaze made me squirm, and I suddenly questioned my choice of attire. "Maybe I should wear something else," I said, heading for my closet.

He stepped in front of me, blocking the way. "No."

"*No*? I can't go to my closet?"

"No, I don't think you should wear something else."

"Well," I said, heat rising to my cheeks, "you're looking at me strangely, and it's making me self-conscious. If you're going to stare that boldly, then so will everyone else. I'm not trying to be a spectacle in this thing—"

"You are a spectacle no matter what you wear," he replied. With the weight of a mountain between us, he took a step closer. I felt like my chest might collapse. "But this," he said, indicating Delphyne's creation, "is the embodiment of who you are."

Another step closer.

Then another.

He stopped only inches from me, his formidable frame looming in the dying light of the sun spilling through my window, and reached into his pocket. "Turn around," he said softly. "*Please.*"

Still nervous, I did as he asked. "What are you doing?"

"I'm adding one final touch."

He stepped closer, his body brushing against mine as he reached around me and placed something in the deep V of my dress. I sucked in a breath as the familiar weight of the stone he'd once given me nestled against my skin where it had always been—where it belonged.

The blood-red stone matched the dress perfectly.

While I struggled to find my tongue, Hemming turned me around in his arms to inspect his addition to my outfit. His hands lingered on my shoulders, the feel of his skin against mine making my heart skip a beat.

"*Perfection...*"

I forced my eyes to meet his gaze. His hold on me tightened.

Then my bedroom door flew open without warning, startling us both. I staggered back a step as Sophitiya came storming into the room. "Ariel!" she cried with joy as she ran toward us. "Auntie said I can come tonight! I can go to the feast!"

"That's fantastic, Soph!"

"I know! And look at what she made me!" She spun in a circle for Hemming and me, her pristine white dress fanning out around her, and I suddenly remembered the present I'd found for her in Daglaar. The one that I'd had fashioned into a necklace.

"You look like a princess," I said, "but I don't think you're quite ready yet." Her beaming smile fell away in an instant, and she watched with sad eyes as I walked over to my dresser and pulled out the Azure of the Sea stone that now hung from a cord, much like mine. Her disappointment disappeared in a flash, and her eyes lit up as I tied it around her neck. "I meant to give you this earlier, but I kept forgetting." I took a step back to get a better look. "What do you think, Hemming? Is she ready to go to the party now?"

He smiled at the sight of the young girl in the sea-blue necklace. "She sure is."

Sophitiya launched herself at me, and I scooped her up. "Thank you!" she said as she hugged me. "I'm so excited!"

"What made your aunt change her mind?" I asked.

She shrugged. "Auntie said tonight was very important to you...that I should enjoy my time with you and Hemming."

I flinched at the implication of her words. Hemming saw my expression change and quickly took Sophitiya from my arms. "We should let Ariel finish getting ready," he said, walking around the bed to the door. "Women like to fuss about such things and don't like to be interrupted until they're perfect."

Sophitiya's brows pulled together with confusion. "But Ariel is already perfect," she argued.

Hemming stopped in the doorway and looked back at me, the weight of his stare as heavy as it had been only moments earlier. "She is. *Always*."

ARIEL

"You look especially mesmerizing this evening," Shayfer said, intercepting me as I went to pour a glass of wine. He put my hand to his lips, and I tried not to laugh. "This dress…it's quite unusual. Harsh, yet incredibly inviting."

"It's a Dawn of Battle dress," I replied. "I thought that would be appropriate, given the situation."

He quirked a brow at me and laughed. "Is that what this is?" He fingered the edge of the skirt where it drifted down from my waist. "I can't help but think it was born of another purpose."

"Like what?" I asked, stepping out of reach.

He laughed harder as his hand dropped to his side. "An invitation for a certain friend of yours."

"Shayfer," I sighed, "we have been over this time and time again—"

"I'm not talking about me, Ariel dear." His gaze drifted

off toward the manor where Hemming stood with Kaplyn, the two discussing something as they watched over the festivities. The sight of them was something to behold, Kaplyn in his golden finery, hair pulled back to accentuate his features, and Hemming clad in black leather from head to toe, armed as if we were going to war at any moment. The pair was a study in contrast, yet complementary somehow, like night and day. Dusk and dawn.

I turned my attention back to Shayfer when I realized he'd been calling my name.

"An invitation for what, exactly?" I asked, trying to ignore the all-knowing smirk on his face.

"Oh, Ariel, have I taught you nothing in your time here?"

"I know which wine to drink with fish and which of the staff are sleeping together."

He rolled his eyes and took my hand in his. "Come dance with me, Ariel. I shall spell it all out for you in terms even you can understand." Without awaiting my reply, he hauled me off to where the others were dancing and started twirling me around. "Allow me to be blunt for the sake of expediency: you are in love with Hemming, and this dress screams 'bed me, Nychteríde war god'."

"It does not!" I argued, slapping his arm.

"It most certainly does, and thank the gods for that. One of you has to make the first move soon, or I'm going to drag you both into bed with me and show you how it's done."

My jaw dropped at the boldness of his outburst. It was brash, even by Shayfer's standards.

He dismissed my shock with a wave of his hand. "Close your mouth, Ariel dear. You look like a fish, and it's killing the effect of your delicious outfit."

"I cannot believe you just said that!"

"Believe it, because it's going to happen…if we all survive this madness tomorrow."

"I feel like that's a threat," I muttered under my breath.

"Oh, I can assure you, it's not. It's a promise. And you'll thank me for it afterward." A wicked smile stretched across his face. "You both will."

He punctuated his statement with a wink. I slapped him again. "You're incorrigible!"

"That I am, but that doesn't make me wrong. You love him, Ariel."

"Of course I love him. I've always loved him—"

"And that love has evolved. Embrace it. Act on it, for the love of the gods. Tonight is a night of magic and mystery in the Midlands. What better night than this to be bold and brazen? To take a chance on something as rare and beautiful as love…" I could feel my cheeks redden, and I tried to look away, but Shayfer wouldn't let me. He caught my chin with his hand and held it gently while he spoke to me with a sincerity I'd never known he possessed. "What I wouldn't give to have someone look at me the way Hemming does you when your back is turned—the longing in those stormy eyes. I'd trade every love affair I've ever had for that."

He stroked my chin then released me, only to begin twirling me across the grounds again.

"Shayfer…I…"

"Do not pity me, Ariel. I have no need for it. But please do me the favor of being honest with yourself."

I closed my eyes as he spun me, my hair falling from where Delphyne had pinned it up. The wind blew it around me wildly, and I felt like I was flying around the mountain just like Hemming and I had when we were young. I could practically hear him taunting me as he chased me through the clouds.

Then I thought about him chasing me around the mountain now, and the image looked very different. My cheeks flushed again. "You're right," I said, breaking the silence. "I do love him."

He leaned in closer. "You need to tell *him* that, Ariel dear. Not me." I moved to strike him a third time, but he caught my hand and twirled me under his outstretched arm. "That's my girl," he said. "Now, will you do me one last favor?"

"Of course."

He paused, and I leaned back to find a wicked grin gleaming in the moonlight. "Be sure to tell me *everything* tomorrow morning."

≈

HEMMING

I wondered if every being in the Midlands was at Kaplyn's that night.

From the top of the steps, I watched as Ariel wove her way through them all, smiling and dancing, a drop of blood in a sea of white and gold. That dress—it was as if Delphyne had wrapped Ariel in the essence of her wings. She looked like a warrior. She looked like a queen. She looked like everything I could ever want. She was so alive— so full of fire, even if her Fireheart was broken. Her fervor didn't come from it. It was who she was and always had been.

And partly why I loved her.

"She's quite special, isn't she?" Kaplyn asked, coming to stand beside me.

"She always was."

"There is such joy in her." He turned slowly to look at

276

me. "Have you ever known joy like that in your life, Hemming?"

I held my gaze on Ariel. "Yes. Through her, I have."

"I wonder what will happen, then, when this is all over and you must return to your home and she to hers."

I looked over at him. His face was impassive, but there was a notable undercurrent in his tone, full of something I couldn't quite place. Mischief? Trickery? Malice? I couldn't be certain.

"And I wonder why you, a fae lord, are so concerned with her plans, as she is old enough to do as she pleases. I also wonder why you are so interested in my happiness."

An elegant shrug from Kaplyn. "I am curious by nature."

"As I am suspicious."

His neutral expression fell. "You doubt that I truly care for her."

"I think you care for her too much..."

A small smile formed at the corners of Kaplyn's mouth. "I think your assessment of our relationship is in error, Hemming. Perhaps you should go drink the wine and eat the food and wait to see if the magic of our lands chooses you— strikes you. Avails your future to you. That is what the eclipse is all about: the magic of your past, present, and future align- ing. If you are one of the lucky ones, your destiny will be made clear."

"And what if that destiny is not what I want it to be?" I asked as I watched Shayfer take Ariel by the hand to dance with her again.

Kaplyn leaned closer. "What if it is?" he asked softly. "I wonder which possibility frightens you more…"

With that, he disappeared back into the manor.

I looked up at the sky to find the moons about to cross paths. The eclipse was moments away, and all I could think about were Kaplyn's final words. With a deep breath, I started down the steps toward the festivities. Ariel was laughing, the soft trill of her voice carrying through the night toward me like an arrow aimed at my heart. The second it struck, her eyes met mine and she smiled.

Then she parted with Shayfer to make her way toward me. "I wondered when you'd join the party," she said, still smiling.

"I had to talk to Kaplyn about something." Her expression faltered at the implication of my reply, and I quickly explained. "Not about tomorrow. Everything is still as planned."

"Oh. All right," she said, trying to brush aside her concerns. "I was starting to think you weren't going to come."

"You know I don't like parties."

"This is true," she said, mischief brewing in her narrowed green eyes, "but you *do* like wine. A lot, judging by the amount you drank the other night under the willow tree." She grabbed a bottle from the table that extended far across the property and pressed it to her lips. Her eyes met mine as she drank, and she must have found something funny in my expression, because a tiny laugh escaped her and she quickly pulled the bottle away. As she fought to swallow the wine before her outburst sent it spraying everywhere, a small drop ran down her chin. I brushed my thumb across her skin, catching the burgundy liquid, then put it to my mouth.

I sucked it clean.

Her laughter ceased in an instant, and she swallowed hard as she stared at me with wide eyes.

"Dance with me," I said, taking the wine from her hand.

"But you don't like dancing, either." Her voice was lower and fuller than normal.

"True, but I *do* like you, and *you* like to dance. I think I can suffer through one or two for your benefit."

A nervous laugh escaped her."How very noble of you, Hemmy."

I took her hand in mine and pulled her close. "It's *Hemming* now, remember?"

Startled, she looked up at me with those vibrant green eyes that shone brighter than the eclipse's blue light. "I'm starting to…"

As I led her toward the crowd, a blast of magic shot across the land. A ripple in the air slammed into me so hard that I felt it in my bones. It coursed through every part of me until I didn't know where it stopped and I began, my feet rooted to the ground where it pulsed through the Midlands. It held me captive as it showed me what it would give me if I accepted it. If I accepted my fae heritage.

One look at what it promised, and I agreed.

Why the magic had chosen me that night, I didn't know. But its message was clear.

I saw Ariel the day she arrived in Daglaar, the frightened girl she was. I saw her in her Dawn of Battle dress dancing through the party, her hair wild and free. Then I saw the way she would look beneath me on the night of our bonding—my name on her lips as she pulled me closer.

Yes, the magic was clear indeed.

Ariel was my past, my present, and my future.

She was my destiny.

41

ARIEL

Hemming's eyes were glowing like the moons above, liquid silver swirling in them like an icy fire. I'd seen it happen to others during the two-moon eclipse, so I stayed still as he stood there, unmoving, and waited for it to pass. I couldn't help but wonder what he was seeing; what the magic had shown him.

I hoped he'd tell me one day.

After a moment, his eyes cleared, returning to their pale grey shade, but he remained still. He didn't say a word as he stared at me. It was only when I touched him that he seemed to come out of his magical trance.

"Are you okay?" I asked, leaning in closer. He went rigid beneath my hand, so I pulled away, fear prickling in my veins. Perhaps he'd seen something terrible—a premonition of what was to come in Daglaar. Maybe I didn't want to know what he'd seen after all. "Hemming…what's going on? Are you feeling all right? Did the magic…did it *do* something?"

"I'm fine. I just—" He cut himself off, staring at me in a way I'd never seen before. Like he was seeing something for the first time and didn't quite believe it.

"You can tell me," I said softly. "You know that, right? You can tell me anything…"

"Not this…not yet." A sad smile stretched across his face. "But maybe after that dance."

Before I could press him further, he guided me into the center of the party where dancers seemed to glide along the ground weightlessly. He gently placed a hand around the small of my back. In turn, I rested mine on his shoulder and let him tuck our joined hands into his chest.

"Do I need to lead, or have your skills improved enough in my absence that you can be trusted with the task?" I asked, looking up at him through my lashes. There was an intensity to him that I couldn't quite weather; a look in his eyes that I couldn't quite meet.

I wondered if it was the look Shayfer was talking about, or if the magic was somehow still at work somewhere deep inside.

"I can manage." He started to move confidently with the music, and I couldn't help but be impressed. His dancing abilities had most certainly improved.

"Are you sure you weren't off practicing with the village women while I was away?" I asked playfully, though the second those words left my mouth, my stomach lurched. The thought of him like this with another woman was suddenly more than I could bear.

I awaited his answer, heart in my throat.

"There were no women," he replied, his words clipped and curt.

Guilt eclipsed my fear as I remembered his earlier words —that he hadn't been allowed near them as part of his punishment—punishment he'd suffered for me. "I'm sorry," I said softly, "I forgot you told me you weren't allowed to go—"

"I wasn't." He pulled away to look down at me. The cautious look in his eyes was a mix of frustration and hurt, and I wanted to kick myself for what I'd said. "Until I eventually was. But I want to make this point clear to you, Ariel: there have never been other women…not for me."

The implication of his words slammed into me hard, but it didn't match the edge to his stare that bored through me.

I felt my defenses rising, though I had no idea why.

"But what about you?" he asked, the steely look in his eyes now mirrored in his tone. "Were you fine-tuning your dance skills with Shayfer and the other fae lords while you were gone?"

My arms fell limp at my sides. "What's that supposed to mean?"

"I don't know," he replied, exhaling hard as he raked his hand through his hair. "You seem very concerned about what I've been doing in your absence and with whom I did it. I just thought I'd show the same level of interest."

His words felt like a slap. "Shayfer is my *friend*—even if that's a blurry line for him at times. And there were no fae lords, or sons of fae lords, or daughters, either, for that matter. No creatures in the Midlands have had my attention, romantic or otherwise, okay? Does that make you feel better?"

A deep rumbling sound escaped him. "*Yes.*"

For a moment, we just stood there staring at one another while the party continued around us as though a bizarre fight weren't brewing in its midst.

"What's gotten into you, Hemming?"

"Nothing—"

"Is this about the magic?"

"Maybe—"

"What did it show you?" I asked, no lack of heat in my tone.

"Nothing—"

"Wrong answer—"

"Ariel, it's nothing," he said, closing his eyes to shut me out.

"That's funny, because it feels a lot like something."

He rubbed his hands over his face and exhaled hard. "Were you always this infuriating?"

"Were you always this stubborn?"

He looked down at me. "I thought you loved that I was stubborn," he said, sounding oddly wounded.

"I did!"

Silence.

"*Did*...or *do*?"

There was a weight to his question, just like there had been when I'd asked him the same one the night we were reunited. It was a pivotal moment. Telling him I'd let him know later wasn't going to work for me as it had for him.

"*Do*," I whispered. "I *do* love that about you."

His body relaxed ever so slightly, and he leaned closer. "But I did *not* love watching you dance with Shayfer tonight."

"Is that what's gotten into you? You don't want me dancing with the gaily dressed fae spy in attendance?"

Another inch closer. "No. Not entirely."

I swallowed my heart back down into my chest. "Are you afraid he might try to have his way with me in the middle of the party?"

He shook his head. "I would never let that happen—"

"And neither would I," I added, folding my arms across my chest. "But this is a party, Hemming. People dance together. If it would improve your mood, I could just dance on my own—unless, of course, my solo dancing offends you too?"

"*Never*," he said as he wrapped his arm around my back again, pulling me into him. "I could watch you dance all night."

The feel of his body pressed tightly against mine combined with the way he was looking at me had me tamping down my nerves. His eyes were so intense that I could barely hold his gaze. Emotions burned brightly within them, and I realized that Shayfer had been right about how Hemming felt, because the look he was giving me said he'd forsake the world to be at my side.

"Will you please just tell me what's going on with you?" My words escaped on a breath as I tried to keep my heart from pounding against his chest and giving me away.

He bent his head toward me until his mouth was at my ear. Every nerve in my body sang as his soft lips grazed my tender skin.

"If you'll allow it, I'd rather show you." His breath tickled my neck, and I pulled back to look at him again. The second his eyes locked on mine, my traitorous heart slammed to a stop. He took my face in his hands and slowly angled it toward him as the blue light of the eclipse filled the sky. But I didn't care about that. All I cared about was the heat in his stare, the proximity of his body, and the way the combination had me coming undone. Then his lips grazed mine, and heat tore through my veins. "I have dreamt of this moment for so long…"

Something deep within me ignited—something that I knew could never be extinguished—and I felt my hand slide along his back until it traced the base of his wing. His body went taut and his grip on my face tightened. His reaction to my touch only stoked that fire further.

"Then perhaps you should tell me how this dream ends—or show me, if you'd rather."

A rumble of approval echoed through his body just before he pressed his mouth to mine. My eyelids slammed shut as his soft lips began to move, his hands drifting into my hair. The feel of his tongue against mine nearly undid me, and I fought hard to stay on my feet. Nothing around us mattered in that moment; just him and me and the bond we shared that could never be broken.

Fire sparked in my chest at the thought of us being together forever, and I quickly pulled away. "Hemming…my Fireheart…I can feel it."

"Good," was his only response before leaning in to kiss me again.

"But what if it comes out *now*?" I argued. "And I can't control it?"

He stared back at me, clearly amused by my flustered state. "I guess that depends on whether you're planning to kiss me or kill me?" I flushed with embarrassment and tried to look away, but his hold on my face was unrelenting. "If you breathing fire down my throat is the risk I need to accept to kiss you, I will." He lowered his face to mine again, our mouths so close they nearly touched. "I survived it once, Ariel. For you, I'm willing to tempt fate."

Whatever momentary fear had held me back washed away in an instant.

I realized in that moment just how long I'd been lying to myself about my love for Hemming, too afraid to admit the truth. But it no longer mattered, because once revealed, there would be no hiding it again. I could tell by the way he held onto me that he'd never let me go again.

I threw my arms around his neck and kissed him with a passion I'd never known I possessed. Insatiable desire consumed me, and nothing seemed to be enough. Not his proximity, or his touch, or the depth of his kiss. All I wanted was to be swallowed whole by the moment and never return.

My legs were around his waist before I realized what I was doing, and I felt a growl tear through his body. His lips retreated from mine, and it felt like my whole world collapsed.

Then I saw the feral look in his eyes as he stared at me, breathing hard, and every nerve in my body came to life again.

"Come with me," he said as he set me down and grabbed my hand. Without explanation, he navigated his way through the crowd toward the far side of the manor as I followed him in silence. He rounded the massive building and continued into the darkness beyond, the sounds of merriment waning the further we traveled. We didn't stop until we reached the willow tree and the privacy its massive trunk and low-hanging foliage offered.

Tucked safely away from prying eyes, Hemming pressed me against the rough bark. I could feel the full weight of his desire against my belly, and it elicited a sound from me that was unrecognizable.

Given the roar that escaped him in return, I knew he approved.

"Ariel," he whispered against my neck as he trailed kisses along the edge of my halter, "my control is waning…and I don't know what will happen to the beast if it does."

"I don't want your control, Hemming," I replied, arching against him. "I want *you*—all of you. Whatever that entails."

A warning grumble echoed around us as he nipped the top of my breast. "Then you shall have it."

His hands slid along my sides to my hips, then around behind. In a flash, he gripped my ass and hoisted me up, pinning my hips against the tree with his own. I groaned at the feel of him between my legs, and his fingertips dug into my leather pants at the sound. Our mouths melded together again with a ferocity I didn't fully understand but never wanted to be without. By the end of the night, Hemming and I would be as one, and nothing could have felt more right.

Friends to enemies to lovers.

A fitting climax to our convoluted journey.

But like the moons had eclipsed one another that night, so did my past overtake the present.

Screams suddenly filled the air, the smell of fire and carnage wafting our way. Hemming's lips ripped away from me, leaving me empty and breathless. He was on high alert before reality fully settled in. It was like being torn from a long-awaited dream and thrust into a nightmare.

"Dear gods," he muttered as he looked past the manor to where festivities were taking place. Then he grabbed me by my shoulders and spun me to look. All I saw was smoke and flame. "We have to go."

With a quick nod to tell him I understood, we took to the air, headed toward the attack. In the distance, I could see the bright wings of Minyades highlighted in the eclipse's light. They were attacking Kaplyn's lands. Their fire was charring it to ash.

"Where are my father and Kaplyn?" I shouted over the din.

"I don't know—I don't see them—but we can't wait, or this place will be burned to the ground. And I only see three Minyades so far. We can take them."

Three…

I quickly took stock of their brightly colored appendages and was struck by a grim possibility. "The prisoners…" I said aloud, not realizing it until Hemming turned back to look at me.

"What?"

"They're the prisoners, Hemming—from the cellar in the

288

mountain. They've come for me. I just know it. But how? How did they get out? Get across the Midlands?"

As I silently tried to answer my questions, a roar from Hemming's beast echoed through the air as he landed amid the chaos with me right behind him. He turned and pinned murderous eyes on me. "They may have come for you, but they will not have you."

He drew two swords from their sheaths and handed me one.

"We have to get these people to safety," I yelled as I scanned the skies for the Minyades. Through a cloud of smoke, the one with bright blue wings dove at the ground, fast as an arrow. A high-pitched scream followed seconds later, and dread shot through me in an instant.

I knew that scream.

I'd heard it once before.

"Soph!" I cried, shooting in the air toward where the Minyade had landed. As I neared, I could see her, captive in his arms. I landed with such force that dust and debris shot up around me, coating my dress in ash as if I'd just walked through fire. And I would, for Sophitiya. I'd raze the world to the ground to keep her safe.

"Come with me, Ariel," the Minyade said, pinning the girl against him with a blade to her throat. The terror in her wide blue eyes made me rage.

"Release her and I'll let you live," I replied, raising Hemming's sword. "*Barely…*"

"We do not have time for this," the enemy hissed, looking to the skies. "They are coming!"

"Yes, they are. Kaplyn, Hemming…my father. They will gut you alive if they catch you, so let the girl go while you can." I flipped the sword's pommel over in my hand as if I were playing around—as if I weren't about to cut him down with it.

"You don't understand," he growled, gripping Sophitiya so hard that her lips began turning as blue as her terrified stare. "The Nychterídes—they know who you are, *Aima Kori*...that you're—"

A blade through the throat cut the Minyade's words short. Sophitiya ran to me the second his grip went limp, and I dropped my weapon to scoop her up in my arms. As she wept against me, I watched the sword pull free from the blue-winged Minyade. His body fell in a heap to reveal Hemming standing there, spattered with blood and breathing hard.

"Is she all right?" he asked, staring at the frightened girl.

Sophitiya looked back at him, then disentangled herself from me. She ran and threw herself at him. He caught her and cradled her tiny body against his chest while she sobbed.

"Take her to the manor," I said as I retrieved my weapon, my gaze fixed on the sky above. I could see my father battling the Minyade with the yellow wings high in the air. I spotted the teal-winged one as he crashed into the woods surrounding the property. It looked as if magic had plucked him from the sky.

I stared at the place where he'd disappeared into the trees.

"What are you doing?" Hemming asked, fear blooming in his stare.

"I'm getting answers." I ran over and hugged Sophitiya before grabbing Hemming's face and kissing him fiercely. "Meet me once she is safe."

Before he could stop me, I took off at a sprint. His shouts were soon drowned out by the wind in my ears. The last Minyade was going to tell me what I wanted to know, provided he wasn't already dead. Father had said not to trust them, but I doubted they were trying to trick me anymore. The one Hemming had killed had seemed far past that point.

I cut through the trees with ease, weaving my way to the place where he should have been, but there was no sign of him. I wondered if I'd somehow lost my direction—or if the Midlands had lost it for me. Then I came to a spot in the ground where the dirt appeared compressed, like from the force of an impact.

I bent down to examine it for blood. That was when I spotted the drag marks in the dirt, leading deeper into the forest.

Then I felt someone creeping up behind me.

I shot to my feet, blade arcing as I spun to face my attacker, but he'd anticipated my move and blocked it, countering with a brutal blow of his pommel to my head. Without my scales, it was enough to make my vision blur and my ears ring. I crashed to the ground in a heap.

"That was easier than I expected," my attacker said, a chorus of laughter following.

My hazy mind grappled with what was happening as I was hauled to my feet, only to be struck again so hard that everything went black for a moment.

"We need to get the Minyade whore out of here now. Kaplyn and the others will be coming," a different male said, though his voice was as familiar as the first.

"Lord Teigan?" I mumbled, my head throbbing.

"Just get us to the border like you promised," the other shouted.

"Gladly," Teigan replied. "And take this piece of refuse with you."

The third blow to my head did me in, but not before realization dawned in my battered mind. In my haste—my need for answers—I'd walked right into a trap. And there was no way I'd be walking out.

HEMMING

I knew something was wrong the second I set foot in the woods. There was an uneasiness there—a wrongness I couldn't shake.

"Where is Ariel?" Kade asked as he ran to my side, covered in the blood of the enemy.

"She's in here somewhere."

Kade's dark eyes met mine. "You left her alone?"

"The Minyade attacked Sophitiya. I eliminated him and took the child back to the house at Ariel's request to make sure she was safe. Ariel ran into the woods to find the fallen Minyade. She wanted answers—answers you wouldn't give her."

Kade snatched my harness and pulled me to him. "If anything happens to her, you will not live long enough to regret it."

"Where's Ariel?" Kaplyn asked as he approached. "I saw her run in here after the Minyade I ripped from the sky." He wiped the blood from his face with a handkerchief, then threw it to the ground.

"I don't know, but we have to find her." I yanked free of Kade's grip and raced further into the woods where I'd last seen her headed. Kade and Kaplyn ran beside me, calling for her, but I couldn't find my voice, my throat too tight with fear to make a sound. I just ran, looking for any sign of her or the Minyade she had come for. I found neither, but what I did find shook me to my core.

In a small clearing, something shiny glinted in the moonlight pouring through a break in the canopy. I bent down and picked up Ariel's blessing stone—the one she never parted with. The one Kaplyn had given her to guide her safely through the Midlands.

"Over here!" I shouted. They were at my side in a moment. "I found this…"

Their faces went pale at the sight of the smooth black talisman.

"It must have fallen out of her pocket," Kaplyn said, reaching for stone.

"We can use it to find her, right?" I asked, panic creeping into my voice. "The Minyade…he must have overtaken her somehow. Maybe they plan to use her to get to you."

Kade nodded at my observation. "Let us hope that is the case."

"Then what are we waiting for? Ariel said the stone could take you to whatever you desire. Let's go!"

"It's not that simple," Kaplyn said. I looked back at his pained expression. Anger surging, I grabbed him by his collar and hauled him toward me. To his credit, he never flinched.

"What isn't that simple, Kaplyn? Don't you want to find her?"

He did flinch at my words. "I love Ariel, Hemming, and I know you do, too. But the stone can't help us find her."

I pulled him in closer. "Why. Not? She used it to find her father—and *you*."

"Because that is how it was blessed—for *her* to find *her* way to what she desired. Not you or me. And though I cast a tracking spell on it that would allow me to find her, it is of no use when the stone is not in her possession." The sorrow in his eyes was plain as he spoke. "If she were my child, I would be able to sense her, but she is not, so I cannot. I'm so sorry, Hemming. Truly I am. We will have to search without the aid of magic and pray it is enough."

"What about him?" I asked, jerking my head toward Kade. "Or can only the fae sense their children?"

Kaplyn's expression grew bleaker. "That trait is not exclusive to the fae," was his only reply. He cast an apologetic glance at Kade, whose body had gone rigid, his face pale.

"Then why are we still standing here? She's your *daughter*," I yelled at Kade, desperation plain in my tone. "Sense her! *Find her*!"

But Kade didn't move.

Neither did Kaplyn.

Rage like I'd never known erupted inside me, the beast's roar cutting through the air. I could feel the change starting, but one word from Kaplyn brought him to a halt.

"NO," he said, voice deep and booming. Sweat rolled down my face. My body felt like it was being ripped in two. All I wanted to do was let the beast out to decimate anything standing between Ariel and me. "The beast cannot find her any more than Kade can," Kaplyn added. His voice was full of guilt and remorse.

I breathed hard, trying to tamp down the beast and ease the pain tearing me apart. "I don't understand—"

"I cannot find her," Kade said, his words sharp and heavy and laced with sadness. I looked up to find tears welling in his eyes.

"Why not?"

"Because I am not Ariel's father—her *real* father."

"*What?*"

"She is not my daughter by blood, so I cannot feel her presence."

His words crashed into me, and I staggered back a step. The beast fell into a dark abyss somewhere deep inside me. I couldn't feel him at all.

Kaplyn took a step toward me and put a steadying hand on my shoulder. "If you were still with her, Hemming, this would be a much easier task, but you are not, so we are forced to split up and search for her."

"All right…"

Kaplyn squeezed my shoulder, pulling my attention to him. "I wish I could do more," he said, hesitating slightly. "I'm sorry…my *son*."

As I stared at him, his final word echoing in my mind, a world of realization crashed down upon me. One with two painful truths.

Ariel didn't really have a father.

And Kaplyn was mine.

43

ARIEL

Another sharp blow to my head landed the second I arrived wherever it was I'd been taken.

Before I could defend myself, a steel mask was placed over my face and secured. Out of reflex, I tried to breathe fire to melt it, but it was steel from deep in the mountain—the downfall of all Minyades. Even if my Fireheart had been working, it wouldn't have mattered. I wrestled against those that held and bound my hands behind my back. Once I was secured, a small door in the mask slid open, allowing me to see.

What it revealed made me wish they'd left it closed.

Warriors I'd grown up around—men I'd thought both supported and respected my father—stood before me, scowling at my presence. Then, just as the surrealness of it all started to dissipate a bit, Baran stepped forward, hands behind his back as always, and smiled.

"Thank you for coming, Ariel. You've made this even easier than I expected."

"Go suck an ox's—" A quick thrust of a staff to my stomach knocked both the wind and my insult from me. I buckled over and fell to my knees, trying to catch my breath. Another hard blow under my chin sent me flying onto my back. I tried to flip to my side to get up as quickly as I could while bound, but Baran drove the staff—*my* staff—into my chest to hold me down.

"Your father isn't here to protect you, Ariel. You'd be wise not to anger me again." With no breath to spare, I didn't reply. "Speaking of your father, he's proven more of a challenge to deal with than I expected, but no matter. His death wasn't integral to the plan—just a pleasant potential side effect. Your death, however, is imminent. Everything is falling into place just as I wanted."

"Really?" I wheezed.

He pushed down harder on the thick wooden rod. "Yes. Really."

"How do you figure? My father lives, and Kaplyn has an army to command. They will come for me, and they will kill you."

The Nychterídes all laughed, as though a fae army descending upon them was no threat at all.

"We have taken care of that possibility." He didn't bother to expand on how. "If your father comes for you, he will find himself at the end of an obsidian sword. He's a traitor, you see. He led his highest-ranking officers into the Black Forest to be slaughtered, all at the behest of his Minyade daughter— the Midlands' spy who poisoned his mind with the help of her mentor and co-conspirator."

"*What?*" The word barely escaped on a breath.

"It's genius, really."

"Maybe, except for one tiny detail," I said, pressing my

298

chest against the end of my staff. "No one will believe that my father would ever turn on his people. That's nothing short of madness. He is loyal to the Nychterídes to a fault. He'd never be led astray."

"This is true," Baran said, crouching down beside me, staff still in hand, "unless they can be convinced that it isn't. I may have given them the one reason—the *only* reason—they would believe he could be turned."

"No such reason exists…"

His smile was cruel. "Oh, it does. Just as you do. And it's as true as the stars in the sky. As real as the fire in your heart. As palpable as the blood in your veins…" He pressed closer, that maddening smile growing wider. "I swear on the bones of your mother and father, my words are the truth."

"My father isn't dead," I growled, thinking of how I could keep that statement a reality when I was incapacitated.

Baran leaned forward, his scarred lips at my ear. "*Yes*. He is. He has been for a long time now." He pulled away enough for me to see the truth in his eyes. "Your father died as your mother did: traitors to their own kind. Kade, weak at heart as he is, did not kill you as he should have when he found you wandering those war-torn streets. One look at you—the product of his brother's twisted love affair—and he couldn't do it. Instead, he brought you home to raise you like you were one of us and, worse still, like the son he'd never have. He lied about who and what you were, and now everyone knows."

"*No…*"

"I was there that night. I tried to talk him out of such a foolish decision, but he would not hear it. He blood-bound me to secrecy to keep you safe, but that blood bond dissolved when you fled Daglaar—when you were no longer his to protect. He put you above the security of his own kind just to keep a piece of his brother's memory alive. A vile piece, but a piece nonetheless."

I felt tears run down my face, but I quickly steadied my emotions. Learning that my father was not my father at all should have broken me, but somehow, it didn't. Instead, it fortified my love for the man who had kept me alive to honor his brother—my father. To give me a life that I would not have had without him. Daughter or not, he loved me.

Enough to send me away to safety.

Enough to trade his life for mine.

It was then that Baran's plan started to solidify in my mind. He would use me as bait to lure my father—a traitor in his people's eyes—to his death.

"When we return to the mountain, you will die a slow and painful death at the hands of those who suffered your presence for far too long, and we will get the leader we've longed for; the one Kade could never be because of his precious truce with Kaplyn and his Neráides."

"He'll kill you all," I seethed.

"We are prepared for what may come our way." Baran stood up and removed the staff from my chest. Then, with a brutal blow, he smashed it against my head, rendering me unconscious. As darkness took me, I prayed that my father and the others would never return to Daglaar—never try to find me.

My life for their safety seemed a fair price to pay.

HEMMING

I stared at my father, disbelief quickly giving way to anger; anger that had been building for over two decades. Anger that he'd said nothing in all this time, when it was clear that he had known. Anger that he'd only told me because he'd been backed into a corner, forced to disclose our shared lineage.

"I didn't want to tell you this way," he said, and my beast roared within me. "I have spent hours and hours trying to think of a way to break this news to you—"

"*Hours*?" I said, my voice so low and menacing I barely recognized it as my own. "You've spent *hours* thinking about telling me?"

"I know that you're—"

"You know NOTHING!" I shouted, the final word coming out more beast than man. "*Years*…I have spent *years* thinking about you—of all the ways I could kill you when I finally met you—"

"You have to understand that I didn't know, Hemming!" he said, palms held up to placate me as I stepped closer. "I never knew you existed—"

"Because you cast my mother aside like a whore!" I yelled, surging toward him. Halfway there, I felt the beast take over, my body shifting and changing along the way.

"Hemming!" Kaplyn yelled, his tone commanding, just like it had been the day I went after Kade. And just like that day, the beast stopped in his tracks as if his body were not his own. That's when I knew it was true. Kaplyn could control him—me—because I was his to control. His son. His blood. His creature.

The beast howled a mournful cry, then relented his position. When I was once again myself, I looked at him, my eyes devoid of emotion. My tone was cold and dead when I spoke. "We need to find Ariel," I said, turning away. "She's all that matters to me."

I took to the air, never looking back. Kade was soon at my side, and together, we searched Kaplyn's lands—my *father's* lands—both ground and sky for any sign of Ariel. I fought back the rage threatening to consume me, the task as futile as trying to find Ariel. I feared she might have already met her fate, which only fueled it further. I cursed the magic of Kaplyn's world—the magic that had shown me a future with Ariel that now seemed doomed from the start. My beast growled at the thought.

As we circled the forest, I saw something in the distant skies—flashes of black cutting across the blue of the eclipsed moons. "There!" I yelled to Kade. The swarm of winged figures was headed west. Toward Daglaar. "Nychterídes!"

"They're heading west—back to the mountain," he said, followed by a growl.

"We have to stop them. If they have Ariel—"

"They will kill her if they know the truth," Kade said

302

under his breath. "If the Minyades told them she is not my blood."

"They'll kill her regardless," I countered. "We need to round up whoever we can and go after her now!"

We turned around and sped back to the manor and the carnage we'd left behind. I ignored it as we landed at the gates—pretended my boots weren't being coated in blood as we ran to the manor. Shayfer appeared at the front door, his fine clothes shredded and bloody.

"The Nychterídes have Ariel. They're headed back to Daglaar," I yelled as we crested the stairs. "We need anyone that can be spared to get her back."

Kade was already storming the house in search of weapons and capable men, but there were few of either. One look at Kaplyn's manor made it clear that it had been ransacked by warriors—Nychterídes searching for Ariel. Anyone who'd remained behind had been either killed or wounded. Our small army had dwindled to nothing.

"There are no others," Shayfer said, confirming my fear, "and we don't have time to hunt down the few that could help us. We must go immediately."

"Sophitiya?" I asked, swallowing back my terror.

"She is safe. I hid her, Delphyne, and the rest of the staff in the wine cellar below the kitchen before the warriors arrived."

I let out a breath of relief as Kade returned with Kaplyn at his side. I stared at my father for a moment, haunted by the truth he'd impaled me with. As if reading my mind, he avoided my gaze, even as the four of us quickly formed a plan to go after Ariel.

"Are you certain they have her?" Kaplyn asked, daring to meet my eyes. The desperation in his tone simultaneously tugged at my heart and crushed it. My father loved her like she was his. His inability to keep her safe haunted him, as mine did me.

But he didn't care about his bastard son.

"No," I said, biting the word out through clenched teeth, "but I suspect they plan to execute her in Daglaar. It would only serve to tighten their ranks, given that they despise all that she is—especially if they now know that Kade isn't her real father." I tried not to let that word sour my tone and failed.

"Then how do we do this?" Shayfer asked, cleaning a blade on his sleeve. His eyes darted back and forth between Kaplyn and me as though he knew what had happened—as if my words had just confirmed his suspicions.

"We will have to sneak in through the wards and the forest to the clearing," I said. "That is where they will sacrifice her." Kade's darkly tanned skin went pale at the thought. I clamped my hand down on his shoulder and squeezed it tightly. "On my life, I will not let that happen."

"If it has not already," Shayfer added softly.

"We must go if we are to get there in time," Kaplyn said, heading for the door.

"We will take you," Kade said to Kaplyn and Shayfer.

The two exchanged looks, then smiled like crazed men about to embark on a deadly mission. "No need, General," Shayfer said, nearing Kaplyn. "I have a faster way."

Shayfer placed his hand on Kaplyn's arm, and the two disappeared in a blink of an eye. Moments later, Shayfer returned, a wry smile tugging at his lips.

"Who's next?"

Kade tamped down his surprise and latched onto the fae spy. The two were gone in a flash.

A tiny 'pop' sound announced Shayfer's return, though this time, I noticed the beads of sweat on his brow. The slight rounding of his shoulders. His deepened breathing.

"Come now, Just Hemming. You should never keep a lady waiting—even if that lady isn't much of a lady at all." I hesitated for a moment when he reached his hand to me. His shrewd brown eyes narrowed. "You may not trust me—may think me devious and insincere—but hear me when I say this: I love Ariel, and if you don't come with me this second, I will leave you here and rescue her without your help."

"No," I said, grabbing his hand and pulling him closer, "you won't."

≈

WE LANDED NEXT TO KADE AND KAPLYN, WHO WERE BOTH pacing the border, awaiting our arrival. Shayfer wiped the sweat from his face, then drew his sword. Kaplyn gave him a wary look, as though he knew just how exhausted his spy was from transporting us all. Shayfer waved him off, then started for the divide between our lands.

"Careful!" Kade roared as Shayfer casually stepped across the border. He shot Kade an incredulous look over his shoulder, then took another step forward.

"I can sense the wards," he said plainly. "No disrespect, General, but they are rudimentary at best. They wouldn't keep but the weakest of my kind out if they wanted to attack."

Shayfer crouched and maneuvered his lithe body until he was standing well inside the forest that led to the mountain. Kaplyn followed his lead, then Kade, then me. Once we were all through, and Kaplyn confirmed that the magic hadn't been triggered, we ran through the trees toward the settlement, Kade at the lead where he belonged. True daughter or not, Ariel was his in his mind, and he would fight for her like any father would his child. For all his faults, I admired him for that. He wouldn't give up on her no matter what—even if we were already too late.

We encountered two sentinels along the way who attempted to sound the alarm, but Kade destroyed them without stopping, the obsidian blade Kaplyn had given him slicing through their necks with ease. We slowed only when we heard a booming voice in the distance addressing a mob barely visible through the trees. And there, strapped to a rocky altar, was Ariel, a steel mask over her face.

I lunged forward, heart in my throat, only to be yanked backward as Kade caught my harness. "Wait," he growled in my ear. "*Listen…*"

We couldn't see who addressed the crowd through the trees, but as we crept forward, his voice became clearer. Shock overcame me the moment it registered. Then the Seer's words ran through my mind. *Not all things are as they seem…and some are exactly as they appear.* Crouched low, we dared to inch closer to the tree line. I needed to see the look in Baran's eyes as he spoke. My trainer. The traitor.

I wanted to wipe that look of smug satisfaction from him when I ended his life.

"I give you the spy who tainted your general's heart, turning him against us. The one responsible for the deaths of Kolm, Adrik, Caelum, Erwan, and Omar. None were spared in the Midlands—Ariel made sure of that. She is a traitor, just as Kade is. They both deserve a traitor's death!" The crowd roared to life at the thought of spilling her blood. "She ran from us and joined the ranks of the fae. Their complicity in this breaks our treaty with them. They will pay for their deceit," he continued, "starting with their half-breed Minyade whore!"

Baran pulled a dagger from his back and held it in front of her face. Her eyes—the only part of her face uncovered—were wild with terror. And hatred.

The delight in Baran's expression as he taunted her made my beast rage. She struggled against the bindings that held her arms high above her head to no avail. Even if she could have called her scales, they wouldn't have been any help. She was vulnerable regardless.

"After her blood is spilled, we attack the fae lords who broke the truce between our lands. They will die, and we will take what is rightfully ours. No longer will we be cursed, relegated to these barren lands. Soon we will live like the Favored Ones!"

"General…" I whispered, the desperation I felt at the sight of her so vulnerable plain in my tone.

"We must move on them," Kaplyn said to Kade.

"I'm going." I gripped my sword tighter as I moved. But a heavy hand fell on my shoulder as Shayfer pushed past me.

"Allow me," he said as he looked back, his expression grave. "To prove my worth—and my loyalty."

Before I could argue, he disappeared in a flash, only to appear next to Ariel, blade drawn. He severed her bindings in a few elegant slashes, then grabbed her by the waist. Seconds later, they were at our sides.

Kade snatched her from Shayfer and practically ripped the mask off her face. She was bruised and battered and swollen, blood caked in her hair and on her face, but she was alive. My hands flexed with the desire to grab her from his arms and crush her against me.

The beast growled his approval.

"*Run*!" Kaplyn ordered, looking back at the army now descending upon the forest.

"Take her," Kade said to me, shoving Ariel my way. "I'll stay behind and fend them off."

"General—"

"Now! That's an order!"

"Here," Shayfer said, taking Ariel's hand. He closed his

eyes, focusing hard as sweat dampened his brow, but nothing happened. With a curse, he broke out in a sprint, practically dragging her behind him. She was weak and wounded, but she kept pace as best she could. If the three of us could buy them time, they would survive.

"You're making a habit of disobeying me," Kade snarled as he raised his blades to the oncoming army. Kaplyn and I took our spots next to him, armed and ready.

"I will break every rule for her," I replied, steadying myself for the onslaught. "*Always*."

"You truly are my son," Kaplyn said quietly, awe in his voice, "and you are worthy of her love. Mine as well—should you want it."

Before his words could settle in my mind, the clash of blades eclipsed them. They echoed through the woods, the start of a battle that I soon realized would not likely end in our favor.

At least Ariel would be safe, I thought as the Nychterídes surrounded us.

That was all that mattered.

45

ARIEL

"We can't leave them!" I yelled at Shayfer as he dragged me through the brush near the border.

"My job is to get you out of here alive."

"But they'll *die*, Shayfer!"

He stopped and turned to me, tears welling in his eyes. "I am aware of the consequences, Ariel. Don't think for a moment that they aren't as well." His words were a knife to my heart. "And don't think that you are the only one who will lose someone they love because of it."

I captured his face in my hands. "We can help them, Shayfer. Give me an obsidian sword and flash us back there, if you can, right now." He stared at me for a moment, considering my words. "I don't want to live if it's at the expense of losing them. Do you?"

He reached over his back and drew a sword for me, then one for himself.

"It has been a pleasure knowing you, Ariel," he said. He

grabbed my face and kissed me—a desperate gesture in a desperate moment.

Then he wrapped his arm around my waist, and everything went black.

≋

WE APPEARED IN THE CENTER OF THE FRAY. MY FATHER AND Kaplyn were holding up well against the onslaught as Hemming's beast ripped through the horde, but even then, they were sorely outnumbered, and I wondered how long they could continue. I tried to ignore the blade I saw jutting out from Hemming's thick hide.

With no time to think, I started carving a path through the soldiers before me, headed for the one behind this madness. Baran would pay for what he'd started. I would gladly be the one to end it.

"Baran!" I shouted, calling him out. Hiding at the back of the mob like the coward he was, he turned to face me, a wicked smile on his face.

"Came back to watch them die, did you, Minyade whore?"

"Ariel?" my father shouted. "Get out of here now!"

"No!" I shouted back at him.

I heard Hemming's beast roar at the realization of my return.

The low-hanging tree branches made it difficult to fly even a little, but I was light enough to stand on them. With a quick jump, I dodged a sword to the belly and hauled myself up into the trees. They were so tightly packed that I was able to jump from one to another, maneuvering my way over to where Baran stood. I would put an end to his reign if it was the last thing I did.

From my vantage point, I could see just how desperate our situation truly was. Shayfer had made his way to Kaplyn and my father, their backs together. As a unit, they wielded sword and magic against the unrelenting Nychterídes. If I was going to help them, I needed to get to Baran. I refocused on that task and ran from branch to branch, swinging myself higher in the trees until I was all but hidden from sight.

Baran, in all his hubris, hadn't bothered to track me.

He probably thought I was already dead.

He stood back and barked orders at his army, unwilling to get his hands dirty. The trainer who wouldn't fight. *Disgrace*, I thought to myself as I loomed above him. With an elegant leap, I landed before him and sliced at his gut.

My obsidian blade shattered on contact.

"Stupid girl," he said, landing a crushing blow to my jaw. "Obsidian no longer works against me." He hauled me up by my hair and punched me again.

"How?" I asked, spitting blood from my mouth. I needed my scales, or I'd soon be beaten to death.

"I made a deal with a fae lord. One as ambitious as I am."

"*Teigan*," I growled, the memory of his voice in the woods when I was abducted ringing through my mind. I blocked a kick from Baran, but the force of it knocked me off balance. His fist connected with my jaw again and sent me flying. I laughed through the pain. "Your fae ally was outed and will be found and dealt with," I bluffed. "You're on your own now."

"Alone?" He pointed to the army behind me. "I have them. They are mine now. You, and your father's treachery, have made certain of that. His lies sealed his fate."

He wound up to hit me again, and a few of my scales dropped into place right where his fist landed. I felt the force, but it was Baran who look pained by the blow. I grabbed a staff from the ground—*my* staff—and spun it in the air in front of me.

"My father lied about who I was to spare me, nothing more. There is no treachery in that."

"Your father put you above all else," Baran countered. "For that, he doesn't deserve his title."

"And you're the one to replace him? The one relegated to training his soldiers? The one no longer fit for battle?"

Baran laughed and swung at me. I narrowly dodged the blow. "Your father made his bed when he kept those Minyades in the cellar. They were very quick to tell me what I wanted to know when they learned of my plan. Of course, I left out the bit about them being used as a distraction—that they would never really be allowed to take you." He smiled at me as he circled, ready to strike again. "Your father's lies were too many for the Nychterídes not to believe he'd turned on them. Once he left for the Midlands, I set my plan in motion. Painting you as a spy was no huge task. Convincing them he was complicit was no harder when the Minyades were paraded before them, telling their tale of a stolen child —one not born of Kade."

I slashed my staff with lightning speed and buried it in the side of Baran's face. He stumbled back a pace or two, and I exploited my advantage, striking him several more times until he collapsed to the ground. Invincible to blades? Maybe. To blows? It seemed not.

"Call them off," I said, hooking my staff under his chin. He wrestled against it, but my grip held firm. "Call. Them. Off."

His voice bellowed through the woods, and the sound of blade meeting blade stopped.

"Tell them what you did, you useless bastard, and I'll be sure your death is clean." My father and the others pushed their way through the crowd until they stood before me, wounded and bloodied. "Tell them now!"

"I already told them the truth: that Kade put a bastard child, not of his own blood, before his people. Refute that, if you can."

"Then tell them how you sent Omar to kill the others in the Midlands. How that entire mission was concocted to make it look like my father and the fae had killed them because I was working with them."

"They won't believe me even if I do." I looked into the hateful eyes of the army before me and saw the truth in Baran's words. "They'll never take the word of a Minyade whore who stole away in the middle of the night with her bastard lover, who killed his childhood friends along the way. Who sold herself to a fae lord to stay on his lands while she plotted her attack on *our* kind."

"Lies!" Hemming roared as he stormed toward Baran in his normal form, his side bleeding. He drew back his obsidian blade and sliced it toward Baran's face. It shattered upon contact, and an army of Nychteríde warriors' eyes went wide.

"He made a deal with Lord Teigan," I explained. "Together, they planned to overtake the Midlands. His invincibility to obsidian seems to have been part of that deal," I said, putting those facts together.

The uncertainty among Baran's soldiers was plain in their confused expressions.

"I sent Ariel away because it was no longer safe for her here," my father shouted to them. "She did not escape in the night to seek refuge with the fae. I took her there myself—to our ally, Kaplyn. He agreed to keep her so that she wouldn't have to suffer at the hands of those who saw her as a target and little more."

"I killed Tycho and the others," Hemming confessed,

"because they crept up on her like cowards and killed Adrik, then tried to kill her just as he'd tried before."

"And she has never whored herself to me for refuge," Kaplyn added. "She is a guest in my home and will remain so until she no longer feels that is her path."

"I saw what Omar did to the others," Hemming continued. "I used fae magic to see through his eyes. I saw him sneak up behind Erwan and Kolm as they slept and slit their throats without hesitation; saw him stab Caelum in the heart. I saw Omar and many others putting this plan into motion over the past few months—*long* before Ariel returned."

"It is true that Ariel is not my child," Kade said, squaring his shoulders. "She was my brother's daughter. He loved her, and he died because of that love. When she survived that attack, I took it as a sign. I brought her to Daglaar to raise her as one of us; to groom her as a warrior against our enemies, not to harbor one among us." He stared out over the men that had once fought for him and saw what I did—a shift in their eyes. His words were swaying them. "I have never and would never put anyone, including myself, above the Nychterídes— not even Ariel. My lies were to keep her safe, not to harm our kind." Once more, he looked upon his soldiers, whose attentions now fell upon Baran. "Take this traitor back to camp," Kade ordered. The set of his jaw dared them to challenge him.

I hoisted Baran to his feet, my staff still crushed against his throat. But my grip was tiring, and he knew it. With a sharp elbow to my gut, he was free, blade drawn, charging at my father, whose back was turned.

"No!" I screamed just in time for Father to deflect the strike from his head to his arm. Hemming and the Neráides moved to interfere, but the soldiers forced them back. If someone wanted to openly challenge the general of the

Nychterídes, that was allowed, though the current circumstances for that challenge were questionable.

The fight was not fair, and we all knew it. Baran had the upper hand because he held two huge advantages over my father: Kade was tired from fighting an army, and no weapon could easily put Baran down. I was forced to watch, helpless. Eventually, Baran would win.

My father tumbled back toward me, his stomach bleeding. The wound Baran had just carved into him was deep, and his life flashed before me. He could not die this way. I wouldn't allow it.

A spark of fire ignited in my blood, and I stoked it further with my anger, begging it to come back to me, if only for one last time. If I never breathed it again, I would accept that fate; but I would not accept my father's death at the hands of Baran. That night, in those woods, I needed my fire to come. To end the madness.

The moment Baran stormed toward my father to finish him off, I jumped in his way. One by one, my scales slowly slid into place.

"This is for my father," I said as I knocked the weapon from Baran's hand and grabbed his face. His mouth opened to speak, and I held it open with my hands. Fire spilled from my mouth, slowly at first. I pushed it hard, my rage fueling every flame, until he screamed and fought against my hold. I felt his stony flesh warming, his body slowly burning from the inside out. Every time the flames began to sputter out, I thought about all the death he'd caused. The havoc he'd wreaked. The loved ones he'd tried to take from me. Hemming, Kade, Kaplyn…Shayfer…Sophitiya. I would have lost them all because of him. With every name that crossed my mind, I could feel my power slipping away, but I held fast. Even as Baran went limp in my arms, the acrid stench of burning flesh surrounding us as the weight of his body pulled me down on top of him, I forced the fire from me with every ounce of energy I had left until there was no more.

Until whatever Fireheart I had left was gone.

Kneeling on top of the charred remains, I turned to my bleeding father. "I love you, Baba," I whispered.

Then I collapsed to the ground.

HEMMING

My world stopped in an instant.
Time stood still.

All that registered was Ariel's lifeless body and the sound of my beast's roar ripping through the forest. Trees exploded at their bases, sending them flying through the air. Kade rushed toward her, clutching his bleeding wound. The beast that threatened to escape howled at me to go to her, to take her. To run her to safety—if a safe place even existed.

I was on the ground beside her, taking her limp body in my arms, before Kade could reach her. She was so cold. She was never cold…

"Shayfer!" Kaplyn yelled from somewhere behind me. "You need to go find the Barterer and bring him here."

"Are you sure?" Shayfer replied, fear in his tone.

"We have no other choice." The resignation in Kaplyn's tone was not comforting. "Do you have the strength to do it?"

Shayfer's eyes turned to Ariel's still body. "I must. There is no other option."

"Is she alive?" Kade asked as he collapsed next to me. A growl escaped my lips, the beast pushing forward again.

I pulled her closer and felt her light exhale on my cheek. "Barely," was all I could manage in response.

"You must go *now*," Kaplyn said to Shayfer. "Meet us at the border. The Barterer cannot come to these lands freely."

"There will be a price to pay," Shayfer warned. I looked back to find Kaplyn staring at him, concern furrowing his brow.

"I know."

The Nychteríde warriors surrounding us parted for Shayfer to pass, but he merely disappeared. The shock on their faces was plain.

"Take her to the border," Kaplyn ordered, staring at me. "I will bring Kade."

Without further directive, I was on my feet, sprinting through what remained of the woods around us. At least a mile of trees had been decimated in the beast's wake.

"Fight this," I whispered in her ear as I ran her to the Midlands. "You cannot leave yet. It's not time. That is not the future I saw…"

She stirred in my arms, and I dared to hope.

As I ran, I did everything I could think of to keep her with me. I told her stories of our childhood as her skin grew icier. I told her how my feelings for her had changed over time as the pauses between her breaths grew longer. Then I told her that the night she escaped Daglaar had been the night I'd planned to tell her how I felt—tell her that I loved her more than anything in existence.

I prayed she could hear me.

When we reached the border, Shayfer was standing there looking grim, his hooded companion lurking just behind him.

I cradled Ariel tighter in my arms. The Barterer was an ominous being shrouded in an aura of nothingness, as if there were a void where he stood—like he sucked up the life around him. Shayfer's unease in his presence was understandable. Even the beast fought the urge to flee.

Kaplyn soon appeared at my side with Kade, whose wound had closed but not fully healed. The moment the Barterer set eyes on the fae lord, he pushed his hood back to reveal a delicate-looking male as pale as Kaplyn's own healer but far more beautiful. He smiled at me, and my body shivered.

"You summoned me, Lord Kaplyn…"

"The Minyade's Fireheart has burned out. Can you restore it?"

His smile widened. "For a price…" The Barterer floated toward me in a smooth motion and reached for Ariel. Instinctively, I pulled her away. "I must touch her to see if she can be saved. Lay her down."

When I didn't move, Kade was before me, his expression stern. "Put her down, Hemming, or give her to me."

Grudgingly, I laid her on the moonlit grass and knelt beside her. The beast paced in my mind, waiting for the Barterer to make one wrong move. He placed his hand on the skin over her heart and closed his eyes. "There is but a spark left."

"Fix her," Kade said, biting his words out through clenched teeth.

The Barterer backed up and searched our faces, looking for something I couldn't comprehend until Kaplyn spoke. "Name it," the fae lord said, feigning indifference. But the frustration in his tone leaked through, betraying his true emotions; the concern he felt for his ward.

"This is no easy task you request. The magic required to repair her is substantial. It requires great sacrifice."

The grass rustled, and I looked down to find Ariel's eyes fluttering. "Ariel?" I said softly. "Can you hear me?"

"It hurts, Hemmy," she murmured, not fully conscious. Her hands flew to her chest and gripped it tightly. I clasped them in mine and held on for dear life, scared hers would slip away if I didn't.

"Tell us what you want before I start removing your limbs to speed this process," Kade growled. He was on his feet, blade unsheathed.

"To restore what has been lost from the Minyade girl— what makes her what she is—will require you to lose that which makes you what you are, General."

I let go of Ariel to draw my sword. She woke up, screaming. The four of us tried to soothe her as best we could, but there was no calming the fear in her eyes when she saw the dust and ash billow from her mouth as she cried out. No telling her it would all be okay.

"What's happening?" she asked, ash smeared across her lips. I wiped it from her mouth, but it was soon replaced with more. She was running out of time, and we all knew it. If there was to be a barter, it would be now or never.

"Enough riddles!" Kaplyn yelled, standing to face the Barterer. "Tell us what you want in exchange for restoring her Fireheart or be gone."

"I want your wings." He turned his gaze to Kade. "Wings for a Fireheart. That is my deal. Do you accept?"

"Baba, no!" Ariel cried, trying to push herself up. Her arms were too weak for the job, and she crashed back down to the ground. "You can't—"

"I cannot let you die," Kade said, fear blanching his skin.

"You'll lose everything without your wings!"

Without hesitation, I was on my feet. "He might," I said, stepping toward the fae, "but I won't." If my wings were the price to pay for Ariel's survival, I would pay it a thousand

320

times over. "I am Hemming of the Nychterídes—one of the greatest warriors they have ever known. Stronger and faster than the others. Heal her Fireheart, and my wings are yours. *That* is the deal."

"Hemming, no—" Kaplyn started before I cut him off.

"That is the deal."

He flinched at the conviction in my voice.

The Barterer's eyes burned with lust, and he licked his lips as he reached for what would soon be his. I didn't flinch at his approach. "A deal, it is," he agreed, drawing a blade from his cloak.

I closed my eyes and tried to block out the sound of Ariel's screams from my mind. I'd traded my wings for her life once before.

I would gladly do it again.

≈

ARIEL

"Hemmy, please don't!" I begged, struggling to sit up. The sad smile he gave me over his shoulder tore my already broken heart in two.

"I've been without them before," he said as I choked back a sob, "and I've been without you. I can live without my wings; I cannot, however, live without you." He turned back to the Barterer. "Do it now."

The fae was upon me in seconds, pushing me onto my back. With Kaplyn and my father holding me down, he placed his hands on my chest and began chanting in a language I didn't understand—had never heard before. The language of the gods. Blinding pain coursed through me, and I nearly passed out. I craned my head back and found Hemming hovering only feet away, the agony in his expression a mirror of my own. But his gaze never faltered. He held me together with those pale grey eyes that I loved.

Then, with one final surge of anguish, it all disappeared. I felt as I had before my mishap in the forest with the Dream-catcher. Before Hemming had tried to restore my Fireheart.

The Barterer stepped away, heading toward Hemming, and I jumped to my feet to stop him. He ran a fingertip along Hemming's leathery appendage and nearly beamed with delight, knowing it would soon be his. When I lunged for him, my father and Kaplyn caught my arms and restrained me.

"He made a deal," Kaplyn said softly in my ear. "He must uphold his end, or it will all fall apart, and you will die."

"No!" I screamed, fighting with all I had to free myself, but their grips were like iron. Neither Kaplyn nor my father wanted me to die. Fire shot from my mouth with every shout and cry and curse, my rage uncontainable. As the trees around us began to burn and the grass scorched to ash, Hemming knelt down before the Barterer, his back to him—his eyes on me. "Hemming!" I cried again, smoke streaming from my mouth as I strained against the hands that held me back. "Hemmy, *please. Please* don't do this."

Tears cut a path through my ash-covered face as he shook his head and stretched his wings wide for the last time.

"I love you, Ariel."

The Barterer stepped behind him, a gruesome-looking blade in his hand.

"With this sacrifice, your debt is paid," he said before that blade sliced through the air, carving through flesh and bone without slowing. Hemming's wing fell to the ground with an unceremonious thud before he repeated the motion again and the other fell beside it. Blood shot through the air, raining down on the fire—my fire—the two forever bound.

Kaplyn and my father released me, and I dove at Hemming just as he collapsed to the ground. There was so much blood. Too much blood.

I turned to the Barterer, murder in my heart. "I will *kill you* for this."

"As well you should, but you will not, for if you do, the magic will be undone. He will regain his wings, but you, little Fireheart—you will die." Hemming's hand tightened on my knee, silently calling me off; a desperate plea to let it go. "If I were you," he said, collecting his prizes from the ground, "I'd stop that bleeding before all this was for naught."

"Go," Kaplyn ordered, his voice teeming with warning.

The Barterer disappeared into thin air without another word. Then Hemming's hand went limp.

"Hemmy?" I called, bending down until my chest grazed the ground next to him. He didn't respond. I looked at his back, the raw, open wounds showing no signs of healing, and knew what I had to do. "This is going to hurt," I told him, my voice cracking on the words.

I sat up and called my fury forth. I breathed fire onto my hands, just as I had when Tycho tried to kill me. I blew until my scales glowed with the heat of a thousand suns. Then I turned to the others and ordered them to pin him down.

"I love you too," I whispered in his ear. "From the day we met until the day I die."

Without warning, I pressed my fists of fire against the flesh where wing had once met body and held them there until he roared with pain. He bucked wildly until he went limp again.

"He will be all right, Ariel," my father said, pulling me away from Hemming's unconscious body. Kaplyn bent down

323

and smoothed Hemming's hair from his damp face before picking him up.

"We should go," Shayfer said, looking around at the flames engulfing the forest.

Kade and Kaplyn nodded in agreement.

Shayfer took Hemming from Kaplyn, who looked reluctant to hand him over, then disappeared in a blink. My father took to the sky, hovering above where Kaplyn and I still stood. Confused at how Kaplyn would return, I reached for him, offering to carry him home, but he shook his head and smiled.

"I will meet you there," he said, dropping the blessing stone into my hand. "And thank you—for loving my *son*."

While that final word ricocheted through my mind, he launched himself into the air, shifting into a massive black-winged bird.

A familiar green-eyed raven.

HEMMING

I opened my eyes to a familiar room with a welcome view. Ariel sat beside the bed I lay face-down upon, her head resting next to mine as she slept. I slid my hand toward her face, careful not to disturb her or strain my back. The pain had dulled, but it was present nonetheless. A reminder of what I'd done. I cupped her cheek—a reminder of why I'd done it—and stroked it with my thumb.

Her eyes opened slowly, and she smiled a sleepy smile. It held no recollection of what we'd just been through. Then realization settled into her expression, terror replacing serenity in a heartbeat. "How are you?" she asked, pushing up onto her knees to assess my back. She turned pale in the scant light of the room and slowly sat back down. Apparently, it looked as bad as it felt.

"I've been better…"

Her eyes went wide before she let loose a sob, thinly veiled with laughter. "Hemming—"

"I know," I said, pulling her forehead to mine. "I know."

"I've never been more terrified in my whole life."

"Me either." I pulled her closer still.

Just past Ariel, on her bedside table, sat a pair of blood-red leather wings, propped up against the lamp. "Sophitiya was here?" I asked. Tears welled in Ariel's eyes as she nodded, knocking the breath from my lungs. "Where is she, Ariel? Shayfer said she was all right. Tell me she's all right—"

"She's fine," she replied, sniffing back her tears. The relief I felt was instant. "She came by while you were sleeping to check on you."

I smiled at the image of the young girl coming to care for her guardian. "She forgot her wings."

Ariel's efforts to contain her emotions failed, and a tear rolled down her cheek. "She didn't forget them—she left them here on purpose. For you." My heart stopped for a moment. "She said you needed them more than she did, so you could have them." Tears now streamed down Ariel's face, and I pulled her closer. "I swear on the bones of my mother and father that I'll see your wings restored, Hemming. No matter the cost."

"Not if the cost is your life."

She pulled away, her eyes searching mine. "How could you do it?" she whispered, her voice tight with emotion.

I pushed her hair back from her face. "How could I not?"

"But you gave up everything! Who you are…your home…"

"I gave that up when I killed Tycho and left with you."

"My father would have set that right upon his return, and you know it. After all you did for him? Surely you knew that."

"I did."

She leaned in, propping her chin on the bed. "Then why, Hemming?"

"I thought '*I love you*' was explanation enough." When I smiled at her, she let out a breath, her lips flapping with frustration.

"You're a fool—"

"A fool in love with you."

Silence.

"Then I suppose I'm an even greater fool for loving you back," she said. My smile grew to a grin. "I spoke to our fathers…" She quirked a brow at me, a playful gesture to belie the pain she felt. "Or I guess I spoke to *your* father and my *uncle*—"

"I didn't know," I said, reaching for her again. "Not until after you'd been taken."

She nodded, a sad smile on her face. "It's all right. You got ambushed by a parental revelation of your own."

My face pressed against the pillow as I exhaled hard. "Yeah. I did."

"How do you feel about it?" she asked, her tone cautious.

"I don't know yet."

"Please don't kill him…"

I looked at her fearful eyes and sighed. "I'm not going to kill him, Ariel. I'm not even certain I could if I wanted to."

She let out a nervous laugh. "What a mess. What do we do now, Hemmy?"

"I have an idea," I said, carefully dragging myself closer to her until our lips nearly touched. Her hands reached for my face, guiding it across the narrow divide until our mouths met, picking up where we'd left off before the world was pulled out from under us. Her kiss was soft and tentative and full of questions I didn't have the answers to. I wouldn't make her promises for our future or happily-ever-afters because there was no way to know what that future held.

Instead, I guided her up onto the bed and nestled her against me. I kissed her gently until her body relaxed into mine and any reservations she had about our decisions the night of the eclipse disappeared into the shadows. I knew they'd be waiting for her when she finally left my side, so I kept her with me through the night, our bodies intertwined like the couple at the bottom of the tapestry hung high above her bed in Daglaar.

The story of her family.

The story of us.

48

ARIEL

Once Hemming was asleep, I slid out of the bed and left the room. He needed rest. And I needed answers.

I searched the house until I found the one I was looking for, standing on the balcony off the dining room that overlooked the front of the property and beyond. His body went tense the moment I spoke. His pitch-black wings twitched in anticipation of a fight.

"I've been waiting for you," Kade said, not turning to face me. "I wondered when you would come."

"I was with Hemming. He's asleep now. His wounds look better, but he won't let the healer tend to him, so it will be a while before they're fully closed."

"What he did—" The general cut himself off. If I hadn't known better, I would have thought emotion had forced him to stop.

"Hemming has always protected me, Ba—" The term of endearment died on my tongue. He wasn't my father. I stood there for a moment, unsure of how to address him. "I...I don't know what to call you now."

While I struggled to find a suitable replacement, he slowly turned to face me, pain etched into his expression. "I may not be your father, Ariel—not by blood—but I am the one who raised you. I have always considered you my daughter, and the fact that you now know the truth changes nothing for me," he said, daring a step closer. "But you may address me however you see fit. I deceived you, and I know that will not rest easy on your mind—or your heart."

I closed my eyes and took a deep breath to calm the muddled emotions rising within me. There were too many to count. Too many to sort through right then.

"Why didn't you tell me?" I asked, my voice meek like a child's.

He let out a breath and came to me, wrapping me up in his arms. "I couldn't—not until I understood more about what had happened. About who you were."

I hugged his waist tighter. "Why did you save me?" My words were muffled by his chest, but he heard them nonetheless. His whole body went rigid, and he pushed me away gently to stare into my eyes.

"The moment you wrapped your tiny arms around me, I knew I could never hurt you."

"What happened that day? You've never told me, and I've never asked because I never wanted to know, but now...now I need to understand."

His hands gripped my shoulders as he struggled to find the words to tell me what he clearly didn't want to. Anxiety spiked in my gut. Either he didn't want to tell me for fear it would break my heart, or because it would destroy us. I could see no other alternative.

"Your village was attacked," Kaplyn said from behind me. I turned to find him standing a few paces away, hands clasped behind his back. He smiled, but it was weary. He looked exhausted, and I wondered just how much of a toll the attack on his people had taken on him. He'd only been able to deal with it upon our return. He'd put me before the others.

A pang of guilt tugged at my restored heart.

"By whom?" I asked. Kaplyn hesitated for a moment, looking to Kade before returning his gaze to me.

"The Minyades."

My brow furrowed in confusion. "But…but that doesn't make any sense. Why would they attack their own people?"

Again, Kade and Kaplyn shared a long, silent look.

"They didn't," Kaplyn corrected. "They attacked *mine*."

"I don't understand," I said, shaking my head.

"Ariel, look at me," Kade urged. "Things are not as you remember. You were so young when I found you. We're still not fully certain exactly how old you are, but you appeared to be around three or four at the time. The village you lived in with your mother was not in Anemosia." He paused for a moment, hoping I would see the truth so he wouldn't have to speak it aloud. When I didn't, he continued. "It was here—in the Midlands. You were to be raised under Kaplyn's protection, hidden among the fae. You and your mother both."

"*Hidden*…?" The word escaped on a breath. Then the memory of that night came into focus, and I wondered how I hadn't realized it sooner. Kaplyn had been one of the men with Kade that night; the golden-haired warrior at his side. I turned to him, my surprise written all over my face, and he nodded. "You…I remember you now…"

"I failed you, Ariel. That fact has haunted me from that day forward." He stepped closer, then stopped himself as though I'd commanded it. "When Kade showed up at the manor with you the night you fled Daglaar—terror in his wild eyes—I prayed I would not fail you again. I vowed to do all I could to keep you safe this time. To train you. To have

Shayfer watch over you. It was my second chance to do for you what I could not do for your mother."

"But why did you have to keep me safe at all? Because I'm a half-blood? Did the Minyades hate my mother so much that they hunted her because of me?"

Kade looked to Kaplyn, and I turned to find the fae lord staring at me intently. "You were in jeopardy because of what you are, yes," he said.

"Is this why the Minyade prisoners came for me? Were they trying to trick me into letting them out so they could finish what they tried to do back then?"

The muscles in Kade's jaw feathered. "*Yes.*"

I thought about all I could remember from our brief encounters—what they'd said to me. The intensity in their eyes when they spoke. Then I remembered the name the one had called me right before Hemming drove a blade through his throat. *Aima Kori...* Those words were foreign to me, but I knew they were important.

"One of the Minyades called me something the night I was taken: *Aima Kori.* What does it mean?"

"Blood daughter," Kaplyn said, his voice as cool and melodious as ever.

I looked at my wings, the color of blood highlighted by the light of the room. "What do they want from me?"

"I don't know," Kade said, "but the Minyades do not know you are here. If anything, they will assume you're still at the mountain where they sent the others to find you. If more come, they will meet the same fate."

"And if they come for you here, we will be prepared," Kaplyn added.

I nodded, mind reeling. "Is that why you kept them prisoner?" I asked Kade. "To find out what they wanted?"

He nodded. "I needed to confirm what they were after—and learn their motives for retrieving you. They would not tell me, no matter how we tortured them. It seems Baran thought to use them as a distraction to get to me through you, though. Clever bastard."

I nodded again.

A knock on the door drew our collective attention, and we turned to find Shayfer standing just inside the room. "I beg your pardon for interrupting, Lord Kaplyn, but Sophitiya has awoken from a nightmare and is quite desperate to see Ariel. Delphyne has done her best to console her, but I fear that only Ariel will do."

"I think we are done here for now, unless Ariel has any other questions." Kaplyn looked to me, an invitation to ask anything else I wished to know.

I took a deep breath and turned to Kade. "Will you tell me about my father?"

His body tensed as he nodded.

Then I turned to Kaplyn. "Will you tell me about my mother? I don't remember her well."

His shoulders slumped, and he rushed over to hug me. He smelled like sun and rain and fresh grass in spring—he smelled like my childhood before I went to the mountain. "I will tell you everything whenever you wish to know it."

"Okay."

"And I will talk to Hemming once he's well enough, though I fear I have few answers for him. I never knew of his existence until he arrived here." He didn't attempt to hide the sadness in his voice as he admitted that truth.

Shayfer cleared his throat, and I pulled away from Kaplyn. "Maybe later?" I suggested.

Kaplyn smiled. "Of course."

I turned to find Kade staring at us, his expression stone.

"I love you, *Baba*…"

His breath caught in his throat. "I love you too, Ariel."

I gave them both a smile before heading toward Shayfer,

who waited for me with patience and grace. But the second we were out of the room, he took me by the elbow and dragged me down the hall.

"I can get there without an escort," I said, attempting to pull free, but his grip tightened as we continued not toward Sophitiya's room, but through the kitchen and down into the wine cellar below. Once he was confident we were alone and out of earshot, he started talking.

"They're lying to you," he said, shaking his head. "Well, not *lying* per se, but they're certainly not telling you everything."

"What are you talking about, Shayfer?"

"'*Aima Kori*' does technically mean 'blood daughter'," he said, his voice hushed as he pulled me closer. "That is the literal translation from the old language—before the lands were divided—but it is not the meaning the Minyades give it."

I stared at him wide-eyed, fear creeping up my spine. "Shayfer. Tell me…"

"The old language lacks terms that have since evolved." His anxiety only increased my own. "There was no word for 'prince' or 'princess', so that was how the Minyades described a child of royal blood: 'blood son' or 'blood daughter'." *Great gods above…* "You never told Kaplyn and Kade about what the witches said, did you?"

"About me being a princess? No, because I thought it was utter nonsense," I said, my chest seizing. "How could the sisters have known in the first place?"

"That's not the point, Ariel. The point is that Kaplyn and Kade know who and what you are, and what you told them today confirmed it. What they *don't* know is that you had already been tipped off about your royal blood by the witches."

334

"I thought the witch was referring to me being *Hemming's* princess—"

"And she could have been. That doesn't really matter now, though, does it? You are a royal in your own right. A royal of the Minyades."

"But the Minyades tried to kill me as a child, Shayfer! Kaplyn and Kade have done nothing but try to keep me safe since that day."

Shayfer pulled away, his expression grim. "Have they?" The uncertainty in his tone gave me pause. "Don't you find it strange that your father—or uncle—just happened to be there with Kaplyn the day your village was attacked? The day your mother died? It seems too convenient to be a coincidence."

"What are you saying, Shayfer?"

"I'm merely suggesting that there may be more going on here than you've considered. Maybe, just maybe, what you have interpreted as them keeping you safe was really them keeping you from returning to your home and claiming your birthright."

My head hurt with all the possibilities; the doubt was undeniable. What had once looked like protectiveness slowly transformed into something more insidious. More malicious. I couldn't help but question whose best interests had been served by keeping me away from the Minyades.

And there was only one way to find out.

"Shayfer," I said, leaning in close, "I need you to do something for me."

"Anything."

"I need you to take me to the Anemosian border."

"Ariel—"

"I'm not asking you to go with me. Just take me there and leave me. I'll do the rest on my own."

A wicked smile twisted his lips. "The hell you will. Why

should you get to have all the fun? Besides, it's hard to get you alone when Just Hemming is around."

He wiggled his brows at me, and I slapped his arm. "You're shameless."

"One of my finer qualities that you adore."

I shook my head and smiled. "It is indeed. And I'll adore you even more if you do as I ask."

All humor drained from his face. "Meet me by the willow after dinner tonight. We leave at dark."

Then he disappeared without another word.

≈

HOURS LATER, I FOUND MYSELF STANDING UNDER THAT TREE waiting for Shayfer to appear. I'd managed to pack my gear without waking Hemming and sneak out of the house without being detected. As soon as Shayfer arrived, we'd be off in a blink. Maybe my idea was reckless; or maybe it was necessary. Either way, we were headed to the land of my people—the ones who had come to claim me years after my mother's death. The ones that had attacked my village and killed her.

I needed answers. And if I didn't like them, I'd get revenge.

Just as Shayfer appeared, weapons strapped to his back and chest underneath his finely embroidered cloak, a voice rang out through the night. "You two wouldn't be going somewhere without me, would you?" Hemming asked, striding toward us.

"Just Hemming," Shafer called. "You should be resting—"

"What are you doing, Ariel?" he asked, ignoring the spy entirely.

336

I was already caught, so I saw no reason to lie to him. I loved him too much for that. "We're going to Anemosia. Apparently, I'm their princess…and our fathers knew this but never saw fit to tell me. All I want is to learn the truth, Hemming. Good, bad, or otherwise."

He stared at me for a moment, then at Shayfer. "This plan is shaky at best. You have no idea what you're walking into—no idea where you're going. You don't know the lay of the land. You don't know who to trust."

"I have to go," I said softly. "It's the only way."

He said nothing for a moment, then pressed his lips into a tight line and nodded. "All right. But I'm going, too." Shayfer and I both broke out in objection, but he silenced us with a hand in the air—just like his father always did. "I go where you go. No more splitting up, remember? It never ends well." I opened my mouth to object again, and this time he stopped me by pressing his lips to mine. I'd never enjoyed being silenced more in my life. "You will never convince me otherwise, so save your energy for our journey, *mikros drakos*. We'll need it."

"Stubborn mule," I muttered under my breath.

He laughed. Shayfer groaned. "If you two are quite finished with your excruciating and bizarre foreplay, I'd like to leave before we're found out." He reached his hands out to Hemming and me, and we accepted.

Whatever fate awaited us in Anemosia remained to be seen, but one thing was certain.

The *Aima Kori* was going home.

ABOUT THE AUTHOR

AMBER LYNN NATUSCH is the author of the bestselling Caged and Force of Nature series. She was born and raised in Winnipeg, and speaks sarcasm fluently because of her Canadian roots. She loves to dance and sing in her kitchen—much to the detriment of those near her—but spends most of her time running a practice with her husband, raising two children, and attempting to write when she can lock herself in the bathroom for ten minutes.

She has many hidden talents, most of which should not be mentioned but include putting her foot in her mouth, acting inappropriately when nervous, swearing like a sailor at inopportune times, and not listening when she should. She's obsessed with home renovation shows, should never be caffeinated, and loves snow. Amber has a deep-seated fear of clowns and deep water...especially clowns swimming in deep water.

amberlynnnatusch.com

MORE BY
AMBER LYNN NATUSCH

The *CAGED* Series
CAGED

HAUNTED

FRAMED

SCARRED

FRACTURED

TARNISHED

STRAYED

CONCEALED

BETRAYED

The *UNBORN* Series
UNBORN

UNSEEN

UNSPOKEN

UNMADE

UNBOUND

The *BLUE-EYED BOMB* Series
LIVE WIRE

KILLSWITCH

DEAD ZONE

WARHEAD

GROUND ZERO

The *FORCE OF NATURE* Series
FROM THE ASHES

INTO THE STORM

BEYOND THE SHADOWS

BENEATH THE DUST

THROUGH THE ETHER

The _WITCHES OF THE GILDED LILIES_ Series
A CURSE OF NIGHTSHADE

The _IMMORTAL VICES AND VIRTUES_ Series
QUEEN ME

Contemporary Romance
UNDERTOW